KILLER
Heart

THE CHAOS CREW
BOOK THREE

EVA CHANCE
& HARLOW KING

Killer Heart

Book 3 in the Chaos Crew series

First Digital Edition, 2022

Cover design: Temptation Creations

Ebook ISBN: 978-1-990338-46-5

Paperback ISBN: 978-1-990338-47-2

ONE

Decima

FROM A DISTANCE, I stalked Damien Malik.

Over the past week, I'd learned a lot about the majority whip, partly with the help of my crew—in particular, Blaze's hacking and surveillance skills and Garrison's ease at charming information out of people. When Malik wasn't in Washington D.C. working with the House of Representatives, he spent most of his time in the smaller nearby city where the Malik family home was located. Unless he had a particularly early meeting, every morning he went for a jog through a local park along a tree-lined pond. Then he stopped at one specific coffee shop to grab a hazelnut cappuccino.

At least two bodyguards stayed with him at all times. I trailed far behind all of the men as I took a little jog of my own. Then I followed them up the stairs into the coffee shop.

When I got up there, Malik was already sitting at his favorite table with his fingers curled around the handle of his mug. The sunlight beaming through the broad windows gleamed off his silver hair, slicked neatly back as always, and brought the hard angles of his polished face into sharper relief.

Now, still-healing scrapes marred the otherwise only faintly lined skin at his temples and jaw. A week ago, just hours before a DNA comparison had revealed that this man was a parental match for me, a lunatic had broken into a late-night planning session at his Washington office and shot two of Malik's staff before blowing himself to smithereens. It seemed clear that the guy the news reports were calling a domestic terrorist had been hoping to take Malik with him.

He'd almost succeeded.

I yanked my eyes away and walked over to the counter to order a small latte. Anything bigger wouldn't be wise. Even a little caffeine got me hopped up with energy until I could have done a fair imitation of Blaze's restless fidgeting.

As I waited for the barista to assemble the drink, my hands clenched at my sides. No matter what the news said, I couldn't help suspecting that the attack had been connected to the household where I'd been held for over twenty years after they'd stolen me from my birth family. My trainer had been keeping an eye on Malik. Their intentions toward him couldn't be anything but malicious.

Had they decided to go after him more overtly now that they'd lost their grasp on me so completely?

I hadn't been here to stop them. I hadn't had any clue that I should be. But now that I knew what Malik was to me—that he was my *father*—maybe I'd be able to protect him if they came at him again.

I'd damn well better be able to.

Sipping the latte and wincing at the bitter flavor, I sat down at a table where I had a view of both Malik and his bodyguards, who gave him a little space by sitting several feet away while surveying everyone who entered the shop. I didn't want to barge right over, but I couldn't wait too long either. I'd promised myself today would be the day I actually approached him. There wasn't anything left I could figure out without speaking to the man himself.

But how would he take the news? Would he even believe me? The story sounded so crazy… and there were parts I couldn't exactly admit upfront. Maybe ever. "By the way, I'm a highly trained assassin with hundreds of murders under my belt," didn't seem like the kind of thing *any* parent wanted to hear.

I'd just have to dive in and see how the first part went.

When I'd made it halfway through my latte and become convinced that I really should have ordered a hot chocolate instead, I noticed the signs that Malik was nearing the end of his own coffee. He closed the newspaper he'd been browsing and sat a little straighter in his chair.

My pulse lurched. I inhaled deeply to steady myself, abandoned my mug, and walked over to his table.

As I put myself in his view, Malik glanced up at me. His expression was mild, not particularly curious but not hostile either. Probably warier than it'd been before last week's attack.

He had a faint bruise on his cheek that I hadn't noticed before from a distance, nearly healed but giving that patch of skin a slightly greenish hue.

I yanked my attention back to my purpose. "You're Damien Malik, aren't you?" I said, as though I hadn't been watching him in person and through screens for nearly every waking moment for seven days straight. I could have recognized him from behind at a distance of a hundred yards at this point.

He put on his practiced politician smile and extended a hand to shake mine. "It's always nice to meet a supporter."

I hesitated and then accepted his hand, giving it a quick shake. I couldn't believe I was actually touching him —my father. The first member of my real family I'd spoken to within my memory. My throat tightened abruptly.

Something must have shifted in my expression that troubled Malik, because he pulled back in his chair as he dropped his hand.

"I—I was hoping I could talk to you about something important," I said, blurting out the appeal faster and more clumsily than I'd intended.

"What would that be?" Malik asked cautiously, his other hand rising just slightly.

I knew what that meant. I'd seen him gesture to his bodyguards before when he felt he was getting too crowded. He was seconds away from summoning them, and then I'd never get through everything I needed to say.

I'd wanted to ease into this, but there was no easy way to manage it.

"Please, don't call them over," I said, sinking gingerly into the chair across from him. "I'm not here to hurt anyone. This is about—you had a daughter. Rachel." My birth name still felt foreign rolling off my tongue. "You think she died in a car crash, but it was a set-up. It was arranged so you wouldn't know she'd actually been kidnapped."

Possibly it was a good thing that I'd blurted it all out like that, because I startled Malik enough that he just gaped at me for a second, his whole body motionless. Which meant he wasn't summoning his bodyguards. But it was only a moment before anger jolted him out of his shock.

"I don't know why you'd come to me with a story like this," he said with an edge in his voice, starting to stand up, "but you should get some help and—"

"No!" I protested, leaping up. "I know it's true. I know —because I recently found out that *I'm* her. I'm Rachel. I'm your daughter."

Malik paused and stared at me again. I knew some of the evidence was right there before his eyes. We'd found pictures of his wife—my mother—back in her college days when he'd first met her, before she'd had the plastic surgery that'd upturned the elegantly straight nose I'd inherited from her and plumped up the thin lips we'd once shared. Our hair was still the same, black and wavy.

He *had* to see the truth. I didn't know how else to convince him. I couldn't exactly tell him I'd broken into a high-security genetics facility with a crew of hitmen to test my DNA.

A glimmer of recognition lit in Malik's eyes. Then he closed them and shook his head. "It's not possible."

"I had a stuffed tiger," I said quickly. I was pretty sure the toy had come from my former life, since it'd already looked worn in the earliest videos of my training sessions, before Noelle had stopped letting me bring it along at all. "Orangey-yellow fur with brown stripes and button eyes. My kidnappers—they let me keep it."

Malik pressed the heel of his hand to the bridge of his nose. As he lowered his arm, he peered at me through his fingers. I thought I saw the doubt in his expression fading.

The tiger hadn't been mentioned in any of the news reports about the car crash. I shouldn't be able to know about it unless it'd belonged to me.

I barreled onward, figuring the more I said while he was listening, the better. The Chaos Crew had helped me construct a story that would fit the timeline and sound plausible without getting into the, well, bloodier parts of my role in the household.

"I had no idea I was kidnapped for a long time," I said. "They told me my parents were dead. I finally figured out that something was wrong a couple of years ago and managed to escape them, but it took me the rest of that time to figure out who my real family was. Where I came from."

Malik cleared his throat, likely trying to gather his

thoughts. Was he going to tell me that he'd finished grieving his long-lost daughter, that I couldn't be her no matter what I said? Would he send me away in disbelief? Anxiety roared through my veins as I waited for a response.

He hadn't called the bodyguards yet. That was a small sign in my favor.

Malik took a few slow breaths. Then he fixed a more piercing look on me than he'd given me before in his initial surprise.

"If you are who you say you are, do you remember what you were wearing the day you were taken?" he asked, his gray eyes that were nearly identical to my own intent on mine.

I couldn't tell whether he really wanted me to answer that question. It'd be easier for him if it turned out I was lying, wouldn't it? He could go back to his normal life where he'd set aside his tragic loss decades ago.

I sucked my lower lip under my teeth. "I was so young. I don't remember my life before the kidnapping at all."

He sighed and leaned back in his seat. I groped for a better answer I could give him, and my mind latched on to my memories of the old videos Blaze had lifted from Noelle's laptop.

I *had* been young in them. In the very first one, I'd been just a crying toddler begging for her mommy and daddy. That image was ingrained in my mind now. The clothes I'd been wearing had been dirty and wrinkled, not like the trim tees and sweats I'd been dressed in later.

Was it possible they'd left me in my original clothes for the first few days while they tried to ease me into my new situation? It was worth checking.

"I did have one old set of clothes—an outfit I don't remember my kidnappers giving me," I added, improvising. "They were different from the others. A little yellow romper with frilly sleeves and a sunflower embroidered over the chest. Was that it?"

Malik's stance went rigid again, but this time there was nothing but amazement on his face.

"And a little bow on the collar," he said, barely more than a whisper.

A smile touched my lips, a wave of exhilaration rushing through me. "Yes."

He brought his hand to his mouth now and then lowered it again. He couldn't seem to peel his eyes away from me. "Rachel?"

The name meant nothing to me now, but I nodded. I could hardly tell him I'd rather go by Dess or Decima, the names the household—my kidnappers—had given me. Regardless of its source, it felt like me far more than "Rachel" did. But he'd hardly understand that.

Malik opened his mouth and closed it again. I'd never seen him lost for words in all the videos I'd watched of his political activities.

His bodyguards must have noticed his agitation, because they strode over to our table, glowering at me. "Is everything all right, sir?" one asked.

"Yes," Malik said, motioning for them to go back to

their seats. "Yes, I think it is." He kept staring at me. "You look exactly like your mother did when I met her."

"I've seen pictures of her in college," I said, glad I could be honest about that. "That's part of how I figured it out."

"You—She'll be so—" He caught himself and composed his expression. His voice came out more measured, falling into professional mode. "I need outside confirmation. I'm sure you can understand. Can I take a strand of your hair—or you could spit in a cup for me—I'm not sure what would work best."

"Well, there's lots of cups here," I said. I'd expected something like this, and it'd work in my favor when he got independent confirmation of our connection. "I guess I'd better use a disposable one."

"Yes." Malik leapt up and hustled to the counter to ask for one of the takeaway paper mugs with a lid. He returned to the table and handed it to me. Feeling a little awkward, I summoned a dollop of saliva onto my tongue and spat it into the cup.

Malik took it from me, holding the cup like it was made out of precious crystal. "I need to go," he said. "But as soon as I've checked—what's the easiest way I can contact you?" He pulled his phone out of his pocket to make a note.

I recited the number from the burner phone Julius had given me, and my father entered it with swift taps on the screen. He tucked his phone away and gazed down at me one last time. Relief was trickling through me that I'd managed to mostly convince him, but my gut twisted at the same time.

It was a lot of pressure, living up to someone's vision of their dead child come back to life, wasn't it? I hadn't totally been prepared for that.

"You're okay for now?" he asked.

"Absolutely," I said. "I've got a job and a place to live, friends who've been helping me out. I just hope we can get to know each other better once you get the results back."

"Of course." He ran his fingers back over his hair and dipped his head to me, a shadow crossing his eyes. "I'll be in touch soon. In the meantime, be careful out there."

I thought about telling him that I could take down a man like his domestic terrorist in three seconds flat if I had to, but that would be revealing a little too much information for comfort. Instead, I smiled at him. "Thank you. I will."

But if any of the people associated with the household came at me or my father again, I was going to make sure they regretted it.

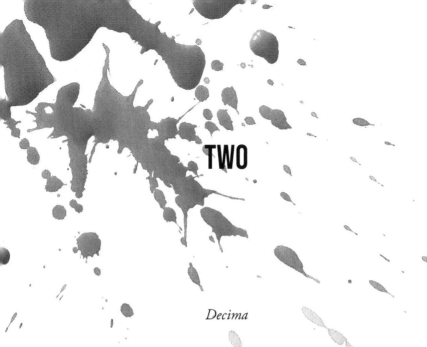

TWO

Decima

AFTER I'D FINISHED TELLING the crew about my first conversation with my birth father, I couldn't stop pacing the room. Which wasn't for the best, because the hotel we were staying in was a converted factory that'd kept many industrial-style features for atmosphere. The ceiling of the large suite held bare heating ducts, two of the walls were old brick... and the lighting fixtures dangled on steel cables at random intervals, just low enough that I could bonk my head on them if I wasn't careful.

I wasn't so sure about that particular design choice.

"It sounds like the meeting went well," Julius said as I dodged one of the dangling lamps.

I peeked at the leader of the Chaos Crew from the corner of my eye, not bothering to say anything. He should have looked intimidating with his substantial height and brawn and the spiky tattoo that showed around the collar and sleeves of his tight-fitting shirt, but I could tell he was hesitant to make a more definitive statement. Julius rarely showed uncertainty, but he cared about us more than he would have openly admitted. The last thing he would have wanted was to hurt me by saying the wrong thing, especially when the stakes were so high.

Garrison, on the other hand, rarely set aside his casually disaffected mask. He shrugged, his hazel eyes cool. "I don't think you could have expected it to go much better, honestly."

I shifted my gaze to the lightbulb that hung alone above my bed, squinting as the brightness seared into my eyes. They didn't understand. With a sigh, I flopped onto the admittedly luxurious mattress. The Chaos Crew always picked high class, if sometimes unusual, accommodations.

"It doesn't matter how well that first chat went," I said. "He knows nothing about me. I could barely tell him anything. He'd never be able to accept who I really am— what I've been doing all this time... He'd probably want me shipped off to a maximum-security prison."

Blaze, in his usual upbeat manner, shook his head with a swish of his pale red hair and moved to sit at the other end of my bed. "I don't think you're giving him enough credit. He *is* your dad. He's finally got you back in his life after thinking you were dead for so long. How could he give that up?"

I turned my head and raised my eyebrows at the hacker. "You know more about his anti-crime policies than I do. He'd like to see small-time drug dealers serving 20 years in federal prison, so how do you think he'd react to an assassin who's murdered her way around the globe?"

Garrison snorted. "Obviously you wouldn't tell him about that part."

"So I'll be lying to him the whole time. And it might come out anyway. Even if I keep it hidden, how could he possibly relate to me?"

Talon, normally a solemnly quiet presence among the others, stepped forward with a flex of his square jaw. "We don't kill innocent people. We take down the same criminals that he wants to put away for life. It's not so different."

I grimaced. "*You* don't kill innocent people. I've been doing it my entire life without knowing it."

"Which is exactly why it isn't your fault," Julius pointed out. "And you've taken up our approach since then. By killing criminals, you're helping his agenda, exactly as Talon said. Maybe you can't tell him that, but you can remember that in a way, you're on the same page."

They were trying to reassure me, but even from the short time I'd been studying Damien Malik, I felt sure he'd never see my situation that way. He'd think I was an even worse criminal than the ones I'd eliminated. If he ever realized what I was and what I'd done, any familial warmth would vanish in an instant.

I'd lose the only real family I'd ever had before I'd really gotten a chance to experience what it was like having one.

And that was if he called me back at all. What if the test he ran on my saliva got messed up and gave him a negative? What if he decided having me back in his life would be a complication his career couldn't afford?

I groaned and flung my arm over my eyes in a way even I knew was overdramatic.

Garrison tsked his tongue at me and headed to the suite's kitchenette with a swipe of his hand through his shaggy blond hair. "It'll be fine. And any part of it that's not fine, we'll *make* fine. I brought a couple of tins of hot cocoa mix with me—including one of your favorites. I'll make you a cup, and you can focus on that instead of this guy who should have jumped at the chance to have you as a daughter."

My lips twitched with a hint of a smile at the understated compliment in his words. Garrison didn't often give out anything resembling praise—and I didn't think he liked sharing his treasured hot chocolate all that much either. Beneath his typical snark, I knew he cared about me too.

The thought of hot chocolate filling my mouth sent a spark of excitement through me despite the uncertainty and stress that had taken over my senses. I shook my head anyway. "I'm still a little jittery from the caffeine I drank earlier," I admitted. "I'll stick with water for now. Why don't you tell me what you and Blaze found earlier? That'll take my mind off things."

I hadn't been the only one at work when I'd confronted Malik. Blaze and Garrison had been continuing their own mission investigating the bombing at his office. If it'd been connected to the same people who'd run the household, we needed to know ASAP—and then we needed to deal with them before they attacked my father again.

Garrison leaned back against the counter, his mouth twisting. "I talked to a *lot* of people. No one saw much other than presumably those who were killed by the initial shots or the blast following it. Everyone seems to honestly believe that Malik was targeted by an extremist who disagrees with his politics, someone acting independently. But none of them had any real proof of that."

Julius rubbed his jaw. "What are they making of Malik's reaction to the attack?"

"If anything, it's bolstered people's good opinions of him," Garrison said. "He's been the perfect boss, accommodating and kind in all the ways that matter. He's visited the families of those who were killed, and he's given a substantial number of extra paid days off for the close friends of those who were lost."

"That seems like a good sign in general," Blaze said. "He cares about the people he works with."

The people he worked with weren't mass murderers, but I didn't say that out loud. "So, you weren't able to figure out much about the bomber from the people you talked to."

Garrison sighed and made an apologetic expression at me. "They didn't have much to cough up. If they'd tried to dodge my questions, I'd have gotten it out of them."

Blaze shot him a self-deprecating smile. "I'd question your supreme confidence, but the truth is, I couldn't find much on my end either. I'd rather believe there simply *isn't* much there to find than that we're both incompetent."

As Garrison glowered at him, Blaze scooped my socked foot into his hands and started massaging the arch absently. I welcomed the gesture, but it wasn't enough to take my mind off the issue at hand. "You couldn't track down any leads at all?" I asked.

"Unfortunately, no," the hacker admitted. "Nothing substantial enough that I'd want to put ourselves at risk pursuing it. I'm still looking at everything I uploaded from his computer. There was a lot to scan through, but so far no indications that he had any idea an attack was coming or records of previous hostility. I tapped into the security cameras in the building where the bombing happened, but with the angle the guy was standing at, the hood of his jacket hides his face. All I could tell you for sure is that it was a man, he was pretty average in height and weight, and no one in the office appeared to recognize him. He was a total stranger."

"That's the same impression I got from the footage," Garrison said in grudging agreement.

I let out a huff of frustration. "Why does this have to be so *hard*?"

"Well, either it was a random lunatic, in which case there's nothing else to find," Julius said with his usual strategic precision. "Or if it was connected to your 'household,' we're dealing with people who have a lot of power and resources. They couldn't have pulled off all this without a hell of an advantage."

"Great," Garrison muttered. "Someone with power and influence right outside of Washington D.C. That sure lowers the suspect pool."

The pressure of Blaze's massaging fingers started to make me tense up more than relax me. I eased my foot away and sat up, my hands curling into the blanket on the bed. There was too much I didn't know, even more questions hanging over me than ever before, and who knew how many lives hung in the balance while we searched for answers?

Talon walked over and rested a hand on my shoulder. "We're not going to get any farther into this right now. Do you want to spar and let out some of that tension?"

I looked up into his steady ice-blue gaze. He was trying to help me the best way he knew how. We'd blown off plenty of tension in the past with our fists, sometimes leading into… other activities that could provide an excellent release. Not that I was feeling at all turned on while I had this ball of stress in my gut.

But it was a good suggestion. Maybe a workout was exactly what I needed—to burn away all of my energy and emotions before revisiting the situation. I needed to think about it with a clear mind, and right now my thoughts were muddled with uncertainty and self-doubt.

I was just standing up when my phone rang. My pulse hiccupped. The number on the display wasn't one I recognized.

My hand shook as I raised the phone to my ear. "Hello?"

"Is this Rachel?"

My immediate reaction was to say no, but I caught myself just in time, recognizing the voice and understanding why he'd used it. "Y—yes. That's me."

The sound of Malik's joy carried through the connection. "It didn't take long for my people to run the DNA test, and the results couldn't be clearer. I'm sorry for keeping you waiting while I verified it. You really are my daughter."

There was so much awe in his words that my chest constricted. I struggled to find the right way to answer. This was exactly what I'd wanted to hear, but now I had no idea what happened next.

"I'm so glad to hear from you," I managed after a moment. "Where do we go from here?"

"We have so much to discuss, and I'd prefer not to do it over the phone. Now that you've come back to us, I want to really be there with you as much as possible. If it wouldn't be too much all at once, I'd love for you to meet the rest of the family. I'll be home for the day tomorrow. Maybe we can spend some time getting to know you and the young lady you've become."

If I'd had any doubts about that plan, the eagerness in his tone—eagerness to get to know *me*—would have dissolved it.

"Yes," I said, a smile crossing my face. "I think I'd like that a lot."

He gave me the address and the time I should arrive. I could barely keep up with his enthusiastic voice when my entire world and everything I knew seemed to be heading in a direction I'd never have expected it to go.

I had a family—one who couldn't wait to meet me. I wanted to believe it would go well, but there were so many factors that could make everything fall apart.

What if I was too awkward after all my time shut away from the regular world? What if they realized that I was nothing like them and hated me?

I dragged in a deep breath as I said my goodbyes and hung up. I had to go and face this new challenge no matter how nervous I was.

But I couldn't shake the looming sense that if I screwed things up tomorrow, I'd lose my family all over again, and *that* would be all my fault.

THREE

Decima

JUST OUTSIDE THE Malik family home, I hesitated.

I knew that I had the right place—a large, two-story home with cedar porch furniture and decorations that looked... cozy. I'd imagined a mansion like the household's or a large, sleekly designed home from a magazine, but this was a more modest building, and one that looked lived-in. Around the side of the wrap-around porch, I spotted a splash of brighter color from beach towels and a pair of swimming trunks hanging over the railing to dry. I couldn't see the pool from the front of the house, but I imagined the porch would lead me there if I continued around.

Instead, I eyed the beige front door, a wreath hanging there with the word "welcome" written in a calligraphic style across the center. All I had to do was knock, and I had no doubt these people would welcome me into their home as if I truly was one of them. But once they met me… would everything change?

I was nothing like the Maliks. I'd never lived in a cozy house with a pool. I'd never had people who loved me the way that a normal family loved one another. I wasn't even sure what love *was*.

I raised my hand to knock on the door, but it opened before I had the chance. Damien Malik greeted me with a wide smile, wearing khaki shorts and a collared shirt with a vibrant Hawaiian print.

Was this how he dressed when he was home with his family? I couldn't remember ever seeing him in anything that wasn't on the grayscale, but all my images of him were from his work life. Apparently the guy knew how to relax a little.

A plethora of emotions flashed through his eyes as he looked me over, likely taking in the dress shirt and slacks I'd worn in a misguided attempt to fit in. I'd assumed that meeting a politician in his home would be similar to doing it in his office, but this was nowhere near as formal as I'd anticipated judging by my father's clothing.

After a second, Malik shook his head. "Sorry, I didn't mean to leave you standing outside. My wife would fillet me for my manners. It's just… it's hard to comprehend that you're really *here*—the daughter I'd spent over twenty years thinking that we lost." He sucked in a deep breath. "Enough of my sappy rambling. I can tell it's making you uncomfortable. Come in, please."

This was the defining moment, so I plastered on my best ingratiating smile and stepped through the doorway.

The inside of the house gave off the same welcoming energy as the outside of it. I walked inside through the entranceway, and despite what appeared to be a coat closet, a few pairs of shoes scattered the entrance rug, and coats hung from makeshift hooks on the walls—over a dozen at least.

How many people had gathered for this get-together?

Malik's hand hovered over my shoulder and then dropped to his side as he thought better of attempting physical contact just yet. "The rest of the family is in the living room waiting to meet you. I hope you won't find it too much. Your mother and I couldn't help sharing the news, and everyone wanted to see you with their own eyes." He chuckled awkwardly. "I promise that none of us bite."

That was such a dad joke—so much of a dad joke that I recognized it as one from my limited knowledge of pop culture without ever having had a dad before—that it put me more at ease.

"I can't wait to meet them," I said, which was kind of true. I did want to get to know my whole family, but I'd expected this first visit to be just Damien and his wife… my mother. I was still having trouble wrapping my own head around that idea.

Maybe it was better to get all the introductions over at once and to get a sense of the overall family vibe. They must be close-knit if they'd all jumped to visit this quickly.

Malik—Damien—my mind balked at thinking of him

as *Dad*—motioned me to a doorway to the left of a broad wooden staircase. "We'll have a little private get-together with the immediate family first. The others can wait. I don't want to drop too much on you all at once."

I dragged in a breath with a little relief. "Okay."

Damien led me into a small sitting room. A woman I recognized as his wife from the photos and an unfamiliar young man who looked to be in his late teens stood up from the sofa at our entrance.

Mrs. Malik froze in place, staring at me with wide eyes. Damien went over to her, and she clutched his shoulder, never tearing her eyes from me.

"My Rachel," she whispered, and pressed her hand to her mouth. She took a step closer, searching my face, and I found myself searching hers too, looking for the college girl who'd looked like me.

I could catch traces of that younger woman in her eyes and the line of her jaw, though the shape of her nose and lips had been altered by her plastic surgery. Fine lines were starting to creep from the corners of her eyes and mouth like they did on Damien. But even with the subtle signs of age, she was beautiful with her naturalistic makeup and striped sundress.

Damien beckoned me over, and I stepped hesitantly toward the two of them. "Mom?"

The word sounded alien falling from my lips, but a beaming smile spread across the woman's face. She wrapped her arms around me in a hug that I had to stop myself from tensing against.

My instinctive resistance only lasted a second. Then I

started to relax into her embrace. It felt… warm. Motherly, even. I laughed inwardly at my little joke and let my arms rise to return the hug.

I had a mother. A mother who'd been missing me all this time.

"Rachel," she murmured, and eased back to gaze into my eyes again, her own shining with joy. "My sweet girl has come back to us. It's a miracle."

A strange sensation swelled in my chest. I'd never felt anything like it before. In all my years at the household—all the years of Ana taking a semi-maternal role—nobody had ever hugged me like this. Nobody had ever shown I *mattered* like this.

I tore my gaze away to glance at the boy who'd stayed by the sofa, where he was eying me skeptically. He had the same storm gray eyes as both Damien and me, but his were lighter than mine, diluted with a touch of green like my mother's. *Our* mother's? He also had the tawny brown hair I'd seen in pictures of Damien when he was younger and a height that matched the older man's, though he hadn't quite filled out that height yet. His limbs were still a bit gangly.

My mother stepped back and took a deep breath, dabbing beneath her eyes with her finger. "Goodness, I'm going to make a mess of myself," she said with a laugh. She reached toward the boy and tugged him over. "You can keep calling me Mom, of course, but if you're more comfortable with first names while you get to know us, I'm Iris. This is our son—your brother—Carter."

Carter gave an awkward wave, and I did the same

thing back. Neither of us knew what to say about that. From the looks of him, he'd been born a few years after I was kidnapped. We'd never existed in the same space until now.

Then the door to the other part of the house flew open, and a short woman with frizzy gray hair burst into the entranceway. She spoke before anyone could get a word out. "Now I know my son told us to stay in there, but I was beginning to think that he was blowing smoke up my ass with the story of his daughter coming back from the dead."

Her presence made the room feel cramped. I took a step back, and more people flooded in behind her. But the plump old lady took all my attention from the others. She was small and wizened, but she bulldozed over Damien's brief protests, and I knew immediately that I *didn't* want to be in her path.

She looked me up and down as she approached, and I wondered what she saw when she looked at me. Her sharp eyes didn't look as if they missed much. A prickle ran down my back

"Grandma Ruby, you're scaring her," Carter said, giving her a playful poke in the arm.

She shot an affectionate glower at Carter, and I could finally breathe. "Now Carter, let me have my fun. She's as much my grandbaby as you are." The woman looked at me and smiled. "Rachel," she said with undiluted affection in her tone, and pulled me into a hug just as my mother had.

I didn't know how to react surrounded by this much affection. It felt like they were excited to see a woman who wasn't here. Who even was Rachel? I knew that'd been my name years ago, but I'd never used it within my memory. Each time they called me by her name, I felt like an imposter. I was Decima, and I didn't know how to be anyone else.

I knew better than to ask to go by the name my kidnappers had given me, though. I could only imagine their looks of horror.

So, I stood there, allowing the crowd to come and devour me with tight hugs. Aunts, uncles, and cousins looked me over, commenting on how much I looked like my mother or father—comments that I knew were more for politeness than anything.

My eyes caught on a few of them more than the others —people who were easier to read, maybe? Maybe their personalities complimented mine, making it easier to meet their gazes. One family in particular—my first cousin, aunt, and uncle on my father's side—drew my attention.

The man and wife each had fiery red hair. Their daughter, who looked around my age or a tad older, had the complexion of a redhead, complete with freckles her foundation couldn't quite hide, but she'd dyed her wavy locks black. My aunt and uncle clasped each other's hands as they took me in, but my cousin seemed almost as interested in her phone as my arrival.

Maybe I should have been insulted, but something about her disinterest reassured me. I wasn't a big deal to everyone. To her, this was just another day. Maybe it didn't have to be such a momentous occasion.

Damien began tossing out names, and I tried to

commit each one to memory. The woman with the dyed black hair was Margaret. Despite her apparent boredom, my father clapped her on the shoulder. "Margaret's twenty-five, so she's the closest in age to you. I'm sure you two will get along great. She and your Aunt Mabel and Uncle Henry come around a lot, so you'll see plenty of them."

He was talking as if I was going to be living here from now on. A prickle of apprehension ran over my skin, even though I knew he wouldn't be taking that step so quickly.

Margaret lifted her gaze from her phone. Her voice came out low and monotonous. "Did they torture you? Like kidnappers in crime shows or whatever?"

"Margaret!" Aunt Mabel said with a gasp.

I wasn't actually offended by the question, but I wasn't sure how to answer it either. I guessed Noelle and the others had kind of tortured me by forcing me to train, but I couldn't say that without getting into the whole "I was raised to be an assassin" thing it seemed better to keep on the down low.

"No," I said, forcing a small laugh. Every pair of eyes focused even more intently on me, curious as to how I would answer her. "No, of course not. I didn't even know that I was kidnapped until recently. They acted like I was a part of their family." A brutally disciplined and distant family, but close enough.

Grandma Ruby was the next to speak. "They kidnapped you. How did you not realize something was wrong? They took you from us, and they never even mentioned that you came from somewhere else?"

I gave an apologetic grimace. Did she really blame me?

"I guess I was so young that after a while the old memories didn't stick with me," I said. "I grew up with them, and they acted like their way of life was normal and that they were the only ones who could protect me from the dangerous world."

And the whole time they'd been the most dangerous people in it. People who'd already torn apart my real family.

"Well, something has to be done about them," my grandmother spat out. My grandfather—Bo, one of the others had called him—came over and slung his arm around her shoulders, but she barely seemed to notice his presence in her fury. "It's disgusting what they did to you and to us."

Her husband looked down at her. "Don't be getting upset. She's here now, and that's what matters the most. Isn't that right, Rachel?"

I nodded, and the smile that had felt forced before seemed to stick in place without much effort now. How lucky was I that I'd found a family who cared so much about someone who was essentially a stranger to them? Even if their questions made me edgy, they only asked because I mattered to them.

If I'd died during a mission for the household, Noelle would have replaced me, and she and her colleagues would all have moved on with their lives. Nobody there would have mourned me.

I was finally a part of something bigger in a good way,

not just a pawn to be maneuvered and manipulated for the sake of someone's selfish ends.

With that thought, the secrets I was keeping to protect myself left a bitter aftertaste in my mouth. Julius's face flashed through my mind. Then Talon's and Blaze's. Garrison's.

They were a family in a way, but they weren't like this one. I was tied to them through loyalty and mutual respect, not blood. But they knew my story and what I'd done with my life. They knew everything about me, and they accepted it all without restraint.

I was going to spend this entire encounter acting like a woman who I didn't know—one who was so far from the woman I had become. I'd created a story to explain the time I'd been away from this family, and if I ever told them the truth…

Well, I didn't know if I could ever tell them the truth about myself. It was hard not to imagine that if I tried, I'd lose them all.

I looked around at all the cousins, aunts, and uncles, then toward Grandma Ruby and Grandpa Bo who stood tall and held her. Then, I turned my attention to my parents, standing side-by-side with Carter in front of them.

Damien's face had become a rigid mask of determination. "We're going to bring the people who kidnapped you to justice," he swore.

My heart skipped a beat as I absorbed that promise. Maybe he knew more about my kidnappers than I'd expected. If it'd been personal—and how could it not be to some extent, with the lengths they'd gone to in order to steal me away—he must know who at least some of his enemies were.

"I don't know how much help I'm going to be in accomplishing that," I said, sucking my lower lip under my teeth. I knew more than I was going to admit, but I couldn't lay everything on the table. Not yet. I needed to know what information would be the most useful in finding the people responsible without jeopardizing my own secrets. "I was isolated from everyone except for the few people who were looking after me, and when I realized what was going on, the situation had turned so dangerous I couldn't stay to find out anything that'd help track them down."

My father frowned. "What about those people who looked after you?" he asked, tightening his jaw, but he loosened it with a deep breath and shook his head. "You were around them a lot. I'm sure there are some things that you discovered, even if you don't realize it."

"Well," I said with a wince, "the woman who spent the most time caring for me was killed by some other group of criminals, so she's out of the picture. That's when I ran. It must have been some kind of gang war or something."

I shuddered, completely for effect. That was how a normal person would react when thinking of a murder, right?

Damien stared off at a place on the wall for a moment, his expression pensive. Was he angry because I couldn't provide him with a lead, or was it more than that? Did he have ideas about who might have been involved that he didn't want to share with me out of fear of re-traumatizing me?

I had to show I was at least a little more resilient than that. "If you have any leads or ideas about the investigation, I'd really like to be a part of it," I said, struggling to hit the right level of enthusiasm. "I want to know the reason I was taken as much as you do."

My father rested his hand on my back with a reassuring pat, though his face was still serious. "There's no need for that. I'm sorry for badgering you about it at all. You've been through enough already. The investigators will want to talk to you, of course, and get any details you can offer, but I'll make sure it ends there."

How did I convince him that I wanted to be a part of this investigation? "I'm honestly happy to help however I can. I want to see these people brought to justice too." Preferably by my own hand, I added silently. "Please don't worry about it being an imposition."

Damien's jaw flexed, but the smile held in place. "Enough on this awful subject," he said, squeezing my shoulder lightly. "Let's focus on everything good that's come out of today. We have you back with us—nothing could be more worth celebrating than that. Why don't we go sit down to lunch and we can talk more there, about lighter subjects."

I couldn't continue pushing without sounding suspicious, so I simply nodded and let my gaze slip over the gathered family members again. "I'm looking forward to getting to know you all better."

As everyone streamed into the hall, heading for the

dining room, I caught a glimpse of another shadow crossing Damien's face, there just for a moment before he caught my eyes and aimed another smile at me.

Something was bothering him. Was it just that I hadn't offered a clear path to finding the criminals he must want to bring to justice more than any before?

Or was there something more going on here that I was missing?

FOUR

Julius

I SWUNG my putter and nailed the golf ball, sending it up the small hill. As I watched, the neon green sphere raced straight toward the hole, ricocheted off the back border, and rolled back toward us, invalidating my entire swing. "Fucking hell," I grumbled, stepping back for Talon to take his turn.

I didn't bother watching him, knowing that if he didn't get an immediate hole-in-one, he'd come close to it. I should have never suggested we join in this mini golfing expedition to keep an eye on Dess and her family, but once they made it deep enough in the course, we would have struggled to keep an eye out without being spotted if we weren't players ourselves.

Dressing like golf-course employees had been the second option, but the margin for error was too high. This place didn't employ that many people. It would have taken only one genuine employee to catch us and kick us off the course.

So here I stood, groaning as Talon sent his ball toward the hole. With a single bank, it clattered in effortlessly. He tugged at the lapels of his polo shirt with a satisfied air.

I glowered at him. "You could at least *act* humble."

A sliver of a smile crossed my long-time partner's lips, and I'd worked with him *so* long that I could recognize it as a taunt when most wouldn't have. "You could act like you know what you're doing," he retorted.

He was the only member of the crew who'd have dared to make a comment like that, and he'd only have made it when the younger men weren't around. I let out a disgruntled huff and lined up my shot before hitting it haphazardly. I knew how to aim guns, not golf clubs.

My ball didn't go anywhere near the hole, but it stayed atop the hill, so we strode up there together, looking over at the next part of the course as we walked.

Dess stood before her ball. She swung the putter with about as much skill as I had, which soothed my wounded ego a little. The ball lifted and soared into the rocks outside the range. Her mother let out a soft giggle and patted Dess on the shoulder with a few words of encouragement. Dess shook herself, and I could see her reining in her natural competitive instincts to plaster an easy-going smile on her face.

I had to restrain a grimace at the sight of that artificial friendliness. She didn't *fit* with this family: her mother perfectly outfitted in white capris and visor, her brother slouching along the side of the course as he leaned on his club nonchalantly, her father completely at ease with his putter as he tapped it on the greenery.

"Must be a rich person thing," I muttered as I eyed them and then my ball. "I'd have thought they'd stick to the real thing, but I guess this is just a mini version of the country club."

Blaze had surveyed this place after Dess had gotten the invitation. I'd wanted to see how her birth family interacted with her for myself, for reasons I didn't feel I needed to spell out. The Maliks did head off to a country club where they had a membership every weekend that Damien was home, but the owner of this miniature course was a donor to their campaign, and sometimes the family came by here to play.

"They're easing Dess up to the full challenge," Talon remarked in his usual unemotional way.

"She doesn't need that kind of challenge. She's got plenty of other things on her plate."

"They don't know that."

"If they had any brains, they'd figure it out." I managed to hit my ball into the hole, finally, and straightened up. Damien was just taking his own turn, easily hitting a hole-in-two. My hackles rose for no reason I could put my finger on. "He's just keeping up appearances by coming here, buttering up the donors."

Talon shrugged. "That's part of his job, isn't it?"

"I don't trust anyone who mostly thinks about what they can get out of the people they're supposedly working on behalf of," I replied.

As we moved to the next part of the course, Talon

spun his ball in his hand and studied me. "He's her father, and he planned a simple activity to keep them entertained."

"His being her father doesn't mean anything. Family doesn't automatically make someone a good person." As Talon should know, although my own sense of personal consideration stopped me from saying that out loud. He didn't need salt rubbed in the wound openly.

From the way my friend's eyes flashed, the remark had hit home anyway. "Playing the role of parents in public doesn't mean much, but he's been good with her so far. She seems happy."

I had to admit, if only in brooding silence, that he was right. I'd thought that seeing her happy would be the only thing I'd want, but as I watched her exchange small talk and the occasional grin with these people, I couldn't shake the feeling that I wished she *wasn't* so relieved to be with them.

I wanted her to have *sustainable* happiness, but the Maliks—and their political lifestyle—didn't seem like a life I'd ever have envisioned for her. Maybe it was the right fit for her and she'd just never had the chance to grow into it, but I had trouble believing that after seeing her in real action.

But I couldn't pretend away the victorious bounce in her step after she knocked her ball into the hole. Or the way she leaned into her mother's hand when the woman touched her hair as if confirming her daughter was really still there. Or her chuckle as she gave her brother a light punch to the shoulder and laughed harder at his playful complaints in response.

God, that laugh could have sent me into an early grave. The sight of her tipping back her head to the sun, delight shining in her pale face and dark eyes, tugged at my heart.

Had she ever laughed with the crew like that? I wasn't sure I'd seen that much joy fill her face when she talked to us. Sometimes she looked mischievous or content. She'd smiled in amusement, but never unadulterated happiness like this.

Would she decide to stay with us when her birth family could give her something I doubted we ever could?

Damien came over and motioned to Dess like he was giving her advice on her swing. My jaw started to clench until I forced it to relax.

"Look at the way he hovers over her," I couldn't help saying to Talon. "He needs to give her some space."

Talon didn't comment, simply getting into position on the next mini green. I watched him line up his shot before I switched to studying the Maliks some more. "It also seems pretty careless to take his family out in public when his life is under threat. Do his bodyguards have any idea how to do their job? We've been behind him the entire time, keeping watch, and nobody has looked twice at us. Shouldn't he be more concerned about protecting his family? Especially the daughter who he just got back."

I narrowed my eyes at Damien. He didn't even bother to position himself to block his family's backs.

Talon raised his eyebrows at me. "Do you actually

think he's being sketchy or are you just bothered seeing Dess that happy with them?"

"Why would that bother me?" I shot back automatically, and then my gut twisted. It had been bothering me. I wasn't going to lie to myself.

"The reporters are keeping their distance because Malik insisted that they give Dess some room without having cameras in her face," Talon said into my silence, pointing to where I remembered seeing them outside the mini-golf place. "That shows that he cares at least a little bit about her healing from her kidnapping."

"It's the least he could do," I muttered.

"He could have been milking the publicity." Talon rubbed his jaw. "And this place isn't *that* public. We walked through a metal detector to get in. The course has a pretty good wall around it. I wouldn't be surprised if it's easier to get into the country club grounds."

"All right, all right." I glowered at him, and he gazed evenly back at me. "*I'm* looking out for her here too," I reminded him.

"And so am I," Talon said. "But the more people who are doing it, the safer she'll be. So far, he hasn't appeared to be a threat to anything except how much time and attention she has left to give us."

He took his swing. The damned ball soared across the green and thumped to the ground right next to the hole, which it promptly rolled into.

I should have brought Blaze. He wouldn't have golfed me under the table.

But Talon had a point. I had to acknowledge that

Malik could have taken the opportunity to advance his political capital and instead had focused on his family's needs. Having a kidnapped child would go a long way to prop up his anti-criminal agenda, and not using the story to his advantage showed a level of commitment to Dess that I couldn't deny.

I wondered if the reason I was so hesitant to trust Malik—the reason I struggled to trust Dess alone with him—wasn't because of Malik at all. I'd witnessed powerful people making decisions that hurt everyone around them plenty of times, and I'd rarely stepped in unless I was getting paid to. The only difference was that Dess was involved, and the thought of something happening to her... Even imagining it for a second sent a jab of pain through the center of my chest.

I didn't have a strategy or any sort of plan to fix this situation if it went sour.

I watched Dess bite her bottom lip as she looked between her ball and the hole. She was so gorgeous she literally took my breath away. She clutched the putter and took a shot that wasn't half bad this time. With a grin I could tell wasn't forced, she bobbed on her feet and glanced at her parents, soaking in their approving exclamations.

Normally I was in total control of my reactions. Why was I letting Dess's association with her birth family get to me so much?

Because every time she stepped out of arm's reach, some part of me screamed that I had to protect her. I'd always treated her as an equal within the crew... but she was more than that. I sure as hell didn't have the same urges and impulses with the other men as I did with her. I wanted her—and I'd also have done anything to know she was safe and happy.

Shit. Was I *falling* for her?

I'd never cared this much about another woman—that much I knew. But as I watched her with her family, I wasn't sure it mattered anyway. She'd eventually have to make a choice. Her father was a criminal hunter, and I was a criminal. Telling her how I felt would only make it harder if she decided to pursue a life with her family. I couldn't do that to her.

I *wouldn't* do that to her. I'd keep my mouth shut until she decided where she wanted to take her life from here.

My phone vibrated in my pocket. I tore my eyes away from Dess as I pulled it out. A text from Blaze had popped up on the screen. I scanned it and then turned to Talon reluctantly.

"Blaze has found a concerning post online that he thinks we should see. It looks like Dess is safe enough here. We'd better check this out."

———

We found Blaze in the hotel room with his gaze skimming back and forth between his laptop and his propped-up tablet. At the pace with which he flicked through the content on both, I wondered how he could read anything they said.

I closed the door firmly behind me, jarring him from

his state of concentration. He swiveled in his seat and then pressed his hand against the spot in his side that still gave him a twinge of pain when he moved too quickly. "I wasn't expecting you back this fast."

"More like you lose all sense of time when you get in that state," Garrison snarked, coming over as we gathered around Blaze at the table. "Are you going to spill the beans now?"

I nodded. "Yes, what did you find that was so important?"

Blaze dragged in a breath. "It could be nothing. But the details, and the way it's written... Well, I'll let you have a look first so you can draw your own conclusions."

He spun toward the devices and clicked on his keyboard. Several windows fell away, leaving one that he maximized on the laptop's screen.

"I have a constant search on the web with several keywords related to our work, and I added some for Dess once we knew her situation. This result popped up today. It's from a DC newspaper."

It was a column of missed connections postings, people searching for someone whose eye they'd caught on a busy bus or across a grocery store. One of the longer posts was highlighted. I leaned closer, squinting at the screen to read it.

Rachel – You got coffee and talked about your accident. You think you've finally come home. There's so much more I need to tell you. Not all the answers are in our saliva. If you care about the truth and not just making a family, please get in touch.

Then there was a phone number.

A chill rippled down my spine. "Could it be someone jerking her around?" I demanded. "How many of those details—the coffee shop, the faked accident, her giving Malik her spit—have been reported in the media?"

Blaze exhaled in a rush. "Good. You don't think it's a coincidence either. The specifics are so on the nose—and most of it *hasn't* been reported. Malik had a blood test done to confirm the result he got from the spit test before they went to the media, and the public stories have only talked about that. And he's never given any details about their first meeting in the coffee shop." The hacker paused, his leg jiggling with nervous energy under the table. "Whoever this is, they were watching Dess when she confronted him. Closely enough to hear at least a little of what she said too."

"And he—or she—thinks they have some important 'truth' to tell her?" Garrison said, scowling. "Why the fuck should we trust this shady creep?"

I folded my arms over my chest. Resolve wound around my chest, stilling the shiver of anxiety inside it. "We shouldn't. But we have to show this to Dess. It's addressing her—it should be her call what she does about it."

"It could be someone who knows something about her kidnapping," Talon pointed out. "Creep or not, we'll want that information."

I wished we could charge in there and demand it ourselves, but as much as I wanted to protect Dess, lying to her wasn't going to accomplish that in the long run. She deserved her freedom after having it denied for so long.

"I'm sure Dess will agree," I said. "We'll fill her in as soon as she gets back, and she'll make the call about what we do next."

FIVE

Decima

I TOOK a deep breath and glanced across the car at Julius, who was poised behind the wheel. A van rumbled by in the parking lot we'd chosen for its central location in D.C. The leather seat felt stiff under my ass.

"Your honest opinion," I said, holding my phone in my right hand and fidgeting with the hem of my shirt with my left. "Is this going to be worth it?"

The leader of the Chaos Crew didn't respond immediately. His hands flexed against the wheel. Then he looked back at me steadily. "That's impossible to judge when we don't know who this person is or what they want."

"It could have something to do with the people who kidnapped me." The organization with the logo like a droplet with a line slicing diagonally through it. The people who'd stolen me from my family and tried to kill the men who'd helped me more than once. "Or the people who hired the crew to kill *them*."

"Even if that's the case, what this means depends on what answers are still important to you. Now that you have your family, how much does it matter to you to understand the rest of your past?"

Maybe it would have been better if I could have simply moved on and forgotten all that. But the urge to find out who'd controlled me so thoroughly for so much of my life nagged at me no matter how many visits I had with the Maliks.

I needed to know why. I needed to understand the reason my life had been rewritten. I needed to be sure the people involved wouldn't hurt anyone close to me ever again.

I wasn't sure I'd ever said anything truer than the words that tumbled from my mouth next. "It's the most important thing to me."

Julius gave me a quiet smile. "Then it'll be worth it no matter what happens, just to know you tried."

Blaze's voice resonated through the headset I was wearing, identical to Julius's. "My equipment is ready. As soon as this person picks up, I can start to triangulate their signal. Be sure to keep whoever it is talking as long as possible. That'll give me the best chance of narrowing down his location."

I nodded. "Got it."

I tapped the number we'd gotten from the strange missed connections ad into my phone and brought it to my ear, easing off that side of the headset. The phone on the other end rang in what felt like slow motion. After the fourth ring, I wondered if anyone would pick up at all. Maybe it'd had nothing to do with me. Just a huge coincidence.

Then there was a click and a momentary silence. My heart jumped. "Hello?"

"Who am I speaking to?" a man's voice asked. It was hoarse. Confident. I got the impression of a fair bit of age in the gravity of his tone.

I almost said "Dess" but caught myself just in time. "Rachel," I said, giving the name he'd used in his ad. "I think you were expecting to hear from me."

There was a faint rustling on the other end as if he'd shifted his position. Blaze's voice carried into my other ear. "He's in the south end of the city." Julius, who was hearing the same report, started the ignition and drove out of the parking lot.

"I'm glad you found my message," the man on the phone said. "You're obviously a sharp one, Rachel Malik."

He knew exactly who I was then, but that wasn't a surprise.

"A friend who knew some of the details of recent events in my life noticed the post and pointed it out to me," I said. I wanted to demand to know what it was about, what he wanted, but Blaze needed this conversation to be drawn out as long as possible. So I stopped there and waited.

The man gave a brief hum. "A friend, not family?"

"I *said* a friend, didn't I?"

"What people say and what they mean aren't always

the same thing, as I'm sure you'll become aware of soon if you haven't already."

"What's that supposed to mean?" I asked, a prickle of apprehension running down my spine.

"I saw you on the news with Damien Malik," the man said, ignoring my question. "Back from the dead. I knew you deserved better than to go in blind. I had to reach out to you."

"And you chose this way?"

He barked a laugh. "We have to be subtle in my line of business."

I frowned. "And what exactly is that? Who are you?" I clamped down on all the other questions that wanted to fly from my mouth.

"I've been investigating the Malik family for some time," he said, again not offering the specific information I'd asked for. "I've turned up some unsettling information. You shouldn't trust them wholeheartedly."

"They're my family," I retorted automatically.

"Not all families mean well. Every villain is part of a family."

I guessed that was true. I squirmed in my seat again, wondering how much longer it'd be before Blaze could home in on this guy even more. I wanted to talk to him face to face, to force him to give me some straight answers.

As if sensing my thoughts, Blaze's voice came again. "I'm closing in on him. Northeast."

Julius nodded and took a turn at the next intersection. I focused on the phone again. "Who are you to be investigating anyone anyway?"

"I'm a special government agent. All politicians have people keeping oversight on them, as I'm sure you can understand. Damien Malik is my assignment."

"And what makes you think there's anything to be worried about with him?"

"I haven't been able to gather enough evidence to prove anything in court," the man said. "You wouldn't believe me if I told you the details. But I know what I've seen. I know you should watch your step."

"This all sounds like a bunch of vague fearmongering to me," I shot back. "Why should I trust *you*? I don't even know your name."

"My colleagues call me the Hunter. And I can hardly jeopardize my mandate by giving away too much to someone who's become so close to the target of my investigation. I simply wanted to deliver the clearest warning I could."

He sounded like he was about to wind up the conversation. Blaze was muttering on his end, obviously still working at tracing the signal. My heart thumped faster. I had to keep this weirdo talking.

"If you're really a government agent, shouldn't you have been able to track down my phone number?" I said. "Why did you contact me in such a roundabout way?"

"I wanted to make sure you were interested in knowing the truth. And that your father wouldn't be hovering over you when we connected."

"Well, you managed that. He's not here now. So why don't you tell me more about whatever it is you think he's done."

Blaze spoke up again with a ripple of excitement in his voice. "I've narrowed it down to a ten block radius. Sending the coordinates for the area to your phone, Julius."

The phone mounted on the dashboard pinged with the incoming transmission. The map we'd already had ready zoomed in on a particular section of the city.

The Hunter, if I really had to think of him by that name, shifted his position with another rustle. "There are a lot of things you don't know."

I gritted my teeth. "Then tell me. Tell me what's so wrong with my family. What have you seen? It isn't much of a warning if I don't even know what to watch out *for*."

"I told you, you wouldn't believe me—not when you're so close to the situation. You'll have to see it for yourself."

"Are you going to show me then?"

"I don't believe it's safe for me to get that involved," the Hunter said. "But now that you know to be cautious, you'll be going in with your eyes open. If I find more evidence—better evidence—I'll share that with you."

His words sounded like a promise of help, but it was only more vagueness when you really looked at it. I was becoming increasingly certain that he had no intention of telling me anything at all. Which probably meant this was all bullshit. But I couldn't stop now.

When I got my hands on him, I'd find out the reason for the bullshit.

Julius took another turn, accelerating as he went. The car swayed lightly under me. I peered out the window at the buildings we were rushing by as he swerved around the sparse traffic.

"Five blocks," Blaze muttered, and the map zoomed in even more. Then he let out a huff of frustration. "Something's interfering with the signal."

I spat out the first question that came to mind that might keep the Hunter talking. "Can't you at least tell me if there's anything specific I should be watching out for? The general type of thing that's made you uneasy?"

"I think you should draw your own conclusions, Rachel," he said. "You're smart enough for that. You'll recognize the rot when you come across it."

Now he was talking in ominous poetry. I groped for something else to say to stop him from hanging up, and Blaze's voice pealed into my other ear.

"There! It was passing through an electric field meant to scatter the transmission, but I modified the search and found it. I've got an exact building now. Probably the top floor."

Julius revved the engine faster. Relief rushed through me. "Well, if you feel like enlightening me more at some point," I said to the Hunter, "you have my number now."

"Indeed I do," he said.

I didn't want to let him go just yet. He'd be more likely to stay in place if I kept him talking. There was no way he could know that we were descending on him right now.

"If I call you again, will you pick up?" I asked. "Or will you be busy with your government business?"

"I suppose that depends on when you call. I'm afraid there's nothing else I can tell you right now."

We'd almost reached the marker on the map. "Wait!" I said. "I need to know—is it just my father you're worried about, or the rest of the family too?"

Julius pulled over to the curb outside what looked like a normal two-story house, a little shabby with pale yellow paint that was flaking off the bricks, but nothing horribly rundown. He jerked his head toward it.

I slipped out of the car, not even shutting the door so I wouldn't make much noise, and darted around to the back door. There were no signs of occupation, no vehicles in the driveway, no lights gleaming through the windows under the overcast sky.

"It's difficult to say without delving in more," the Hunter said. "But for now I'd be wary of all of them."

He was just a bucket of joy, this guy, wasn't he? I whipped out my lockpicks and had the back door open in a matter of seconds. After I'd eased it open, I padded silently through the first-floor hallway, confirming there was no one in those rooms before heading up the stairs.

"Even my brother?" I prodded, letting skepticism color my voice. "The kid's only eighteen."

"I've met killers who were twelve," the Hunter said. "Don't put much stock in age as an indicator of innocence."

The idea of my grumbly teenage brother being on the same level as a killer—a killer like *I* was—nearly made me snort. I swallowed the sound and darted along the upper hall to the room at the front of the house. The door was ajar.

I didn't bother to say anything else into the phone. I sprang into the room—

And found nothing but a vacant chair with a folded paper sitting on it.

A low chuckle reverberated from the phone as I picked up the note. *Nice try*, it said in neat letters.

Amusement colored the Hunter's voice. "It seems you're good at this, Miss Malik, but you need to be ready in case someone turns out to be even better."

Then the line went dead.

My fingers dug into the paper, creasing it, as I lowered the phone. "What happened?" Blaze asked through the headset, but I didn't know what to tell him. The Hunter's last words were still whirling through my mind.

He'd been here. Obviously he had—who else would have left this note? But somehow he'd either faked his signal or managed to get out of here just before I'd arrived without any of us noticing.

And now he knew that Damien Malik's recently rediscovered daughter was more than just a restaurant hostess with a fraught past—that I had the skills to track a man like him down.

A chill tickled over my skin. Just how much about myself had I inadvertently revealed to this man with his tricks and his warnings? About the *real* me, not Rachel Malik?

SIX

Decima

THE SPREAD of food across the Maliks' outdoor dining table looked more like a Thanksgiving feast than a basic luncheon with close family, although the options were more suited for a summery meal than a fall one. Chunks of watermelon and pineapple lay in large ceramic bowls next to sweetly creamy dips. Sandwiches cut into bite-sized pieces stood heaped on platters. Each placemat had a glass on the top filled to the brim with what looked like a frozen red juice.

It was all so… extravagant. But then maybe my frame of reference was off considering that I'd only ever eaten alone for all the meals I could remember until just a few weeks ago.

"Did you bring a bathing suit, Rachel?" my mother asked, following behind me and Carter as we approached the patio table.

I eyed the large pool and the stone patio surrounding it. Lounge chairs and pool inflatables littered the patio. From the new assortment of towels draped over the porch railing, it looked like the family had made use of the pool earlier this morning in the late summer warmth.

"I don't really swim," I admitted.

I *could* swim, of course. It'd been a part of my training with Noelle. But if I wore a bathing suit, way too many of my scars would be exposed. I wondered how my mother would react to them, no matter what excuses I came up with to explain them away. I'd told the Maliks that the people who'd kidnapped me had treated me like one of their own, and it would be suspicious to change up the story now.

I was wondering a whole lot of things, really. After my phone call with the man who called himself the Hunter, it was hard to take this cheery family get-together at face value. *Had* he discovered something about the Maliks that should make me concerned? What could they possibly be up to?

Or had he just been trying to create tensions for his own bizarre agenda? I had no idea who that man was.

Of course, the truth was I barely knew who any of these people were either.

I glanced at Grandma Ruby and Grandpa Bo, the only other Maliks in attendance today, who'd followed us over to the table. Grandma Ruby had her nose turned up at the feast waiting for us as if she found it wanting. I couldn't imagine what it was missing, but then, Damien's mother seemed to enjoy criticizing whatever she could. And she got worse on days like today when her son had been called into work. I wasn't sure whether I felt more or less at ease without my father among us.

"Well, everyone take a seat." My mother pointed to one of the trays of small sandwiches. "I made sure to have some pepperoni and cheese sandwiches made special for you, Carter. Rachel, do you have a sandwich preference?"

I wanted to laugh. I'd never been offered options. At the household, they'd given me whatever they pleased, and I was expected to eat it or starve. With the guys, I'd grabbed whatever I found in the refrigerator or what Steffie, their housekeeper and general assistant, made for us.

"I'm not picky," I said with a small shrug. "I'll eat pretty much anything."

Did Carter make a bit of a face as he sat down? I hoped he didn't think I was implying anything negative about him having his own favorites. His shoulders rounded into their typical slouch in his chair, and I hesitated before taking the seat next to him. Sometimes he joked around with me a little, but sometimes he seemed like he'd rather I wasn't around.

It had to be pretty weird having a big sister drop out of the sky without any warning. I couldn't blame him for being a bit awkward.

"Maybe I'll try the pepperoni and cheese if you can spare some," I said to him, shooting him a smile. "I do like pizza."

The corner of his mouth twitched into half a smile.

"These are the closest things I can get to it at one of these dos."

Our grandparents sat across from us, and my mother sank down at my other side. She looked around the table, and a smile stretched across her face. "Wow. I could have never imagined this in my wildest dreams. Sitting at lunch with my family, my daughter at my side. My son a seat down. Damien's parents across from us. I'm so grateful."

She sounded a bit choked up by the end of that speech. Even if the Hunter had sown some doubts in my mind about the Maliks in general, I was completely sure that my parents were grateful to have me back in their lives. Iris got close to tears at least once during every visit, and I could never tell what the best response would be.

Today, I ventured a touch of my hand on top of hers. She flipped her hand and squeezed my fingers, and I knew I'd judged the situation correctly. The physical contact put me a little on edge, but it seemed to soothe her as she took a deep breath.

"I don't think any of us could have predicted how happy we'd be, Iris," Grandma Ruby said, piling watermelon on her plate and sprinkling a generous amount of salt on top. Her gaze veered to the garden. It was full of blooms with narrow yellow petals around a dark center. I didn't know much about flowers, but they appeared to be in excellent health to me. Vibrant in a wild sort of way.

"You need to get out there and pull those weeds," my grandmother remarked. "They're taking away the effect of the black-eyed susans."

"I think it looks really nice with a little wildness in there," I said, trying to offset the criticism of her statement.

My mother waved my protest off. "No, she's right. I haven't been out to pull weeds in the flower beds for a couple of weeks. It's about time."

"You don't have a gardener?" I asked.

I never would have imagined my mother pulling the weeds from the garden on her own. I glanced over at her perfectly manicured nails—not a chip in sight.

She laughed. "Oh, we do have a groundskeeper who sees to all the yard work, but that garden is an important symbol to the family. I like to handle it myself. Black-eyed susans symbolize justice, you know, and so much of our work—especially your father's—goes toward bringing more of that into the world."

"Look at how well they grow for our family," Grandma Ruby said, gesturing to the lush garden. "We're clearly doing a good job of it. They couldn't be in better bloom." She paused. "Well, maybe a little better without the weeds."

"I'll get on that this evening, Ruby," mom said with a genuine smile. She must be used to the nagging after nearly three decades of marriage into the family.

Other than the nagging, all of these people seemed so… nice. Even Carter's awkwardness came across as more shy than hostile. Maybe it was *because* the idea of them having some nefarious side seemed so absurd that I couldn't get the Hunter's warnings out of my mind.

If he'd been lying, why? Why would he have it in for

the Maliks? He hadn't appeared to know anything about my past, so I had no reason to think he was connected to the household, but a man as high up in politics as Damien Malik could definitely have made more than one enemy.

As I chewed on one of the pepperoni and cheese sandwiches, which actually were pretty good, I considered how I could get at whether the family might be aware of this man's vigilance.

"I heard some people talking about hunting when I was at a corner store in town yesterday," I said, making up the story as an excuse to broach the subject. It seemed like something Garrison would do to get people talking. If the gambit worked, I'd have to let him know his influence had rubbed off well on me. "Is that a common hobby around here?"

"Oh, sure." Grandpa Bo nodded, speaking up for the first time. He mostly seemed to let his wife do the talking between the two of them. Given her personality, maybe that wasn't surprising. "Every couple of years I go out with a few of my buddies, and we bring back a buck or two."

Carter grimaced and gave a little shudder, and my mother shook her head. "Let's not discuss that at the table while we're eating." She glanced at me. "Carter saw him bring back one of those deer when he was younger and just thinking about it makes him queasy."

"I'm fine," Carter mumbled, but he did look a bit green. "I just prefer my animals either alive or already in a form where you can't tell what they were before they made it to the grocery store." He waggled his sandwich in the air to indicate the pepperoni.

I raised my eyebrows slightly. "I guess you all don't spend a whole lot of time with avid hunters then." I motioned to Grandpa Bo. "What are your buddies like? The hunters who go with you? I've never known anyone who was into that kind of pastime."

Grandpa Bo chuckled. "Between you and me, they're all old men who like to shoot their mouths off more than they like to hunt. One is nearly deaf, and one can't walk through the woods for more than ten minutes without needing a breather. The two of them live in Ohio, so they only come around when we plan a trip."

I resisted the urge to clench my jaw in frustration. The man on the phone had shown no sign of hearing problems, and he'd seemed very familiar with the city. He also hadn't sounded as old as my grandfather.

"Does Damien—my dad—ever go with you?" I had to ask.

Grandpa Bo laughed again and patted Ruby's hand. "My son has never been interested in hunting, and he certainly has never asked to go with me."

Well, it was totally possible that the Hunter's moniker had nothing to do with any interest in hunting animals, only his penchant for hunting down information. I switched tactics. "I guess Dad has to stay pretty conscious of the image he presents even on his down time. Maybe all of you do. Do you find you're under a lot of scrutiny because of his political career?"

"Oh, it's nothing we can't handle," Iris said quickly. "We're proud to see how much he's accomplished." Then she paused. "But you've been thrown into the mix out of the blue. If you find anyone's bothering you, you only have to let us know. We can help you navigate those waters. And I know your father has already been working to ensure no one intrudes too much on our privacy despite the investigation into your kidnapping."

"He has," I acknowledged. "I've actually been okay."

Members of the FBI had questioned me, and I'd given them an expanded version of the story I'd told Damien, saying that I had no idea where I'd been held and that I'd escaped when my usual caretaker had taken me on a trip and our van was attacked. It was an easy way to avoid having to point to any locations where I'd supposedly lived. I didn't want them digging too closely into the real details of my life, or they might uncover more about me than I was ready to share.

My mother had seemed awfully eager to respond to that question, though. And Grandpa Bo had been quick to dismiss my inquiries about hunting. Was it possible they didn't want me digging too deeply into the inner workings of the family?

I shook myself mentally. That was ridiculous. The Hunter's words had gotten under my skin and made me overly suspicious.

"If you feel it'd be easier living closer to home..." my mother ventured. "I realize you might not be comfortable moving in here, although of course you'd be welcome. But we could see about setting you up with accommodation closer by. I'm not sure how nice a place you've been able to arrange on your own."

"Oh, you don't need to worry about that," I said. "I'm happy where I am."

"I just know that hotels can be so expensive around here, and not always all that comfortable. And we've gone years without being able to support you the way we should have been."

"Most of the hotels around here are shitholes," Grandma Ruby announced. "Your mother's just too polite to say it outright. You really should be with family."

Iris winced. "Ruby, language."

I wanted to laugh at the way she looked offended. The curse word had flown right by me, especially after spending so long with the Crew. The foul language that came from *their* mouths would have sent my mother into an early grave. I made a mental note to make sure nothing similar fell out of my mouth around her.

"I'm only saying the truth," Grandma Ruby said with a huff.

"I promise, I'm fine," I said before the conversation could become a full-out argument between my mother and her mother-in-law. "I enjoy where I'm staying. And I… I'm proud of how I pulled myself back onto my feet when I escaped the people who took me, and I prefer to have some independence for now. I went too long without having any."

It was immediately obvious that I'd played the right card—so obvious a jab of guilt hit me in the gut. My mother's eyes clouded with grief before she nodded. "I understand that. If you need anything, though, please don't hesitate to ask."

I gave her a grateful smile. "I appreciate that." The emotional direction our talk had taken left my skin itching. And I still hadn't found out anything that could convince me one way or another about the Hunter's intentions.

I had one more strategy I'd meant to employ, one that didn't involve any talking at all. "Would you mind if I went inside and used the restroom?" I asked.

"Oh, by all means. You remember where to find it, right?"

I stood with a bob of my head. "I believe so. I'll be right back."

Thankfully, no one offered to join me on my trek into the house. The second I stepped past the door, I darted down the hall to maximize the time I had before they started wondering why I was taking so long.

First I closed the door on the downstairs bathroom so it'd look like someone was inside. Then I slipped up the stairs. I'd already seen all of the rooms on the ground floor, but there were a few upstairs that I hadn't been shown into. My parents' and Carter's bedrooms I wouldn't expect to get a tour of, but what was behind the third?

The door at the front of the house led to the master bedroom, and Carter's had a cheeky DO NOT ENTER sign pasted on it. I'd bet Iris just loved that. But hey, he was a teenager. Pissing off his parents was his job, as far as I'd gathered from my limited TV and movie consumption.

I never really had the option to piss anyone off while I was a teenager living in the household. Not that I'd had parents there anyway.

Two doors down from that was one of dark wood with a knob that jarred at my twisting hand. Locked, as I'd expected.

Because I'd expected it, I'd come prepared. I pulled two small pins from my hair—an excellent hiding place for these basic tools—and stuck both into the lock, using one for leverage. I felt my way around the mechanism in a matter of seconds, jerked one of the pins, and the contraption gave with a click, the bolt sliding over.

I palmed both pins and pushed the door open.

The sharp smell of masculine cologne wafted over me, and I recognized the scent my father often wore. It lingered in this room as if he spent a lot of time in it.

Which I'd guess he did. The space was clearly a home office, with built-in bookshelves along two walls and a sturdy mahogany desk stacked with papers—a little more haphazardly than I'd have imagined my straightlaced father would have stood for. I glanced over them carefully, getting a sense of a personal system of organization that I couldn't decipher immediately.

The wall behind the desk held several framed photos, a few of family, others of important work events, including one where Damien had met a previous president and shaken his hand. I took out my phone and snapped a few pictures as my gaze skimmed over them. My attention settled on a larger frame to the right of the photos.

This frame held a piece of parchment that was yellowed with age, though otherwise in excellent condition. It held a column of writing in brown ink, most of the characters symbols I didn't recognize. Next to those symbols were an ascending sequence of four-digit numbers: *1903, 1904, 1905…* all the way to *1928*.

Were those years? Why did my father have a paper about something from a century ago in his office? Did it have some political or historical significance? Nothing about it made sense to me, and that unnerved me just a little.

I took a picture of that document too, just in case the guys knew what to make of it.

I only spent another few seconds scanning the surfaces in the room before backing into the hallway and relocking it. I was running out of time, and I couldn't risk someone finding me snooping around. I padded back down the stairs quietly and turned toward where my family waited for me outside, taking a brief detour to open the downstairs bathroom again.

The sunlight had just started beaming straight through the bathroom's large, glazed window. It streaked across the hallway on an angle. As I walked through the swath of brighter light, my eyes caught on a detail on the floor that made me pause.

Something about the carpet by the wall just a few feet down from the bathroom was… different from the surface around it. Just a tad flatter than the rest. A slight indent that was a ghost of the more obvious wear in front of the bathroom door I'd just left behind.

As if there was another doorway here that had seen periodic traffic.

All I could see next to that spot was a seamless wall with its striped red-and-gray wallpaper. I frowned, tilting

my head to the side as I stepped in to take a closer look—
and my mother's voice echoed through the house.

"Rachel, are you all right?"

I jerked back my reaching hand as if I'd been burned. I
couldn't delay here any longer. Besides, there might not be
anything unusual about the spot I'd noticed at all. Maybe
a piece of furniture like a side table had once stood there,
and it'd caused the wear.

"I'm coming," I called, forcing my voice to sound
friendly. I turned on my heel and strode back toward the
lunch my family had prepared for me.

I'd found nothing. Nothing to prove the Hunter's
warnings right, and all possible evidence that I had a
loving, concerned family.

I couldn't let myself get so paranoid that I wrecked
everything good I'd found for myself over the ravings of a
stranger.

SEVEN

Blaze

THE COMPUTERS WERE ACTIVELY SCANNING, but it felt wrong not to work alongside them and check for leads as they were split into the backup folders and categorized. If the Maliks posed any kind of threat to Dess, every second could be of the essence.

For every twenty potential leads my searches had turned up so far, I found that only one seemed even semi-relevant, and it led to a dead end that had nothing to do with Damien Malik or his family. I didn't know whether to be frustrated or relieved that I was turning up so little.

Could anyone really be that clean? There wasn't even a speeding ticket on his records, and no more than vague murmurs of overstepping his role or hypocrisy with nothing to back them up—by all appearances the disgruntled rumblings of political opponents.

I was *definitely* frustrated that I'd made no headway into deciphering the symbols on the document Dess had taken a picture of in Damien's home office. They didn't match any language or code I'd encountered before, and apparently the internet had never encountered it either. I scowled at the empty folder still waiting for a real match.

As for the Hunter himself, I'd found nothing tying any government agent or otherwise suspicious personality to the number he'd given Dess or the house his signal had led us to. Unless Belinda Mitchener, 92-year-old grandmother of six and great-grandmother of nine, was simply wearing an old lady suit and faking her severe arthritis, the owner of the house definitely wasn't our man.

Finally, I pushed myself away from the hotel room desk with a restrained growl. I was failing the only job I could do to keep Dess safe—failing miserably, even.

I glanced across the room at where Garrison sat by the large window, tinkering with the miniature-sized telescope that he'd insisted on bringing with us. On the other side of the room, Julius had laid out a few of his army figures on the suite's dining table. I couldn't tell what exactly he was trying to strategize as he moved them back and forth across the top of it. He'd just completed his meditation for the day moments before, and Julius liked to follow his meditation with plan-making.

Talon sat on the other end of the sofa, knitting what was either the sleeve of a sweater or a very puffy scarf with brisk motions of his needles.

"You look pissed off, man," Garrison said, and I

realized with a start that he'd abandoned his telescope to join me and peer at the blinking screen of my laptop.

"It's just…" I paused. I didn't normally like to show any weakness around Garrison, since the guy took every opportunity he could to heckle me about stuff, but after seeing him with Dess, I knew better than I ever had how much the snarky persona was for show. I didn't really care if he took a jab at me. Maybe that would even jostle my mind out of this gloom. "From the start, everything around Dess's situation has been nearly impossible to crack."

He leaned against the nearby sofa. "Couldn't that just mean there's nothing *to* crack? I'm not one to trust any politician, but I trust weirdos who give silly code names and lead us on wild goose chases around the city even less."

I took a deep breath, but that didn't stop my knee from starting to bounce of its own accord. "Maybe there's nothing on Malik. Maybe he really is that clean. But I haven't been able to piece together anything all that useful about the organization behind the household. I still have no idea why they kidnapped Dess or what beef they had with the Malik family. Or who hired us to attack *them*. And now I'm coming up empty with this Hunter prick and the crazy secret code too."

"I think the word you're looking for is 'we,' not 'I,'" Julius said from across the room without looking up from his army men. "None of us have been able to come up with any answers. Including Dess. She's not going to blame you."

I'd blame me. I balled my hands to stop them from fidgeting, grappling with the emotions coursing through me.

Garrison shrugged. "From where I'm standing, things are looking pretty good. Maybe we don't have all the answers, but we've made progress. We found her birth family. She's managed to reunite with them. We got all those mercenary groups off our backs. The rest is just a matter of time."

How could he be so confident? But then, that was his constant persona, all cocky assurance. He might have been just as torn up as me underneath and simply choosing not to show it.

Sometimes I might have envied his carefully constructed masks just a little.

"But what if I'm missing something?" I said. "What if the Maliks *are* a threat, and she's walking straight into some kind of trap?"

Garrison arched his eyebrows, and I immediately felt how ridiculous that idea sounded. Dess's birth family had been nothing but welcoming to her. Why would they have an evil agenda against their own daughter? It made no sense.

"I mean, I don't think she should go mentioning the whole criminal career thing to them," Garrison said. "And she probably shouldn't bring us around while publicizing that we make a living offing people. But as things stand, she's been pretty happy with them. She wouldn't keep spending time with them if they were rubbing her the wrong way."

That was true. She was off at her family home right now for another visit. And something about that fact niggled at me just as much as my lack of progress.

"I know," I said. "I like seeing her happy." When she came back to the hotel after a visit with that new light shining in her eyes, when she talked about her father or mother or brother with that hint of excitement she couldn't totally hide, the thrill of having that family at all… I wasn't sure I'd ever seen her that delighted before. She was usually so serious. "I just don't want her to get hurt."

Garrison cocked his head at me. "Is that all? You're not at all bothered by the whole her-family-would-hate-our-guts thing?"

I scowled at him. Of course he'd pick up on the emotions I was trying not to feel as well as the ones I was talking about. "It's a reasonable concern. If he finds out everything about *her*, he could turn his back on her and break her heart."

"Oh, so it's *her* heart you're worried about?"

"Of course," I grumbled. "Whose are *you* thinking about?"

To my surprise, Garrison's mouth twisted at an angle that looked genuinely conflicted. I rarely saw him drop the confident front. I didn't totally know what to do with a glimpse of vulnerability from him.

"Look," he said. "I'll make it easier for you just this once. I think we're all aware that the more entwined she gets with the Maliks, the harder it'll be for her to stay close to us. I'd love it if you dug up some dirt on these pompous pricks that shows they're not such a model of familial joy after all. But if it's not there, it's not there. Dess isn't the kind of woman who'd let anything get between her and something she's set her mind on. If she wants a family…"

Then she'd stick with that family. Yeah. He'd laid it out more clearly than I'd let myself even in my head.

I swallowed against the tightness in my throat. "I know that too. But there's nothing wrong with making absolutely sure that she knows what she's getting into, right?"

Garrison snickered, back to his usual obnoxious self. "Nothing at all. Just don't blow a circuit trying to make it happen."

Maybe he was right to hassle me about this. How could I say that all I wanted was for Dess to be happy when at the same time some part of me was desperately hoping I'd come across evidence that would destroy the image of the happy family she'd thought she'd found? Just so that we wouldn't lose her.

So that *I* wouldn't lose her. I sure as hell didn't know where I'd find another woman to match her. But I'd let her go if I had to. I just wouldn't like it.

My laptop dinged twice with an alert I hadn't anticipated. It had nothing to do with my searches for information but instead the temporary security systems I'd put in place in the neighborhood of the hotel.

I snapped to attention, leaning close to the screen. My fingers flew across the keyboard as I checked out the movements it'd picked up on nearby streets. A group of men had walked by one of my surveillance cameras, half of them with obvious guns protruding from the backs of their jeans.

They didn't appear to be heading in our direction. Who the hell were they that they'd saunter around so casually while armed? With those tattoos and piercings, they definitely didn't look like cops. Normally regular citizens were a little more discreet.

Furrowing my brow, I dove into the data further to try to trace their path into our neighborhood and figure out where they'd come from while still keeping an eye on their path through the city as they passed us by.

Garrison stepped closer. "Why so serious?"

"Serious gets the job done," I retorted.

"Not for you. You're usually cracking a million jokes a minute while all our lives hang on the line." He folded his arms over his chest. "Seeing you all somber is kind of scary."

I rolled my eyes without meeting his and confirmed that the armed men were still heading in the opposite direction from the hotel. Whatever they were up to, it definitely didn't appear to have anything to do with us.

But we couldn't be too wary. I had to be strong to protect Dess properly, and maybe that did mean I should let go some of my usual carefree approach. Jokes weren't going to deflect bullets aimed her way.

Whether she stayed with us or moved on, I'd never forgive myself if something happened to her that I could have prevented. Even the thought of her taking another wound, physical or emotional, made an ache form around my heart.

The men with the guns had shown up on one street cam outside my private surveillance network. When I tried to trace their path farther back, I didn't spot them. It appeared they'd gotten out of a vehicle hidden somewhere within a gap in coverage.

They'd gotten out just a couple of blocks from the area I was monitoring, and then walked right through the edge of that area with weapons on full display before sauntering on out of that area again.

My instincts twitched with apprehension. That didn't feel right at all. It was almost as if they'd purposefully come through to catch our attention…

And draw it away from what?

Panic flashed through my nerves. My hands leapt across the keyboard. In a matter of seconds, I'd brought up the feeds closest to the hotel building.

Just in time to spot several forms in normal clothes with no overt equipment that would have alerted my systems converging on the building with a purposefulness that had me jumping to my feet. Even as I opened my mouth, all those feeds blinked out into static.

"We're under attack!" I hollered.

The words had barely left my mouth when the windows along the side wall exploded with a hail of glass shards and intruding bodies.

EIGHT

Decima

MY MISSION TO make my brother more comfortable with the surprise sister who'd fallen into his life currently involved a game of 20 Questions while we basked in the backyard in the warmth of the midday sun. The game meant I had to do a fair bit of lying, but I did want to smooth over any awkwardness between us if I could.

And having Carter on my side would make fishing for information about the family much easier.

"Are you a DC or Marvel girl?" he asked for his eighth question, stretching out his lanky legs in the lawn chair. My mom and grandmother sat at the outdoor dining table a few feet away, carrying on with their own conversation about gardening and cooking, which I couldn't say I'd have had much more to contribute to.

I thought back to everything I knew about those

specific franchises. Noelle had sometimes included superhero movies in the rotation of media available to me, but I'd only watched a few. She'd cautioned me that they gave an over-the-top impression of the world, and that was exactly why I'd never totally connected with them. I knew how nitty and gritty tackling your opponents actually was. And you definitely didn't get points for flashy costumes.

I didn't think Carter would appreciate that answer, though. I considered the films I had seen and the bits of pop culture I'd managed to absorb over the years. "DC, I guess. I like Batman." At least he had the sense to keep his costume black, even if the cape and the pointed ears were a bit much. And he used training and gadgets rather than superpowers.

My brother crinkled his nose. "Really? More than Iron Man? Or Black Panther? Or Thor and Loki?"

I shrugged. "I'm not much of a superhero fan in general. But maybe I've missed some good ones. What about you?"

He let out a scoffing sound that had Iris glancing over as if worried she might have to defend me from his teenage scorn. "I'm a Marvel fan, obviously," he said as if the question wasn't even worth being asked. "But you know the rules. You have to come up with original questions."

"Do you prefer baseball or football?" I asked, referencing what seemed to be the two most common sports in the country. From what I'd seen, they appealed to very different people with different temperaments—levels of patience, enjoyment of physical aggression.

He opened his mouth to reply at the same moment as my phone released a loud chime in my pocket. "Baseball," he said as I reached for the device. "I played in middle school, but Dad didn't want me to be out in public without bodyguards so much, and it started to feel weird having them tagging along for the games in high school, so I just stopped."

I made a sympathetic face. Even in this family, my life wouldn't have been completely my own. At least Damien hadn't tried to enforce that level of security on me so far.

"That must be really hard," I said. "Does it bother you?"

"Meh. It was just for fun, not anything really important. I had lots of extracurriculars closer to home. Graduated near the top of my class and got a spot at my top pick college, so it all worked out in the end."

I would have asked more about his plans for college, except I looked at my phone then, and my heart stopped. Blaze had texted me a brief message. *Attack at hotel. Stay alert.*

An attack in our hotel? Was it happening *now*? I had to assume that if Blaze had been doing anything other than fighting for his life when he'd composed that message, he'd have explained in more detail—or outright called me. Shit.

"Hold on a second," I said to Carter, and dialed Blaze's number. My heart thumped as the line on the other end rang, but he didn't pick up. When I tried Julius, I got kicked to voicemail too.

My chest was constricting. The Chaos Crew was under

attack while I was sitting here making small talk and sipping lemonade. Who the hell had come at them now?

I stood from my chair with the burst of adrenaline and anger, maybe faster than was wise. Grandma Ruby went quiet as I stepped back and away from the table. "My goodness, Rachel."

"I need to leave," I blurted out, and scrambled to compose myself slightly more with an appropriate excuse. "A friend of mine had her boyfriend break up with her suddenly. She's a mess." Personal issues, especially dating ones, seemed to get the most sympathy from the average person.

"Oh, I'm sure she'll be all right," Grandma Ruby said. "At your age, the men come and go."

Iris shot her a look. "At Rachel's age, I was engaged to Damien." She nodded to me. "We've been monopolizing a lot of your time. If your friend needs your support, you should be there for her."

Her understanding response added a pang of guilt to the whirlwind of emotions inside me, but protecting the guys came before anything else. "Thanks. I'll call when I have the chance."

I managed to keep a measured pace as I walked around the house, but as soon as I was out of view of the backyard, I bolted down the street and across it. When I spotted a car in a secluded enough spot that I could break in and hotwire it without being seen, I dashed to it. There wasn't time to wait for an Uber and another driver's law-abiding approach to the rules of the road.

I had the door open in a matter of seconds and the

engine running in several more. As I tore out of the driveway, my teeth gritted.

Who would have attacked the crew here? We were so far from home that none of their usual enemies would have been close enough... although I supposed I didn't know how many enemies they might have made during their missions across the country.

Was the organization behind the household making another stab at capturing me? But then, why wouldn't they have come at me here at the Maliks' rather than attacking the guys?

Whoever it was must have had a death wish, because when I found them, they wouldn't stand a chance. If they harmed a single hair on the guys' heads, I would end their lives slowly and painfully.

Nobody messed with my men.

I tore through the city, cutting off other vehicles and racing through red lights until I finally reached the hotel. After slamming to a stop around the corner, I yanked up the parking brake and hurtled inside.

I rushed into the hotel and past the receptionist, who greeted me with a smile, having no idea that an attack was happening in this very building. If it was contained to our suite, it was contained intentionally, either because our enemies were trying to avoid drawing outside attention or because the guys didn't want to put unnecessary people in danger by making it a spectacle.

It could have been either option, I realized. I had no idea who they were facing or what I'd be walking into. I was nearly unarmed and certainly unprotected with no bulletproof vest or padding to speak of. I was about to rush into a potential bloodbath with only the small blade that I always kept at my hip.

There wasn't any question that I would, though. The only weapons I really needed were my bare hands.

I didn't bother waiting for the elevator. Dashing into the stairwell, I stormed up all five flights to the penthouse we'd taken over. The guys had picked this building carefully for discretion, and the soundproofing between the floors was good enough that I didn't pick up the sound of gunshots until I was bursting out into the short hallway that led to the suite entrance.

At least they *were* still shooting. That meant someone was alive.

The damn apartment door was locked. Swearing under my breath, I fished out my key card, jabbed it into the slot, and barged inside into what could only be described as chaos.

Several bodies already slumped on the floor in the suite's living room, but there were still more attackers grappling with the Chaos Crew around the room.

My gaze caught on Talon first. He was whipping back and forth between three opponents, fending off their weapons. If he'd had a gun to begin with, he'd lost it in the fray. Right now he was fighting with... knitting needles.

I'd have laughed if the situation hadn't looked so dire. His expression was taut with strain. I jumped in, clicking open my small knife as I leapt. I plunged it into the back of the nearest man, jabbing it deep enough to pierce his heart through his ribs. I'd never carry a knife too small to accomplish that.

He crumpled, and the man next to him spun with a gun raised. In the instant before Talon leapt to my defense, the other man... hesitated, staring at my face. He could have taken a shot—and I would have dodged it—but it was almost as if he didn't think he should.

Then Talon was snapping the guy's wrist with a crack of shattering bone.

As I whirled, I spotted Blaze holding his own against two men near the sofa. Another man barreled into view and paused at the sight of me, a lot like the gunman had.

What the heck was up with these guys? Had they never fought a woman before?

Well, they were about to find out that I was an equal opponent.

I whipped the knife I'd withdrawn from my first kill through the air, and it hit the man right in the middle of the forehead. As he slumped over, Blaze managed to get in a shot at one of his attackers, who stumbled backward clutching his gut.

I glanced past Blaze and found Julius fighting three men, Garrison at his back fending off another. Four more men were just clambering through the shattered windows that let in a brisk breeze.

I didn't know who to help first. All of them were getting overwhelmed, and I'd given up my one weapon.

I dropped to the ground and grabbed at the waists of the corpses for anything I could use. My groping hand found a gun. I quickly checked the magazine before pulling back the slide and finding one bullet already in the chamber. Two remained in the magazine. Three bullets total. I'd need to be so careful about how I used them.

A loud groan from across the room caught my attention. I watched as Julius fell to his knees, holding his side as one man circled behind him with a blade and another withdrew a pistol from his hip.

A silent wail of protest filled my head. I didn't think. I reacted.

I lifted the gun I'd pilfered and fired at the man with the pistol. The bullet lodged itself in the side of the man's head. I took down the man with the knife a second later.

Then a body slammed into me from the side. But even as I fell, I saw that Julius had heaved back to his feet. He'd be okay.

I rolled as I toppled and yanked my gun hand around with good enough aim to fire a shot into my attacker's chest before he could do any more damage. He went limp on top of me. I shoved him off, snatching the knife he'd held and swiveling to prepare for another onslaught.

My efforts to thin our enemies' numbers had helped. No new attackers careened through the window, and the men were making short work of the remaining foes. I slashed one man who was raising his gun toward Blaze across the throat and stabbed the knife deep into the back of another's head. A few more shots rang out, and then it was just the five of us, a little bleeding and battered, standing over a heap of corpses.

Garrison caught my eye with a quick nod and a grimace that could have either been acknowledgment of the shitty situation or his disgust at all the gore. He crouched to sift through the men's pockets. "Let's see if we can find out who these assholes are and why they came after us."

"Check fast," Julius demanded. "We're leaving in five minutes. Get your shit so we can get out before the cops get here."

His hand was clamped to the wound on his side. Blood seeped across his shirt. His gaze caught mine, and my heart lurched all over again at the thought of how close he'd come to dying.

"You should bandage that," I said. "No good avoiding arrest if you bleed out."

"I'll be fine," he said with typical unshakeable confidence, but he did march into the bathroom and tear a strip off one of the towels to tie around his waist.

Blaze was grabbing his laptop and assorted other devices off the desk, shoving them into a large satchel. "I texted you so that you could keep an eye out for danger and *avoid* it where you were," he said to me, his tone dry but with a hint of frustration.

"Well, I'm happy I came back," I retorted, "or you all could have been killed."

He made a face, but none of them disputed that fact.

I only had a small bag of belongings that I refused to leave behind, so I rushed to the side of my bed, stepping over corpses as I went. I always kept my things ready to go at a moment's notice anyway, so all I had to do was sling the bag over my shoulder.

"You don't have any idea who these people are?" I asked over my shoulder.

"They're no one I recognize," Talon muttered.

"And they didn't stop to introduce themselves first," Blaze added. "Very impolite."

"I have a hunch." Garrison lifted a phone in the air. "Because there's an interesting text message on this man's home screen."

I hurried over. "What does it say?"

Garrison cleared his throat. "*Don't touch the daughter.* Who do you think that could be?"

I stopped in my tracks. Obviously I was the only person who usually hung out with the crew who could be anyone's daughter. And the way some of the men had shied away from attacking me loomed large in my mind.

Our previous attackers had sometimes gone easier on me, but only because they'd been looking to take me captive rather than murder me. One of the men from the household's organization had outright told me that they had permission to kill me if I proved too difficult to take alive.

This was different.

"Who would have wanted to kill all of you and not hurt me?" I said, and then the thought clicked into place in my head at the same moment as the guys' expressions stiffened with similar realizations.

"Who would think of you foremost as being a 'daughter'?" Julius said. "Does your father know where you've been staying? Has he given any indication that he knows you've been staying *with* other people or that he's concerned about the company you're keeping?"

I shook my head, my pulse kicking up a notch all over again. "No, I haven't gotten any impression of that at all." But Damien Malik did hate criminals, and he was determined to protect his long-lost daughter. Still… "It doesn't totally make sense, though, does it? It's pretty convenient that the guy left that text visible on his screen. Every other time we've been attacked, our enemies have been more careful not to have any identifying info on them."

"That's true," Blaze said, but he was frowning. "Sometimes people make mistakes, though. And if these people came from Malik, they'd be a different breed from the mercenaries who took us on before."

I rubbed my forehead. Adrenaline was still surging through my veins, making my thoughts race back and forth through my head. I didn't know what to make of this when I could barely focus on anything at all.

"It doesn't matter right now," Julius said firmly. "We'll figure this out, but we need to get out of here before someone finds this mess."

"Where are we going to go?" Blaze asked, holding his satchel and suitcase.

Julius took a deep breath before he spoke. "We'll want someplace more secure than a typical hotel. There's a local group that owes us a favor. We'll go to them and see what they can do for us."

NINE

Decima

I DIDN'T KNOW what I found odder—the guys who showed us the house or the house itself.

The house had a... unique security feature, as it had been built into the side of a rocky hill on the outskirts of town—going as far as to use the rock as a structural feature. The back half of the house was embedded in stone and not accessible by intruders, so we only needed to worry about the front.

I ran my fingers down the rocky face on the inside, finding it cool to the touch but polished pleasantly smooth. I wondered how they kept spiders and other insects out of the house when half of the building was built using nature as its guide. Hopefully they'd put a little thought into that. I could handle bugs, but I'd rather not have them crawling on me in my sleep, thank you very much.

The brothers who showed us the place gave off a similarly weird vibe, a mix of warm exuberance that reminded me of Blaze in his typical state and cool competitiveness that came out at unexpected moments.

"We built this place from scratch," the taller, seemingly older brother said, patting the slightly shorter of the two on the back.

His brother scoffed, poking an elbow into his brother's abdomen. "*James and I* built this place from scratch. You supervised when you felt like it."

There were actually three brothers. We'd met James briefly when we'd gone to see about calling in Julius's favor after patching up the guys' injuries from the fight. Warmth had definitely not been in *his* vocabulary. The youngest of the three siblings had simply glowered at us before slouching away.

Now, the older of the two apparently non-identical twins shrugged. "If you'd come out of Mom first, maybe you'd have been given the role of supervisor."

"I'm happy I didn't come out first. I'd probably be as fat as you."

Garrison's snort sent me over the edge where I'd been balancing, and I covered my mouth to silence my laugh. Neither of these men was fat by any means, but the "second" twin was certainly the fittest with lean muscles covered in dark ink down both arms and across his chest.

The younger twin dodged the older one's attempted slap, raising his hands in a feigned defensive maneuver. Was this the kind of relationship I might one day have with Carter? It was difficult to picture.

"Anyway," the older twin said to the rest of us, ruffling his brother's hair in a way that looked more affectionate than hostile, though still aggressive, "you can have the run of the place while you're in town. I think that should make us square, don't you?"

Julius inclined his head. "It'll do very well. We appreciate the hospitality."

"We'll leave you to it then."

As they ambled out the front door, Blaze let out a dramatic sigh and flopped onto the leather sofa. He didn't waste a moment before digging out his laptop.

"Comfortable?" Garrison asked with an amused smirk.

"I'll be more comfortable when I'm sure we're not going to find ourselves under siege again," the hacker muttered. His usual jovial air had dampened quite a bit since the attack. Noticing that sent an uncomfortable pang through me that I didn't know what to do with.

I distracted myself by exploring the rest of the house. I'd want to know all the entry and exit points in case it did come to another battle, after all.

With the wooden walls that expanded out from the stone face at the back, the building looked like a rustic mountain cabin, even though the low hill it was built into was the highest peak around this area. A fireplace stood across from the sofa in the center of the room, constructed of decorative stone that rose all the way to the high, wood-beamed ceiling. A bearskin rug covered the floor.

For all the cabin-like décor, it was all clearly top of the line. To rent this place on the open market I'd guess would have cost at least triple what we'd paid for that already upscale hotel. I was guessing Julius hadn't mentioned the possibility of violent invasion when he'd called in this favor.

Or maybe people in our line of work simply took it for granted as a risk.

"Is trading favors a typical thing in this industry?" I asked. "They're happy to just give us this place for as long as we need it because you helped them somehow in the past?"

"Yep," Garrison said, poking around in the kitchen. "The most successful of us in the underworld have more than enough money, so cash payments are actually less appealing than goods or services we might be able to provide. We've all got different skills, after all." He stepped away from the counter toward the front door. "Speaking of which, I'm going to go and see if I can pick up any word on the street about who might be targeting us locally."

Blaze shot up, wincing slightly at either the old bullet wound that had nearly healed entirely or the bruising he'd gotten from the most recent fight. "Can I get a ride? Some of my equipment was damaged in the fight, and I need to replace it. Plus there are a few new security measures I'd like to put in place, mountainside or no mountainside."

Garrison sighed, but there wasn't much animosity in it. "I suppose I can put up with your company a little longer. Anyone else wanting to hitch a ride? Going once… twice…"

"I'll reach out to the local supplier and stock up on

more ammo," Talon said, striding over. "If things keep up like this, we'll need it."

Those words and the sight of the three of them about to step out of view made my pulse stutter. What if our enemies came at them again? Who knew what they might face out there?

It was ridiculous. The Chaos Crew had gone off on all kinds of errands and missions since I'd met them and before then too. They could obviously look after themselves. But in that moment, all I could think of was how close they'd all come to taking a bullet in the brain just a few hours ago.

How empty my life would feel if I lost them.

The words tumbled out before I could catch them. "Can't some of that wait for tomorrow? It'd be nice to get settled in here first."

I cringed inwardly as soon as I heard myself. Garrison would get the best gossip on the day of the attack, and picking up ammo and security equipment weren't optional. We couldn't wait another moment to have all of these things taken care of.

Garrison had raised his eyebrows, his expression turning a bit concerned. Before he could respond, I covered my awkwardness with a laugh. "Never mind. I'm just tired. I think *I* need to get settled in—and maybe take a nap. Go get what you need."

They had each other, after all, and they'd kept each other alive long before I'd been in the picture.

The three guys marched out through the door, and I stayed where I was until the growl of the car's engine faded away outside. Then I took a deep breath and stepped back, sinking onto the sofa. It *was* pretty comfortable, but the buttery leather did nothing to relieve my skittering nerves.

Julius loomed over me, but these days, his commanding form was reassuring rather than intimidating. "Something's wrong," he said. "Were you hurt during the fight? You don't get to brush off your injuries when you insist on us taking care of our own."

"I'm not injured." My gaze dropped to his side, where his shirt now covered a more normal bandage that he'd applied after we'd fled the hotel. The cut he'd gotten had been fairly shallow, nothing remotely life-threatening.

Just enough to throw him off for a few crucial seconds while a gun had whipped toward his head.

My stomach turned. I focused on the man in front of me—the living, breathing man who I had to convince myself was stronger than anything this life could hurl at us. A desperate urge rose up in me to *feel* just how alive he was, to take all that strength into me, to know beyond a doubt that I hadn't even remotely lost him.

A strange heat kindled low in my belly. I pushed myself to my feet and reached up to touch his chest, holding his gaze.

"I'm not totally all right, though. I need you to show me just how okay *you* are. In every possible way." I slid my hand down his solidly muscled chest, more heat spreading up through my abdomen. My voice dropped. "Do you think you can help me with that?"

Lust flared in Julius's eyes. He lowered his head, his

breath tickling over my forehead, and set his hands on my shoulders. "I think I could manage that."

"Good," I whispered, pulling my shirt over my head without a moment's hesitation. "There's only one rule. *Don't* be gentle."

Julius's eyes flashed, and his grin turned feral as he slid his hands down to grip my hips. "I don't do gentle."

I pushed myself up on my toes to meet his lips, but Julius had different ideas. He marched me backward and shoved me onto the sofa. It slid back a couple inches as we crashed into it. I barely had a chance to catch my breath before he grabbed my thighs and pulled them toward him.

The smooth leather cradled my back as Julius yanked his shirt over his head and tossed it to the ground beside him. He reached for his pants. I pushed myself up on my elbows, licking my lips as he dropped his jeans, leaving only his boxers behind.

My eyes moved up to the bandage at the side of his abdomen. The recent wound had to hurt. Maybe this was a bad idea.

Julius caught my gaze and must have guessed my thoughts. He braced himself over me, pinning me between his brawny arms and with his dark blue gaze.

"Just a scratch," he said. "It'd take a lot more than that to slow me down." He tapped the edge of my lacy bra. "Take it off."

I peered at him through my eyelashes. "What if I want you to do it?" I teased. I needed him to touch me and surround me. I needed *him.*

"Fine." He knelt over me, grabbing the bra from the

front. Before I could open my mouth to speak, he jerked, and the fabric tore from my body.

He reached for my pants and tore them open as well. The button popped right off, flying across the room as he peeled the pants off me. I lifted my hips, and he bent forward, licking a line between my breasts. He moved to the side, and without a moment's hesitation, he tugged my nipple between his teeth and pulled it. A gasp jolted out of me.

His mouth moved down the center of my stomach, straight to my core. He devoured my sex so forcefully that I jerked from the sofa, his hands on my hips the only things that kept me still beneath him. He didn't stop there, utterly wrecking every part of me with his mouth.

"Julius," I moaned, and my voice did something to him. It added a sense of urgency as he tightened his grip on my thighs and plunged his tongue even deeper inside me. Pleasure throbbed through my core, blazing into an inferno.

He nipped my clit and plunged two fingers into me where his tongue had just penetrated, and I came undone. Stars burst behind my eyes as I bucked my hips and panted.

As the afterglow rolled over me, my need was barely sated. I looked down at him and found him eyeing my reaction with an expression of complete satisfaction.

"Fuck me, Julius," I said roughly. "I want you inside of me *now.*"

I reached between his legs to emphasize my point. A second before my fingers closed around his rigid erection, he grasped my hand. Taking charge, exerting control. A giddy quiver ran through me as I let him place my hand against him and show me exactly how he wanted me to stroke him up and down, fast and hard. His cock felt like silk-sheathed steel.

"Condoms are in my suitcase," he said with a rasp.

I didn't want to let go of him. I didn't want anything to break this moment. I tightened my grip behind his guiding hand and studied his face. "I have a birth control implant, and I'm clean. I haven't been with anyone but the four of you, and that was always with protection. If you're clean too…"

A low curse spilled from his lips. His mouth collided with mine, hot and rough. He lifted my hips and lined himself up against me, first letting the head of his cock rub over my clit.

I let out another moan, clutching his shoulder. My sex outright ached now.

"Let me fuck you," I begged, imagining how it would feel to ride him to my orgasm.

Julius's laugh was dark and full of promise. He shoved a decorative pillow under my ass. "I'm the one who does the fucking here," he announced. "Don't think that will ever change."

If I hadn't been ready before, those words sent tingles straight through my body. Then he was plunging into me, and I almost came just like that all over again.

I tipped my head back into the soft leather, reveling in the feeling of him filling me, stretching me, claiming my body in a way I was only too happy to accept.

"Please," I murmured, not entirely sure what I was begging for.

Julius was here. He was *right here*, as close as he could possibly be.

He thrust in and out at a pace that soon had us both sweaty and panting. Bliss radiated all through my body as I rocked with his rhythm, and somehow I kept soaring higher and higher. The pressure of my building release was almost as torturous as it was thrilling.

"I promised I wouldn't be gentle, didn't I?" Julius murmured, and bucked into me even harder than before. My body trembled with the waves of pleasure he was sending through me. I rose up to meet him, digging my fingers into his back, and he angled me against him so some part of him brushed my clit.

With a cry, I shattered beneath him. As the flood of ecstasy rolled over me, I opened my eyes, and I found him staring down at me. His own eyes glazed over as he worked to find his own pleasure.

I couldn't help lifting my hand to his face, stroking his cheek. His breath stuttered. He tipped his head back and increased the intensity of his thrusts even more, sending fresh pulses of pleasure through my already giddy body.

"Come for me, Julius," I whispered, my voice hoarse from my orgasm.

He came so hard that a roar left his lips, the single hand on my thigh tightening to a near bruising grip. Then he bowed over me, his chest grazing mine but not crushing me as it could have with his full weight.

I pulled him down over me, wanting to feel all of him.

The smell and the press of his body replaced the vision of the gun rising to his head.

Now, all I wanted to do was find the people who thought they could do this to us. I wouldn't be distracted by the thought of what could have happened. I *would* find and kill whoever had attacked my crew.

Julius held me in his powerful embrace for a moment longer and then rolled to the side, withdrawing from me. He brushed a careful hand over the sweaty hair that'd become stuck to my forehead. "Better?" he asked with a gleam in his eyes that told me he'd enjoyed the encounter just as much as I had.

I grinned up at him. "Just what I needed." I pushed myself into a sitting position and reached for my bag so I could retrieve some clothes to replace what he'd ruined. "Now let's get to work figuring out what assholes we need to make pay and how they're connected to me."

A chuckle tumbled out of Julius. He shook his head, but there was nothing but admiration in his gaze. "You're some woman, all right."

"And don't you forget it," I said tartly.

Julius wrapped an arm around my waist and held me in place just for a moment. I couldn't stop myself from gazing down at his nakedness. God, he was an impressive specimen of a man, wasn't he?

"We're going to find out the truth, Dess," he promised. "It doesn't matter what it takes. We're going to dig right to the bottom of this mess so we can fully protect you."

I raised my eyebrows at him. "Since when do I need

protection?" I asked, gesturing to the bandage at his side to remind him of exactly *who* had needed protection the last time we'd tangled with these pricks.

"I didn't say you *needed* protection." Julius tugged a lock of my hair and then squeezed my shoulder. "But you have to know by now that we're going to protect you every way we can anyway, because we want to. That's what people do for family."

TEN

Talon

I SHOULD HAVE KNOWN BETTER than to rebandage my wounds with the bathroom door even slightly open. I didn't think the minor scrapes and cuts were anything to fuss about, but after I'd peeled off my shirt and paused to study the marks in the mirror over my shoulder, Dess peeked in.

"Do you need some help with those?" she asked, nodding to the ones on my back. "You'll have trouble reaching them on your own."

Blaze tsked his tongue from the room behind her. "Don't be shy," he teased. "You're just looking for excuses to grope all those muscles."

"Oh, hush," Dess said, rolling her eyes. I had a feeling she'd have had a harsher retort if it'd been Garrison who'd made the comment. Our hacker tended to bring out the softer side in all of us... just like our chameleon tended to do the opposite.

I looked down at myself and decided that patching myself up would go a lot faster with help, even if I didn't like to ask for it. She'd volunteered, after all. And I didn't particularly mind the idea of her hands on my muscles, whether Blaze had only been teasing or not.

"Come on in," I said. "I've already disinfected the ones I can reach."

She slipped into the bathroom with me and positioned herself next to the stone basin that served as a sink, where I'd set out my supplies. I applied fresh bandages to the minor cuts on my shoulder and my chest while she dabbed antiseptic cream on the marks down my back. They stung more now than they had when I'd gotten them yesterday—I'd barely noticed the swipes of the enemy knife in the midst of the surge of adrenaline that'd gotten me through the fight—but Dess kept her fingers light.

"You have almost as many scars as I do," she murmured.

I gave a faint hum. "And you've had about half as much time to build your collection."

"Oh, I don't know about that. When did you start this kind of training?"

The words came out before I'd thought them through. "The earliest ones aren't from any kind of training."

I hadn't meant to bring up my past. It wasn't something I liked to discuss with anyone, and I sure as hell didn't need to drum up sympathy from Dess of all people.

But she'd clearly caught my insinuation even from that brief statement.

Her hands paused over my broken flesh. "I'm sorry. I didn't know."

"Of course you didn't," I said. "How could you have? It isn't important now anyway. And even with that, you've still got me beat."

I wasn't any kind of jokester, but I must have managed to work enough dryness into my voice that Dess's mouth twitched with a hint of a smile. To my relief, she laid the subject to rest. Instead, she patted the polished stone of the sink as she reached for the bandages. "This house is… interesting, isn't it?"

"You mean the way it's practically a cave?"

She snorted. "Yeah, that part. It's a little closer to nature than I'd generally prefer to live. I swear I saw a centipede as long as my hand run across my bedroom floor last night."

"Don't tell me you're afraid of bugs?" The thought of Dess, the famous Ghost assassin, being scared of anything that small and weak amused me.

"I wouldn't say *afraid*," Dess said. "More like disgusted. No living creature has any business growing that many legs."

Her fingers brushed against my skin as she fixed the bandages into place, so careful to avoid putting any pressure on the wounds themselves. Even Julius with his medical training didn't offer this light a touch. Maybe the real contradiction was how such a skilled and ruthless killer could be so gentle when the situation called for it.

"I guess I can agree with you on that," I said. If I saw a centipede in my room, it'd be mashed into the floor in two seconds flat.

"There. I knew there was a reason I liked you. We can hate on bugs together."

Dess's tone was playful, but her touch stayed soft and careful. Something about the tenderness of her attentions brought an unfamiliar warmth into my chest. It unfurled further with each graze of her hands. I found myself closing my eyes, wanting to focus on nothing but her soothing presence behind me.

I'd never had a woman look after me like this. Never had a woman who cared enough and understood my kind of life enough to want to. In that moment, I'd have killed anyone who so much as looked at her wrong.

She was *my* woman. The rest of the guys' too, but still mine. I wasn't used to this possessive sensation either, but it felt right somehow.

Some part of me wanted to bundle her up with all the same tenderness she'd shown me and hide her away until all the danger that lurked in this city had passed. Be a shield between her and the rest of the big bad world.

But Dess didn't need that, didn't *want* it—and I wasn't sure I could be tender anyway.

"There. All patched up." Dess stepped back, and I turned to face her. Her brightly affectionate smile provoked a flutter amid the warmth that had filled my chest. A fucking *flutter*.

What the hell was I supposed to do with that or all these other emotions I wasn't used to feeling? My heart had been as much of a cave as this building was before she'd come along—an empty cave. And suddenly it was buzzing with way too much feeling that I had no idea how to adjust to.

One impulse rang through all the rest—one thing I did know how to do. I *was* going to defend her every way I knew how, every way she'd let me. And that included figuring out how much danger she was in from the man she'd accepted as her father.

"I'd better see if Blaze is ready to head out," I said.

Her smile dimmed a little. I didn't know whether she was more concerned that we'd find something damning about Damien Malik or that we wouldn't and it'd turn out we'd violated her family's trust unnecessarily. I guessed both made sense. Neither were impressions I associated with my own family one bit.

"Right," she said, putting on her determined face. "You're ready to go."

———

I didn't really have a clue how anything Blaze was planning to do at the Malik home worked. It was all buttons and wires as far as I was concerned. But I didn't need to know. That was his job, and mine was keeping watch and being ready to leap into action if he ran into trouble.

Sneaking around a large house with two people inside wasn't particularly difficult. But the Maliks didn't give us a problem even when they came outside. Iris Malik walked along the porch collecting old beach towels without even glancing toward the garden shed we were using for shelter. Her son—Dess's teenager brother—sauntered around the pool and then back into the house with equal inattention.

I grimaced to myself. One thing was obvious: Dess didn't have a lick of protection from the people living here. No wonder Damien needed professional bodyguards.

When Iris had left for work, leaving just the boy in the house, we slunk across the lawn to the back wall. Blaze stalked along the perimeter, holding a device that beeped faintly, while I peeked through the windows. Dess had told us where her brother's bedroom was, and we were heading in the opposite direction, but we wouldn't want to be spotted from the common rooms.

Blaze paused partway down the east side of the house, where the device had started beeping faster. He spoke under his breath. "The router's around here." He glanced up. "Probably on the second floor."

I cocked my head as he pawed through his satchel for some other electronic box that looked almost the same as the other one to me. "And this is going to let you tap into their internet?" I murmured.

He nodded. "I didn't have the equipment to manage it before—and even now, I need to get this thing very close. Give me a lift?"

I moved without hesitation, bending down and offering my interlaced hands for a boost up. My muscles only strained slightly hefting the slim man's weight. I raised him to the level of the second-floor window above us.

Blaze gripped the ledge for balance. Peering inside, he

let out a soft whistle. "Holy cow. They've got a whole games room—this kid has everything. Systems, special controllers, fancy sound system, the works."

A whole room just for playing around? I wondered if the teenager who lived here had ever known a hardship in his entire life. I'd enlisted in the military the second I was old enough, and he had what were likely the most expensive consoles piled recklessly in a room.

It wasn't anger that I felt, and it wasn't jealousy, but when I considered Dess being surrounded by this spoiled family, it just seemed… wrong.

"Bingo," Blaze said. "There's the modem and the router. No wonder I couldn't get into this thing without being closer. It's state of the art."

I held him steady, keeping my ears pricked. Blaze got to work attaching his device, which was about the size of his palm, to the siding next to the window. He'd painted it the same color as the siding ahead of time, and it was so small it'd blend in easily, especially tucked against the protruding frame. I barely noticed it when I looked up, and I knew it was there.

Would we find anything useful from his efforts? I wasn't sure I believed that the Maliks would say anything incriminating even in the privacy of their own internet network. They might not have been great at physical surveillance, but they struck me as awfully cautious about appearances, even with each other.

But this wasn't my wheelhouse anyway. Blaze thought the attempt was worthwhile, and he'd had plenty of brilliant brainstorms to earn the right to experiment.

The hacker was twisting another screw into place when he froze above me. I tensed too.

"Shit," he whispered. "The kid just walked into the room."

He flattened himself against the outer wall. I eased closer too, my pulse speeding up just slightly. I'd have yanked Blaze down, but the thump of his landing seemed like more of a risk for drawing the boy's attention than the chance that he'd crane his neck around looking out the window.

What exactly would we do if he did spot us? Two strange men forming a tower against the side of his house... There was no way it wouldn't be suspicious. I'd been prepared to eliminate any guards who came at us, but Dess's brother himself?

My stomach twisted. The seconds slipped by, both of us waiting in rigid silence. Then Blaze exhaled in a rush.

"He went back out again. I'd better finish this quick. Are you holding up all right down there, Talon?"

"I've carried guns that were harder on my arms than you are," I muttered at the slender man, and he chuckled lightly.

"Just have to get this last screw deep enough in so it stays in place... There." He tapped a few buttons on the outside of the device and nudged my hand with the toe of his sneakers for me to lower him. As he hopped out of my grasp, he aimed one of his broad grins at me, his brown eyes sparkling.

"We're in."

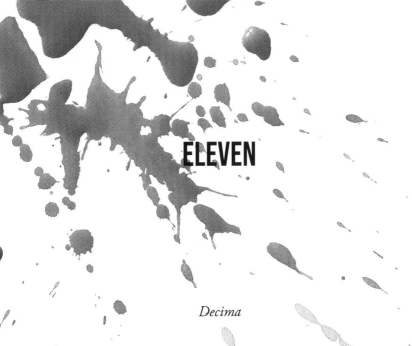

ELEVEN

Decima

"YOU SAID you could stop by for a visit on the weekend?" my mother asked outside the restaurant where we'd just had dinner with most of the extended family.

I dragged in a breath as my Uber pulled up next to the curb. I was getting used to the smaller family get-togethers, but having the attention of ten or more people on me for hours at a time still exhausted me. I guessed that wasn't surprising when for most of my life, I hadn't interacted with anyone other than my trainers. I was used to long stretches with only myself for company, not extended conversations full of small talk and family gossip.

But I did want to be a part of this family. It'd get easier over time, right?

"Bright and early," I replied with a smile I had to force a bit. "See you then."

I ducked into the back of the Uber, and the immediate

silence greeted me like a warm blanket. The driver pulled onto the road with a rumble of the engine. As I sank back in my seat, tipping my head against the warm fabric, I caught a motion of the driver's hand. He was setting a phone on the passenger seat next to him and hitting the speaker button.

I sat up straighter, frowning, just as a low voice carried from the phone's speaker. "Hello again, Rachel."

My stance stiffened. I'd recognize that slightly hoarse tone anywhere even after only one previous conversation with the guy. My gaze flicked to the driver, but he stayed focused on the road now. What the hell was going on?

"I know you're there," the Hunter said on the other end of the phone line.

"How did you know I'd be here?" I snapped. "Why are you bothering me again?" I glanced at the doors, wondering if I should make a run for it. I didn't like the idea that I was in a vehicle probably controlled by this strange man with his unknown agenda.

But so far the driver appeared to be taking the correct route back to the house in the hill. And I did want to see if the Hunter would reveal more than he had before. The need for answers warred with my sense of caution.

"That doesn't matter," the Hunter replied. "You're still playing happy family with the bunch of them. I thought you'd have smartened up by now."

I glowered at the phone, not that he could see my reaction. "I've done some investigating of my own, and I haven't seen any reason to think they're doing anything wrong. And since *you* won't give me any specifics, even tell me who you really are, I'm going by my own judgment. If you don't like that, maybe you could give me more to go on."

The Hunter let out a faint scoffing sound. "You have the inside access. You obviously haven't dug very far. Maybe you don't actually want to know the truth. You'd rather live in a happy delusion."

His accusation raised my hackles. "The only one avoiding anything is you. If it's so important to you that I know the 'truth,' you could tell me what you know. The fact that you won't seems like pretty solid proof that you're just trying to stir up problems for the hell of it."

"Oh, the problems in this situation aren't of my making."

"There you go again," I said. "All vague, ominous statements. I don't know you, and I have no reason to trust you. So I'm done with this conversation if that's all you've got to say for yourself. I'm smart enough to realize when someone's just jerking my chain."

I didn't actually move toward the phone. As frustrated as I was, there was a chance that he'd reveal something—at least about his motivations—now that I was turning the conversation around on him.

He chuckled darkly. "Chains. That's a good one. Fine. Listen carefully. There's more digging you should do. There are answers in the soil if you know how to read them. And that family does love its garden."

"What?" I demanded. The remarks sounded like more creepy vagueness. When the Hunter didn't answer, I unclasped my seatbelt and lunged forward in my seat.

"Stop the car!" I shouted at the driver, gripping his shoulder hard enough to hurt. I snatched at the phone with my other hand.

As the driver jerked over to the side of the road, I picked up the phone, scanning the screen for any details about the caller. But it'd gone blank. The Hunter had hung up on me.

I swiveled toward the driver, still clutching his shoulder hard. His face had gone white. "Who was that?" I said. "Why did you set me up like this? Do you work for him?"

"I—I don't know anything about it," the man stammered, looking so terrified I believed him. "I'm sorry. This woman paid me to take the phone and pick you up— she said it was a surprise and that I should stay quiet. I didn't realize—I don't even know who you are! I've got nothing against you."

I eased back my hand, worrying at my lower lip. That did sound like how someone like the Hunter would operate. Missed Connection columns and now this. He liked to put as many layers as possible between me and him. That only made his intentions more suspect.

Or maybe it proved he really did feel he had to be careful because of the danger surrounding the situation.

"The woman," I said. "What did she look like?"

The man rubbed his hand over his face as if trying to produce the memory with the gesture. "Blond hair. A lot of makeup. Honestly, I was more focused on the cash she was offering me."

Blond hair and a lot of makeup. That wouldn't get us

very far. The makeup might disguise her true appearance and mess with any chance of Blaze using his facial recognition app against her. But we could still try, if the interaction had been caught on a street cam. Which I had to admit, I didn't think was very likely given the Hunter's usual meticulousness.

"Where did she approach you?" I asked anyway.

"Just around the corner from the place where I picked you up," the guy said. "Outside the shoe store."

"Okay." I shoved the phone into my pocket just in case the tech genius could determine something from it. Sitting back in my seat, I debated my next steps for a moment, but the guy already had the address I'd been going to, which meant the Hunter would have it too. There was no point in trying to hide my current location now. "Take me home. As fast as you can."

The drive passed in what felt like seconds as I stewed in my thoughts. The moment the driver pulled up outside, I leapt out and burst into the house.

All four of my men were in the living room, Blaze alternating between watching his computer's screen and tossing darts at a makeshift board he'd put together. Julius and Garrison were handling the dishes from their own dinner in the open-concept kitchen. Talon looked like he'd just come out of a shower.

They all went still and silent when I barged in. I held up the Hunter's phone and tossed it to Blaze, who caught it easily.

"I had an interesting conversation on my way here," I said. "The Hunter wanted to check in on me."

Julius stepped toward me, his expression darkening. "Are you okay? He obviously upset you."

"Oh, I'm pissed off all right. Mostly he just wanted to needle me about not listening to his vague bullshit as much as he liked." I marched into the kitchen and grabbed the milk and chocolate syrup. I needed a hit of cocoa to finish processing everything that'd just happened. "He's still insisting that there's some dirt on the Maliks that I haven't found. Actually, he mentioned the literal dirt. The soil in their garden. Like I'd find something there if I 'read' it."

Garrison knit his brow. "Like a soil analysis?"

"I guess. Hard to know with him." I paused, stirring the syrup into a glass of milk. The thought of poking around in my birth family's affairs, trying to find some reason to distrust them, brought an ache into my stomach that had nothing to do with hunger.

But what if the Hunter really did know something? He watched them closely enough to know how they felt about their garden. Wouldn't it be better to check and know for sure than have his insinuations hanging over me?

If I could prove to myself that he *didn't* have a case at all, maybe I could let go of that niggling worry completely.

"None of you have found out anything concerning so far, right?" I said.

The men all shook their heads. "Damien Malik runs a tight ship—and a clean one," Julius said. "But that doesn't mean he couldn't have secrets."

Garrison grimaced. "On the other hand, this Hunter prick is shady as fuck."

Talon gazed at me steadily. "What do you want to do, Dess?"

I groaned and flopped onto the sofa, pressing the heel of my hand to my forehead. "I mean, it wouldn't be *hard* to take a little soil from the garden. And it wouldn't hurt anything to check it even if it turns out he's just jerking me around. But if the dirt turns up nothing, then I'm done talking to that weirdo." I opened my eyes to glance at Blaze. "Could you do this soil analysis thing?"

He made an apologetic gesture. "That's outside my domain—all of our domains."

I thought of the way we'd obtained this house, how we'd gotten my DNA sequenced back home to connect me to Malik in the first place. "Then we need to find someone else who can. Someone who won't ask questions about it… I don't have much in the way of money, but maybe I could set up an exchange of favors like you have before?"

Garrison nodded slowly. "I've heard of a woman out in New York who handles a lot of things along that line— chemicals and environmental hazards. I've never dealt with her directly before, but from what the people who've mentioned her have said, she seems to understand discretion and to stick to her word."

I nodded. "Great, reach out to her as soon as you can. And find out what she'd want from me in return."

"From us," Julius put in. "Whatever she wants, between the five of us, I'm sure we can manage it."

A rush of affection filled my chest at his automatic offer of support, not that it should have surprised me after everything else he'd done and said before. But I found myself shaking my head, resolve wrapping around my heart.

"No." I caught Garrison's gaze. "Make sure it's something I can handle on my own. The Maliks are my family, and the Hunter came to me. I should be the one 'paying' to fix that problem."

"We really don't mind," Blaze started.

I cut him off with another jerk of my head. The Hunter's words from our first conversation came back to me, echoing up from my memory. *You still need to be ready in case someone else turns out to be better.*

"I might have been respected as the Ghost, but no one except the four of you knows that the Ghost is me—no one has any reason to respect me as Decima. I need to be able to stand on my own two feet in this world, and that means I have to prove myself on my own. If I want respect, *I* have to earn it."

Garrison gave me a small smile that I thought was approving. It sent a tingle of heat between my legs more intense than anything his usual smirks could have provoked.

"You've got it, sweetheart," he said. "One return favor, catered just to you. It's not like you can't blow them away without any help from us."

TWELVE

Decima

I PAUSED JUST inside the restaurant, taking in the posh surroundings. Crystal glinted everywhere, and the tablecloths shone bleached white. Subdued classical music tinkled through the room. My skin immediately started to itch.

I'd spent time in places like this before to get at various targets, but I'd never enjoyed it. At least I'd known how to dress for the part. I'd selected a modest purple evening gown that hung just below my knees. The neckline wasn't necessarily revealing, though it wasn't prudish either, dipping into a V that just barely accentuated my assets. To top off the look, I'd paired it with a gold necklace and earrings to match a shiny clutch I carried.

From the way the crew's gazes had clung to me as I'd headed out, I knew I'd pulled off the look all right, even if I was way more comfortable in tees and sweatpants.

"There you are." Damien Malik came up beside me, resting his hand briefly on the small of my back to guide me with him. "You look lovely, Rachel."

My father looked taller than usual in his fitted black suit, with an air of authority I hadn't seen him exercise all that much among family. Maybe he was displaying it now because of the company we'd have for this dinner. He'd just gotten back from a longer than usual stint handling political work in DC, and he'd wanted to introduce me to a couple of his close colleagues from the capitol.

I couldn't say I was looking forward to meeting even more strangers, and these ones people I wasn't even related to, but I could tell it meant a lot to my father. And it was part of really becoming Rachel Malik, if I wanted to fully embrace that role.

I just hoped the role of Rachel started to feel more like *me*.

"Just be yourself," Damien assured me with a fatherly smile as we headed toward a table near the back of the room. "They'll go easy on you. I think it'll be good for you to have a deeper understanding of the work that occupies so much of my time. It affects the family in so many ways."

"That makes sense," I said. And it did affect all of the Maliks quite a bit. Like Carter deciding to give up baseball. Like the times when Iris was left to fend for herself when my grandparents visited, because Damien was out of town for the week. But Damien's standing also supported that big house with its expansive property and all the activities that happened in and around it.

We stopped at a table where two men were already sitting, though they got to their feet to greet us. Both were a good match for my father: white, middle-aged, with an air of importance around them as if it never occurred to them that they might not get what they wanted, one way or another. An awful lot of my targets for the household had been people like that.

My skin itched again with that thought. I could only imagine what my father's colleagues would think of *my* line of work.

Damien set his hand on my shoulder. "Clint, Gary, this is my daughter, Rachel. I'm so glad you're finally getting to meet her at last."

Clint, a portly man with bushy eyebrows and a beakish nose, dipped his head to me. "So am I. Such a lot of trouble and trauma on the way to you getting back to your family." He smiled with what looked like genuine sympathy, but I couldn't help feeling there was a patronizing edge to it. Like he thought I'd gotten myself kidnapped as a toddler out of some oversight of my own.

Gary, slim with a short, pointed beard, held out his hand for me to shake it. His grasp was as firm as I'd expect from his confident stance. "It's a pleasure. I can already see the apple didn't fall far from the tree, regardless of how you got there. Nature over nurture!"

"I'd like to think so," Damien said with a chuckle, and we all sat down.

"So, you work with my father in Washington?" I ventured, feeling like I should make some effort to add to the conversation and show an interest in the two men.

"For well over a decade now," Clint said, clapping his hand to my father's back. "Couldn't ask for a better ally among all the goons out there. Hard to find men with real integrity these days."

I thought of the Hunter and all his insinuations, and then mentally kicked myself for giving that stranger's accusations any space in my brain. Garrison hadn't yet confirmed the exchange of favors that'd let me get the Maliks' garden soil analyzed, but at this point, there was no reason to think it'd reveal any horrifying secrets.

"But I'd like to hear more about you," Gary spoke up, tipping his head to me as the waitress went around filling our water glasses. "As much as you're comfortable saying. Have you been able to settle in with your family all right after all this time?"

I would have bristled at the private question if he hadn't spoken so gently. But then, he was a politician, so framing things in the right way to get the answers he wanted must have been second nature to him.

"I think so," I said carefully. "We've only really just gotten started."

My father patted the back of my chair. "I'd say that Rachel has been fitting in exceptionally well, considering the circumstances. She's incredibly resilient."

He didn't even know the half of it, but part of me lit up at the praise despite myself. Noelle had barely acknowledged the strain she'd put me under. She'd taken it for granted that I'd get through everything she threw at me and every assignment I was sent on. But I *had* survived a hell of a lot.

Clint offered a sympathetic grimace. "You'd have to be. You've been through far more than any young lady—than anyone at all—should have to."

"And let's hope we see the perpetrators of that crime duly punished," Gary said. "Thanks to your father's work over the years, they'll face more jail time than they would have when you were first taken. Although some feel even that isn't enough. What are your thoughts on capital punishment?"

I held back a laugh. It hadn't taken long for them to transition from personal condolences to political agendas, had it? I guessed that was probably how things worked in Washington.

I'd never really thought about whether I believed in the death sentence before. Legal forms of murder had been far removed from my existence. I'd have been much more likely to get killed by the people I was intending to do the same to myself than to be caught by law enforcement and sentenced.

But then, what did the Chaos Crew do—what did *I* intend to do from now on with my skills—other than dole out capital punishments of our own?

"I can see some cases where it might be necessary," I said, still picking my words cautiously. I wasn't sure where even my father stood on this subject. "The criminal world is a violent place. Anyone who gets all that involved must know that's a risk they're taking."

Clint nodded. "I couldn't agree more. Although there is some debate about which approach actually puts more strain on the taxpayer."

"And the problems of false convictions," Gary pointed out. "Can't come back from a lethal injection if new evidence comes up later."

"Well, you know that doesn't happen very often."

I cleared my throat, feeling the need to add a little of my own perspective… especially because in their eyes, my men and I were probably among the kind of criminals they'd imagine would get a sentence that severe. "I do think the evidence should be clear. And also the person's motives need to be taken into consideration. Why they did what they did. What the consequences were."

Gary hummed to himself, and I couldn't tell whether it was approving or skeptical. His tone didn't give much away. "You're thinking of those hypothetical 'stealing bread for the starving family' situations."

Well, no, I'd been thinking about the very non-hypothetical "assassins who take out fellow criminals" situation, but I wasn't going to tell him that.

Before I could figure out how to answer, Damien set his hand on the back of my chair again. He'd been watching the whole conversation thoughtfully, and his gaze lingered on my face for a moment before he spoke, as if he was evaluating what he'd seen from me so far. A nervous twitch ran down my back.

But all he said was, "Let's not heap too much shop talk on Rachel all at once. She's here to meet you as friends, not to have her political stances dissected."

"What good are friends if you can't talk politics, huh?" Clint winked at both of us. "I'm sure you must at least share your father's stance on cracking down hard on the criminal element, especially after what you've experienced."

Did Damien's gaze get even more intent as he waited for my answer? My throat constricted just for a second. I did feel put on the spot now, and he wasn't rescuing me this time.

"I'd definitely want to see the people who kidnapped me punished with the full force of the law," I said. My law, delivered by my hands. "No one should steal a child from their home. It's unforgiveable."

Gary chuckled. "Only bread thieves can get off."

I shifted in my chair, trying not to outright squirm. "I don't know. I just think it depends on the crime and the reasons for it. Isn't there a saying about how the punishment should fit the crime? It's hard to make a blanket statement about all of it."

But it did seem like my father believed you could. He wanted every criminal treated more harshly. I wasn't sure he'd ever understand my perspective. Crimes had two sides, and I didn't think Damien Malik had ever been put in the position to see the side opposite his own.

But then, after losing me the way he had for so long, maybe his vehemence was understandable.

"Absolutely," he said now. "The trouble is that the laws have been too lenient across the board. The people who get away with too much vastly outnumber the few who were truly acting with what they thought were good intentions. Take theft—of anything, not specifically bread.

Did you know that people don't usually get more than five to ten years in jail for that crime? They're taking away someone's livelihood or rightfully earned belongings, and that's all they face. I'm pushing for double that at *least*."

I swallowed hard, thinking of the car I'd stolen—and then crashed—as I fled the household that first night. The one I'd grabbed in his own neighborhood to reach the crew in time to help defend them from the surprise attack? Would he have spoken that firmly if he'd known his daughter was a thief too?

Probably. He'd have excused my crime away thinking I'd needed to do it to save my life and those I cared about, that I was one of those rare exceptions. It was everything *else* I'd done in my life that he wouldn't be able to explain away.

Trying to come up with an answer that would satisfy him and hopefully end this line of conversation, I thought of the criminals I'd encountered over the past few weeks. The drug dealers who'd eagerly been packaging their product for the addicts they'd hooked. The movie-making gangsters who'd talked gleefully about murdering some guy for his camera equipment. The attackers who'd tried to kill the crew more than once, as recently as last week…

The man next to me *couldn't* have hired paid killers, could he? Not with attitudes like the ones he was expressing now. It didn't make any sense.

But why would someone else have wanted to murder the men of the Chaos Crew but not "the daughter"?

I shook those thoughts away and focused on my

frustration with the underworld we'd come up against. "There are definitely a lot of people getting away with more than they should. I'd like to see a world where fewer innocent people get hurt."

That response seemed to please Damien. His smile grew, and he nodded emphatically. "Exactly. I knew you'd understand."

Just then, the server arrived with the appetizers we'd ordered. I couldn't have been more grateful for the excuse to focus on doing something with my mouth other than hashing out the flaws of the justice system.

Thankfully, my father and his friends veered into other topics during the rest of the meal. Clint and Gary inquired about everything from my sports interests to how much of the city I'd seen, offering tips of landmarks to check out when I admitted I'd barely explored DC. "Don't let them keep you holed up in your father's hometown," Clint said with a wave of his fork. "You've got the chance to see the world now."

If only he knew how many countries I'd already visited. I'd probably been more places before I'd turned eighteen than he had in his entire life.

When all the food had been polished off and the check paid, we waved goodbye to the two men and I summoned an Uber, the nearest one a few minutes away. My father sat on a bench outside in the warm evening air to wait with me for it. He crossed his legs at the ankles and leaned back, looking more relaxed than I'd seen him all evening.

"You did great in there," he said as he gazed at the

passing cars. "I know they can be a bit overwhelming. I hope you didn't feel cornered at any point."

I shrugged. If I had, it was for reasons he couldn't have predicted and I couldn't admit. "They weren't that bad."

"Your brother hates things like this. Not that he doesn't agree with the policies we support; he just doesn't see the point in talking about it. More of a doer. Which is important, but you can't get permission to do without knowing how to talk the talk first." Damien shook his head. "Your mother—she has a real knack for playing politics. I can tell you're her daughter." He glanced over at me. "You're becoming an integral part of this family, aren't you?"

Somehow that question felt more momentous than the actual words he'd used. "I'd like to think so," I said. "It's been wonderful *having* a family, a real one."

As soon as I said those words, guilt stabbed through my gut. Julius had referred to me as part of the crew's family. Maybe I wasn't connected to them by genetics, but my bond with them was at least as real as anything I shared with the Maliks.

"I'm glad you feel that way." Damien paused for a moment as if deciding what to say next. "We have a long-established legacy among the Maliks, one that goes back generations. I hope that as we become closer, that's something I can introduce you to. We'd be honored to have you be a part of it."

Something about his tone set my nerves prickling. I was already part of the family, wasn't I? The way he phrased it made it sound almost like a cult or something that I'd be indoctrinated into.

He couldn't mean it like that, though, right? He was just passionate about the family and what they stood for. I'd seen how close-knit and supportive the Maliks were.

"What kind of legacy?" I asked, watching him closely.

"Mostly in standing up for the innocents who need our protection, a lot like you said in there." He smiled at me. "Dedicating ourselves to the public good has been an ongoing tradition that means a lot to us."

Was that what the Hunter wanted to warn me about —that my family was dedicated to doing good? Inwardly, I rolled my eyes at that hoarse voice on the telephone with its ominous warnings. Sure, I'd still take a look at the soil, but there'd been no other indications of any kind of threat around the Maliks. Blaze hadn't even found anything suspicious digging through their internet activity.

"Well, that sounds like the kind of legacy I could get behind," I said, and my mind leapt to one specific crime I'd hoped he'd have more details about after all his time away from home. "I don't suppose the investigation into my kidnappers has turned up any new leads? There's still so much about that situation that I don't understand." And still so many people who needed to pay for the lives they'd upended.

My father sighed. "Unfortunately, the path seems to be very cold. Since you escaped without knowing where they'd been holding you before your trip, I think the investigators are stumped on where to even start. And your kidnappers were very effective in covering their tracks."

His mouth twisted. "The worst menaces in society are getting increasingly difficult to pin down. All the more reason we need to crack down on them more than before. Make it clear that the consequences aren't worth it, to stop others going down the same path. People who do such horrendous acts should never be allowed out of prison. They should rot and die there."

Even though I wanted to destroy the people who'd wrenched me from my original life and forced me to become their tool, the vehemence in Damien's voice made me tense. I couldn't blame him for being angry, could I? He'd had his daughter ripped away from him, had to think I was dead for all these years. I wanted the people who'd orchestrated that loss dead too.

But there'd been a viciousness that'd crept into his tone that didn't fit with the upstanding politician he usually presented himself as. He might talk as if his policies were for the greater good, but for him, it was clearly very personal as well. And I got the impression he wasn't only talking about the specific criminals who'd taken me but all of them.

Including people like me and the Chaos Crew.

I didn't have time to think of an appropriate response, because my Uber pulled up across from us just then. Damien walked me over and opened the door for me, getting a promise out of me to stop by the house for Sunday brunch. He was the total picture of a reserved gentleman again. His fond wave as he saw me off felt so normal it was hard to believe he'd been wishing death on the entire prison population just minutes ago.

He couldn't realize how close his claims hit to home, and I hoped he never would.

My phone dinged, breaking me from my reverie. I glanced at the screen and found a text from Julius. *Garrison's contact is willing to meet with you. It's time to swap some favors.*

THIRTEEN

Garrison

AS THE TRAIN roared along the tracks toward New York City, Dess kept her usual calm, cool poise in the seat across from me, but I knew her well enough to mark the signs of tension in her shoulders and her jaw. She ran her finger across her lips, drawing my attention to where it really shouldn't be while we prepared for this detour of a mission.

She'd wanted to come alone, but Julius had insisted that I come along, since I was the one who knew the most about our contact and had handled the negotiations as a middleman. *You'll still be delivering the favor and earning hers on your own*, he'd told Dess. *But it's important to us that everyone knows the Chaos Crew has your back.*

Dess must have been a little nervous, because she'd agreed without any further argument.

"Anthea Noble," she said now, adjusting her position

as she turned the woman's name over on her tongue. "And she specializes in discreet crimes?"

I nodded. "The word that's gone around is that she's the one to turn to if you need a murder set up to look like an accident or an innocent illness—or if you need to investigate an accident or illness that you think might have actually been murder. Checking the chemical compounds in a soil sample, especially for anything that hints at a crime, fits right in with that. I heard that one time she took down an enemy by lacing his rosebushes with some kind of undetectable poison."

Dess grimaced. "A gun to the head or a knife to the throat is much simpler. Clearer. Are you sure we can trust her?"

I shrugged. "As much as we can trust anyone in this world. She's well-established and connected—the aunt of the head of a major gang in a county called Paradise Bend that's a few hours away from New York. And she seems to care about her reputation, which is that she's cutthroat when she needs to be but fair with those she feels have earned her loyalty. I don't think she'd stab us in the back for no reason. If she does... I'd bet you can deal with her."

A glint of humor lit in Dess's eyes. "I can definitely shoot her before she can slowly poison me."

I let out a laugh. "And good thing, too. But I really don't think it'll come to that. She knows you come with the Chaos Crew's support, and we've got quite a reputation too. The best-connected people don't turn down new connections among the upper echelon. They've gotten where they are by forging solid alliances. She'll see us as just as useful to her as she is to us."

"And this gang she's associated with? Are they going to want a cut?"

"She didn't mention anything about that. It appears that she mainly operates independently, without needing permission or guidance from them."

"All right." Dess leaned her head back in her seat with a sigh. My gaze was drawn to the soft, pale stretch of her neck with the urge to run my mouth across it, but I doubted she'd welcome a PDA.

Was she worried more about the stranger we were going to meet or about what that stranger might tell us about the Maliks?

I didn't know how to ask her that, so I settled for a teasing question instead. "So, here you are about to embark on your first solo mission without the household behind you. No cold feet, I hope?"

Dess let out a dismissive huff. "I was always alone in the household anyway." Her eyes went momentarily distant before refocusing. "They might have funded and backed my missions, but they weren't there to make sure I survived. I relied on no one but myself during those operations just as I'll be doing on this one."

"You're getting to call the shots about what and who you do this time, though. Moving up in the world."

She glowered at me through narrowed eyes. "Are you trying to pump me up or take me down a peg?"

I grinned. "Can't it be both at the same time? We wouldn't want your head to get too big."

She patted her hair. "I think it suits me just fine as it is."

The truth was, I was going easier on her than I might have if I couldn't have told that she wasn't totally confident in this new role. It *was* the first time she'd taken on a solo job as a totally free agent.

And really, she should feel proud of where she'd ended up. She'd endured trainers who only cared about how well she could use the weapons they'd put in her hands, no family to speak of in her entire living memory, and death-defying missions from her childhood. But those trials had only honed her into the strongest woman I'd ever known. Even now, knowing what she did about her past, she hadn't let it shake her all that much.

The sudden urge gripped me to open up a part of myself as deep and painful as the losses I knew she'd faced. My chest constricted at the thought. I *never* let down all my walls, never let the all-too-real agony spill out of me.

But I could give her *something* real. Something I could say honestly without sarcasm or jokes to deflect the impact.

I drew in a breath and steadied myself, forcing my voice to come out with genuine warmth rather than its usual wryness. "I'm looking forward to watching you kick ass on this mission without the pretense of anyone controlling you. I can't wait to see what you'll do on your own."

Dess looked at me, and the softness in her eyes showed that she knew how significant those words had been. She leaned toward me in a burst of motion, taking me by surprise as her lips collided with mine. Her hand wrapped around the back of my head and tugged the hair at the base of my skull.

She didn't really do gentle, not when it came to physical intimacy. From the hints she'd dropped when we'd hooked up that one evening, I knew the reason was something that'd make me want to tear apart the world to avenge her.

But she hadn't shared the details, so I wasn't going to pry. Not yet, anyway. I just kissed her back with equal passion. My hand fell to her thigh and squeezed, and she let out a muffled moan.

Then she pulled back. The passengers across the aisle from us were watching, not that I minded. Let them see how much I cared about this woman and how much she wanted me.

A playful smile crossed Dess's lips as she ran her fingers through her dark hair. "I'm glad you're here with me," she said. "I *can* do this on my own... but it's better knowing that I don't have to be. Maybe you'll get to find out just how much the Ghost can pull off when she's in her element."

I gave a soft chuckle. "Oh, I think I have a pretty good idea already."

The tension clenching my chest had eased. The world hadn't ended because I'd gone for sap over snark just this once. Dess hadn't shunned me. Everything was still on its proper course. I actually felt a little lighter than I had before. Freer.

Would it be so bad to let my walls down more often?

Well, with her, at least. Not with the guys or anyone else…

No, I still needed those inner protections. They were my armor. I couldn't let myself get complacent, or I could screw everything up for both me and the people who stood with me.

———

It was night by the time we reached the city. We eased through the shadows of the trees in Central Park, veering off the main paths. People were usually warned not to wander around in this place after dark, but I didn't think anyone would bother us. If they did, we could quickly clear up any misconceptions about who the real predators were here.

We stopped amid the brush behind the Civil War Memorial statue, just a few minutes before our arranged meeting time. Dess peered at the branches that loomed overhead. "What are the odds that we have a sniper on us right now?"

I raised an eyebrow. "I don't see anyone close enough to pull off a shot through all this vegetation without the most incredible aim in the universe."

"And why would I want to have someone ready to shoot you anyway, when you're here to give me something *I* want?" a dry voice said.

A woman emerged from the forested terrain to meet us. At the first sight of her, skepticism shot through me.

She was slim and petite, a full head shorter than I was,

with her bright red hair coiled elegantly behind her ears and tumbling down to her shoulders. The traditional style matched her subtle flower-print dress, which looked like something a '50s housewife would have worn. But even though she appeared to be no older than her early thirties, she seemed totally at ease with the old-fashioned vibe.

Could this really be the infamous Anthea Noble?

"From what I understand, it's supposed to be a trade," I said. "We're not here to pile gifts at your feet."

A sharp, sly smile crossed the woman's lips, and just like that, I could see the renowned schemer within the domestic homemaker package. "What a shame. I like presents. But I'm not one to expect that kind of generosity from strangers. I'm fully prepared to repay your help with help of my own. Hard to turn down an offer from an associate of the havoc-wreaking Chaos Crew."

"I understand you lean toward a subtle approach," Dess said, folding her arms over her chest. "I promise my methods are less bloody than theirs… unless bloody is what you want."

Anthea's smile grew. "Exactly what I like to hear." She paused for a moment, studying us both, and my skin prickled with the sense that she saw much more than she was commenting on. This definitely wasn't a woman to tangle with—but that meant she could be a very valuable associate if we played our cards right. I was always glad to make a new connection myself.

"We appreciate you taking the time to meet with us and consider our proposal," I said smoothly. "Your reputation precedes you too. And the task we'd like to employ you with shouldn't require any significant risk on your part."

"You have a boring job for me, do you?" She clucked her tongue teasingly and focused on Dess. "I'm afraid I can't say the same, although maybe you'll be happier that way. I've gathered that you specialize in taking down targets that most assassins wouldn't be able to reach—and without leaving any evidence behind."

Dess raised her chin. "That's right. You might have heard of me before. Apparently a lot of my killings have been attributed to 'the Ghost.' That would be me."

I caught the brief flash of surprise that widened Anthea's eyes before she schooled her expression back to its previous unreadable state. "Fascinating. I'd imagine this shouldn't be *too* much trouble for you, then, if you're willing to take the job on."

"What exactly would you like her to do?" I asked evenly. I wasn't going to be pushy about it, but I did want her to get to the point.

Anthea ran her fingers along a branch that dipped low alongside us. "There's a mark I'd like killed. He's tricky to get to—lots of security and very cautious. He's evaded my own resources more than once, and I'd like to simply get the job done once and for all."

"You want me to get to him and kill him," Dess clarified.

Anthea rubbed her fingers together, and her face hardened just for an instant. "I want you to kill him, yes, but not just that. I want him to die in a particularly horrible way. And no one can know that you were involved or that I hired you."

"That shouldn't be a problem," Dess said, but then she hesitated. "Why do you want him dead?"

I understood immediately, with a pang that resonated through my heart. She'd spent too many years blindly killing for someone else's sake. The household had never given her a choice in who she killed, leading her to believe she was eliminating criminals and harmful figures when really she'd been fulfilling their own selfish agenda, whatever that'd been.

But Dess didn't revel in killing for the sake of killing. She wanted to know her targets deserved it, just like we did. She was determined to make her new path a just one as long as she had the choice. Of course that didn't change even when she could gain something from bending her personal ethics.

Anthea's eyes flashed, and her voice came out taut. "This man raped a few teenagers who've since come under my protection. I want to make sure he's never in a position to do the same to any others."

Dess's posture straightened, her mouth pressing flat. Resolve radiated off her as she held out her hand for Anthea to shake. "I look forward to wiping him off the face of the earth. Point me at him, and he's good as dead already."

FOURTEEN

Decima

THE POLYESTER HOUSEKEEPING uniform itched at my arms. I resisted the urge to scratch them as I wiped down the benches at the edge of the hotel lobby. The desk clerk had even made a comment to me about how the one near the door needed a lot of work, so I knew that at least she didn't recognize me as an imposter. The position also made it easy to keep my face at an angle where it'd never be caught on the security cameras.

I didn't normally like to do a lot of playacting for a mission. I'd rather have slunk in unseen, relying on stealth and strength rather than pretense. But Garrison had pointed out to me that while he was here, he might as well help pave the way to completing Anthea Noble's job. My pride had wanted me to say no, but practicality had won out.

Better to do everything possible to ensure the

operation went off without a hitch than to insist on doing it totally solo.

Right on cue, Garrison sauntered into the lobby as if he were meant to be there, wearing a dark leather jacket, sunglasses, and a chip on his shoulder larger than the massive hotel. He strode through the lobby and stopped before the farthest elevator—the one labeled PRIVATE. The two guards stationed there stopped him in his tracks.

"This car goes to the penthouse only," one said, placing a hand on Garrison's chest and nudging him a step backward. "There's nothing you need here."

Garrison's dramatic gasp echoed through the lobby. "Do you know who I *am?*" he asked, and I held back from chuckling at the clear change from the voice I was used to. He spoke with a high-pitched, whiny tone that would have had Blaze in hysterics.

"Doesn't matter. Mr. Fitzgerald doesn't have any appointments."

Garrison removed the sunglasses he'd been wearing and placed them atop his head. "He does with me, but what would you know about his schedule? You're just the help."

He made as if to waltz past the men, and one of the guards pushed him backward more forcefully. "I can double check if you're going to make a fuss about it," he grumbled. "But he doesn't like being interrupted unnecessarily."

"Oh, this is absolutely necessary," Garrison insisted.

The guard whipped a phone out of his pocket, but before he could dial, Garrison snatched it out of his hands.

"I think *I'd* better do the talking," he said, and dashed for the front doors.

I was already ambling across the lobby with my head low, as if I hadn't noticed the altercation. Garrison ran past me, and the guard hurtled after him. I placed myself in just the right spot that he couldn't help bumping into me at the speed he was going.

"Watch where you're going," he spat at me, staggering, but his attention was still mostly on Garrison. I scrambled out of the way, and the guard hurtled out of the building after the phone thief.

The desk clerk stared at all that wide-eyed. "Should I call the police?" she asked the remaining guard.

He shook his head, looking bored. "Heath can take care of it."

That's what he thought. I meandered on in the general direction of the private elevator, tucking the keycard I'd picked from the first guard's pocket into a pouch sewn on the inside of my sleeve.

It was only a few more seconds before Garrison dashed back in—alone. Somehow he'd made his face go pale as if in a panic. "He's having some kind of fit," he said to the remaining guard. "I don't know—I didn't mean to get him so worked up. Does he have epilepsy or something?"

"What the fuck?" The second guard barged toward the doorway to find out what was going on.

I had no idea how the rest of Garrison's scheme would play out, only that he knew what he was doing. It was time for me to take care of my part.

The instant the second guard had barreled past the

lobby doors, I darted to the elevator and swiped my sleeve past the scanner pad. The key card activated through the fabric, and the doors slid open. I slipped into the car and jabbed the button to close the doors before anyone could return and try to stop me.

The elevator car vibrated around me as it ascended. I kept my body turned away from the security camera, my head still tipped down. If anyone checked the footage later, they'd see nothing more of the murderer than the maid uniform and the brown wig I'd pulled over my hair.

Mr. Fitzgerald, the owner of this hotel, lived in the penthouse suite, and he had around-the-clock guards at every potential entrance for his safety. According to Anthea, there were none *inside* the room because he preferred a certain level of privacy. Naturally that also meant that once I got inside, I didn't need to worry about cameras.

He was careful, sure, but I'd dealt with far more difficult targets.

As I neared the top floor, adrenaline began to course through my veins. How long had it been since I'd been out on an assignment, preparing to take down a target as only I knew how? The danger around me and the certainty that I could see this kill through exhilarated me in a way nothing else—not even chocolate—could. I'd forgotten what that feeling was like after the way my discoveries about the household had soured my memories of the work I'd done for them.

The thrill was momentarily dampened by a jab of guilt. Maybe those memories *should* have been soured. The people I'd killed… For a second, I pictured my father's face if he knew, taut with disapproving horror.

But this mission wasn't about Damien Malik or my birth family. This was about eliminating a man who absolutely deserved it. And there was no one better to fulfill that duty than me.

The elevator opened into a small foyer that led to the main penthouse. Another guard was stationed there.

The instant the doors parted, I sprang into motion. There wasn't a second to waste if I wanted to stop him from raising the alarm.

The guard had inadvertently positioned himself right where I could take full advantage, standing facing the elevator with a gun in his hand and a frown on his face. I sprang at him, jerking sideways to throw him off, kicking the gun from his hand, and swinging out my arm with the knife I'd retrieved from my pocket on the way up.

The blade caught him across the throat before he had a chance to do more than draw in a breath to shout. I sliced through muscle and cartilage, severing his neck all the way down to his spine and shoving him away from me.

Blood spewed out across the floor, only a few flecks catching on the dark fabric of my uniform. As the guard crumpled to the floor, his head lolling on his nearly severed neck, I rubbed the droplets in so they wouldn't show.

Mr. Fitzgerald's closest bodyguards had stood by while he'd raped who knew how many girls, ignoring everything they'd seen and heard. Even if they'd been able to convince themselves there wasn't anything outright violent involved, they'd known their boss was fixating on underage teens. Anthea hadn't asked me to give this man as thorough a punishment as his boss, but I didn't feel any regrets about his death.

The boss was so cautious that no one had the key to the penthouse door other than him. But he also had old-fashioned tastes, preferring to trust actual keys over digitized cards. I couldn't have said he was wrong. If it'd been Blaze coming for him, the hacker probably could have found a way to hack an electronic lock in less than a minute.

Instead, I brought out my picks. The door had a complex mechanism, but I felt my way around the tumblers through the pounding of my heart. A push here and a twist there…

The lock clicked open. I eased the door open an inch, listening at the gap.

No one reacted on the other side. The sound of a TV show—a news report, from the staccato voice reaching my ears—carried from a more distant room. I caught a faint rustling as if someone had moved on a bed.

Perfect.

I closed the door behind me and slunk through the opulent penthouse to the master bedroom. The trappings of luxury often worked in my favor. The rug was so thick it absorbed my footsteps without much effort on my part.

The door stood halfway open. I peeked inside. A stout, doughy-faced man lounged at the edge of his king-sized bed as he watched the TV. I noted the steel chain of his necklace with a panic button on the central link. I had to work fast before he had a chance to press that.

I judged the distance and the height of the bed. Then I waited until he glanced away from the TV at the wall opposite the door.

The moment there was no chance of him seeing me, I sprang through the doorway. My first few footfalls were so silent he didn't even realize anything was wrong until he turned back and I was nearly on top of him already.

A startled yelp jolted out of him, and his hand flew toward the panic button. But I was prepared for that. My first move was to snatch both his wrists, snapping the narrow bones as I yanked them over his head. When he fell back on the bed, I pinned his forearms under my shin and rammed the side of my hand against his throat.

The louder shout he'd been summoning died with a pained whistle. I'd crushed his windpipe to a sliver of its former self. He could still breathe, so he'd be alive for the vengeance Anthea had asked me to carry out, but he wasn't going to be doing any hollering ever again.

It would have been easier to simply kill him outright, but I found I liked the idea of stretching out his suffering on Anthea's orders. It still wouldn't be anything close to the way his victims must have suffered—must still be suffering.

He started to flail against my hold, making little squeaks of pain when he strained his broken wrists. I put an end to all that struggling with a few plastic zip ties that I'd concealed in my uniform. I hauled him up the bed and attached his arms to the wrought iron headboard. Then I bound his ankles together and ran a rigid line between them and a post at the foot. It stretched him so tightly that he couldn't bend his knees or his waist.

Mr. Fitzgerald stared up at me, wheezing, as I flashed my bloody knife. I jerked open his shirt, letting the buttons pop, and applied the tip of the blade to his flesh like a pen.

"This is for Mika," I said, carving the full name Anthea had given me deep into the skin over his ribs. "And for Carmen, and for Tonya. You're never going to violate anyone like you did them ever again. I'm turning the tables on their behalf."

A whimper worked its way from his battered throat. Blood seeped from the wounds. His muscles twitched as I dug the blade in again and again, drawing every letter that told the story.

I didn't let him bleed enough to lose consciousness. When I finished my etching, I held up the knife again and yanked down his pants.

The man's face was already drenched in sweat and sickly gray. Now he made one last, futile attempt at escape. I shook my head as he jerked this way and that.

"If you lie still, it might hurt a little less," I informed him. Not that I cared how much it hurt.

He didn't heed my advice. He was still wriggling away when I slashed right through the base of his dick. Then a thin wail carried from his throat, only cut off when I finished the last piece of Anthea's request and shoved his member down his throat to cut off his air completely.

It was vicious, but when I sat back and watched his

body shudder and sag, there was a certain artistry to the act of justice. I was *proud* to have dealt it out.

My heart kept thumping on with the rush of adrenaline. Mr. Fitzgerald's eyes stared blankly at the ceiling now. A smile crossed my lips. I stripped off the housekeeping costume to reveal the tight black stealth clothes underneath, retrieved the thin but sturdy rope I'd had wrapped around my waist underneath, and went to the balcony.

It only took a minute to rappel down to the ground through the cover of the night. Then I was darting away into the shadows like the ghost the criminal underworld had seen me as for years.

The wig went into a restaurant dumpster around the corner. By the time I reached Garrison where he was waiting outside a bar three blocks away, all my tension had melted away, leaving only the giddiness of the task I'd just fulfilled. I couldn't help smiling again. Garrison took one look at me in the hazy light of the streetlamps and chuckled under his breath.

"Faster than I even expected. And I can tell you got the job done."

"Hell, yes," I replied, falling into step with him as we started walking down the street.

He looped his arm casually around mine. "I could do this every day if there were enough missions to keep us that busy. Such a fucking thrill."

"Yeah," I agreed, with a swell of emotion that had nothing to do with the job itself.

Who else had I ever known who'd really understood

that feeling? Even Noelle had been more interested in my results than how I experienced my success.

How lucky was I that I'd found my way into the midst of not one but four men who could relate to the deepest, darkest parts of my heart?

FIFTEEN

Decima

FINALLY, my hands were empty, and all that was left to do was wait for Anthea's results.

I'd dropped off soil samples from a few different sections of the garden—soil that I'd stealthily scooped into little baggies while I'd wandered along the beds of flowers, pretending to be crouching down for a closer look and sniff. Once I'd left the house, I'd packed the samples carefully and sent them off by courier so Anthea would get them later today. She'd said it'd take a day or two for her to produce her results.

When I made it back to the house in the hill, the sun was waning, casting the entire world in a golden light. I found the guys all huddled around the sofa, flipping through channels on the TV and looking like they'd just finished squabbling over who would hold the remote. Unsurprisingly, Julius was the current victor. But the moment they heard me enter, he clicked off the screen and they all turned toward me.

"There she is," Garrison said with a clap of his hands. "Is everything taken care of?"

I nodded and flopped into the space in the center of the sofa that was just big enough for me, right between Julius and Talon. "Anthea promised that when the courier got the samples to her, it would go to the top of her priority list."

"You know, this is how Talon and I tested out new members of the crew," Julius said, letting his fingers brush over my knee in a way that sent sparks right up my leg. "Set them up on a trial mission that they have to handle on their own."

"I wasn't completely by myself," I felt the need to remind him. "Garrison helped with the diversion."

Garrison rolled his eyes. "I hardly did anything. Without me, you would have easily handled the guards. Drawing them away was easy."

"Still, I didn't do it alone."

Blaze cut into the conversation. "Were you alone in the room with the target?" I nodded and opened my mouth to counter, but he stopped me. "And you passed the other guard without a problem?"

"Okay, fine," I said. "But it's not like it's the first operation I've carried out alone anyway."

Julius smiled. "It's the first one you've gone on since you took up with us, and you completed it much to your 'client's' satisfaction and without any blowback. I think that means you're officially part of the crew now."

There was a mildly teasing note in his tone. I elbowed him gently. "Are you saying I wasn't already?"

"I don't know," Garrison said with mock-skepticism. "Should it really count when we weren't the ones who picked the scenario?"

As I debated whether there was something in easy reach that I could throw at him, since I didn't want to leave my cozy spot on the sofa, Blaze tsked his tongue. "Maybe it wasn't our call, but it *was* ten times harder than the trial mission I got sent on. Pretty sure yours didn't involve a nearly unreachable target either."

Garrison leaned back in his chair. "Well, there you go. It's not fair that she got such an exciting scenario for her trial run. I think it's only fair if she does a boring mission like the rest of us before we fully initiate her." His lips twitched with a hint of amusement.

Talon patted my thigh, sending another wash of heat through my body. "I think Dess deserves a promotion for taking on a harder job than the rest of us did," he said in his usual deep, emotionless voice, but when I peered up at him, I caught a glint of humor in his cool eyes.

I stretched out my legs over the bearskin rug. "I guess I'll take Julius's place if you're offering."

Julius snorted and gestured to the rest of the crew. "If you think you can keep them in line better than I can, more power to you."

"Hmm." I tapped my lips. "As my first order as queen of the crew, I demand that you bring me all the chocolate in the city."

Blaze burst out with a laugh, and Garrison's and

Julius's guffaws quickly followed. Even Talon let out a chuckle. He stroked my thigh again, and I found myself thinking about things they could do that would be even sweeter than procuring chocolate.

As I looked around at the four of them, basking in the warmth of their admiration and comradery, a surge of affection swelled in my chest. I *had* gotten incredibly lucky to find these four men who complimented me so perfectly. I cared about all of them more than I'd even known I was capable of. If I believed in a higher power, I'd have been thanking it right now for bringing them into my life.

But I didn't believe in that. I was the highest power I believed in. And maybe it was time I showed them all just how much they meant to me.

I reached over and teased my fingers over Talon's thigh in turn. He swallowed audibly, shifting just a tad into my touch. My gaze slid over the other men gathered around me.

I'd been with all of them individually—and Talon and Julius together once—but we'd never come together as a crew, as a *team*, in the most intimate way.

Would they even want to? They did just about everything else together, but Julius and Garrison had gotten pretty uptight at first about the idea that I wanted all four of them in any way at all.

They'd gotten over that hesitation, though. And we should probably find out if we could be a team like this too.

I trailed my hand further up Talon's thigh, skimming

just shy of the fly of his jeans. "Actually, I have a better idea. I just want all of you. In every possible way."

The temperature in the room seemed to rise five degrees in an instant. Four gazes burned into me. "*All* of us?" Blaze repeated with an eager light in his face. I should have known he'd be enthusiastic from the start.

"If you think you can handle that," I replied.

Talon answered by gripping my wrist, taking control just how he knew I liked it. He set my hand right on the bulge of his already hardening cock, letting out an approving grunt when I gripped him through the fabric. He showed no sign at all of embarrassment at being fondled like this in front of his friends.

"I'll take you any way you want," he said, his voice gone a little rough.

Garrison got to his feet, an unfamiliar wildness in his eyes. It didn't look like a refusal, at least. He stepped across the rug and grabbed my other hand. "You don't have enough holes for all of us, sweetheart," he said, bringing my knuckles to his lips.

I cocked my head as I held his gaze, swooning silently when he sucked my forefinger right into his mouth and then nipped the tip. "I think I can manage. I've got two hands as well. And hopefully sometime in your lives, you all have learned the basics of taking turns."

Julius led his pack of chaos in this scenario like he always did. He stood and took my hand from Garrison, pulling me to my feet. As his deep blue eyes bored into mine, smoldering with desire, lust pooled between my thighs. Right then, I knew we were really going to do this.

"Which one of us do you want to fuck you first?" he asked in a low voice full of so much promise I soaked my panties. But that wasn't the right question.

"I was hoping you could make a collaboration," I replied. "I thought I made it very clear that I'm not interested in choosing when it comes to the four of you."

I stepped away from him and slid my fingers along the hem of my shirt. The guys all watched me as if I were an exotic animal they couldn't believe they were getting the chance to capture. I raised the hem of my shirt an inch and then another, meeting each pair of eyes that stared at me as I claimed all of their attention with just the faintest lift of my arm.

A smirk crossed my lips as I finally tugged the shirt over my head and tossed it aside. Next I reached for the button on my pants, popping it slowly.

Talon sank back into the sofa's padding, the movement drawing my attention to him. He unzipped his jeans and freed himself, stroking his hand up and down the thick shaft I'd felt through the fabric just moments ago. His eyes stayed fixed on me. Cool and blue, they drilled into me and urged me to continue exposing myself to him. To all of them.

I could hardly look away while I slid my pants down my waist. My breath snagged in my throat as he parted his lips slightly, watching me.

God, I couldn't handle his gaze—not yet. He could finish me with mere glances, and I needed to pace myself if I hoped to satisfy this many men.

My gaze flew to Blaze, standing rigid at the side of the

sofa, just as fixated by my movements as anyone. I bit my lip and unclasped my bra, allowing my breasts to fall free.

"Blaze," I ordered, "come here and lie down."

He was the safest, even if the passion in his eyes enflamed me. Talon could finish me with a look, and Garrison could finish me with his cunning words. Julius… God, Julius would unwind me the moment he touched me. But Blaze could take orders. Blaze could take it slow and help me put on a tempting show to get us all on the same page.

Of course, he could give orders too. "Condoms," he demanded as he strode toward me, whipping off his shirt as he came. My mouth watered at the sight of all that lean muscle on display.

Julius tipped his head to one side in a subtle question aimed at me. "I don't think we need them."

I licked my lips, reaching for the waist of Blaze's slacks. "You're the main ladies' man around here," I said, ignoring Garrison's noise of protest. "Are you sure you're clean?"

His pupils dilated, and I'd swear I heard his breath hitch. "Yeah. It's been a little while—and I've always used protection—test results just a couple weeks ago were clean."

"Anyone else have any reason to think they should wrap it up?" I asked the room at large. "I've got an implant, so I'm covered in that area."

"Fuck," Garrison muttered, but there was nothing but desire in his voice now. "I'm good to go. Whatever you want, sweetheart."

Talon's cock twitched in his grasp. "There hasn't been anyone but you in a long time," he said quietly.

Oh, fuck, now I was even more turned on. My panties, the only piece of clothing still on me, had to be absolutely drenched at this point.

Blaze kicked his pants to the side and tossed his boxers after them. He hooked his fingers into the waistband of my panties and tugged me toward him, eyeing me like I was his next plate of pasta to devour. "Where do you want me?"

"Right there," I instructed, pointing at the thick rug beneath our feet.

He lowered himself to his knees, pulling down my last article of clothing as he went, never once breaking eye contact. Then he eased onto his back, propped up on his elbows. His cock jutted into the air, beckoning me.

I sank down over him, watching the other men's expressions as I did. Blaze gripped my hips, giving me a little of the forcefulness I loved. I ground against him, a shaky breath spilling out of me as his cock slid against my slick folds.

The anticipation of having him ram right inside me was torturous, but somehow that made the pleasure even more exquisite. I tipped my head back and rocked over him, drinking in the stutters of his breath and the way his length hardened even more as he rubbed against me. Then my eyes met Garrison's.

As if the colliding of our gazes was a signal fire, he moved toward me, positioning himself next to Blaze and tangling his fingers in my hair. Then he knelt down and claimed my mouth with all the fiery energy that called to me in him. I fumbled with the buttons on his shirt, wanting to bare his well-toned body as well.

Garrison pulled back just enough to shed it, chuckling under his breath. "Are you going to fuck Blaze or just tease him until he explodes?"

A moan escaped me at the insinuation of those words. Blaze adjusted himself beneath me, and I decided I'd teased *myself* long enough. I fit myself against him and fell down onto him, letting his cock spear right into me with the most delicious friction.

The hacker groaned, bucking his hips to meet me and massaging my hips where he was still clutching me. As I raised and lowered myself over him, taking him deeper with each bob of my body, Garrison straightened up again. He undid his belt and let his pants fall before grasping my hair with one hand.

"Let's see how well you can handle two at once."

He knew how to bring the roughness too. As Garrison tapped the head of his cock against my lips, my pussy clenched around Blaze, the rush of my impending orgasm building inside me. I opened my mouth obediently and flicked my tongue around the other man's shaft. Garrison muttered a curse.

"That's right," he said. "Take me right down like I know you can."

Oh, I'd show him what I could do all right. I sucked him into my mouth, wrapping my lips tightly around his cock and swirling my tongue around him. Then it was Garrison's turn to groan.

I kept bobbing over Blaze, propelling us both toward our release, and Garrison rocked into my mouth at the same time. Just like when I'd taken Julius and Talon at once, there was a special thrill to mastering these two talented men. Making them both come undone at the same time when they rarely made themselves vulnerable to anyone.

I set one hand over Blaze's where he was squeezing my hip and clasped it as if to say we were in this together. I gripped the base of Garrison's shaft with my other hand.

We moved together like some kind of blissful machine. At the pumping of my hand, Garrison's breaths started to fracture. I worked him over faster, sucking harder, and he came with a cry and a flood of salty cum in my mouth.

The taste of him and the urgent pace I'd set with Blaze tipped me over the edge. Bliss crashed over me, and I released Garrison's cock to cling to his thigh as I shuddered with the sensation. Blaze's fingers dug into my flesh, and the hot spurt of his own release filled me.

"So fucking good," the hacker mumbled, stroking me with gentler fingers as I lifted myself off of him. My legs wobbled, but only in the best of ways. We weren't anywhere near done. I still had two other men I hadn't gotten to play with yet.

I glanced down to take in Blaze's sated expression and found that Talon had already made plans of his own. He'd gotten off the sofa, and as Blaze scooted out of the way, the dispassionate killer nudged my shoulders down. "On your hands and knees," he ordered. "You're not done until you've screamed."

A giddy giggle tumbled out of me. "And I suppose you're the man for that job."

"I think we're all going to get you there together. So it'd better be a good scream, or we'll just have to keep working you over."

When he rubbed his palm over my ass with those words, I couldn't say his threat frightened me. What woman in her right mind would say no to that?

"Ass up," Talon demanded. I arched my back, giving him the reins. He gripped my hips with those strong, solid hands and tugged me backward.

In a second, he aligned himself and thrust into my pussy so fast a gasp tumbled out of me. Even with my channel relaxed and slicker than before, Talon's cock stretched me, wider than any of the others.

As Talon pounded into me, making stars spark behind my eyes and propelling more whimpers from my throat, Blaze tugged my face around to capture my mouth. He kissed me long and hard, drinking in my sounds of pleasure, and then gazed at me with heavy-lidded eyes. His attention shifted to the last of the four men who'd just approached.

Julius loomed over me, unfastening his pants. As I swayed back and forth with the force of Talon's thrusts, the leader of the crew crouched down in front of me. I lowered my head even more to lick the tip of his erect cock. Julius growled in approval and tugged me down to take him fully into my mouth.

As I was filled from both ends again, another heady thrill racing through me, Blaze and Garrison refused to be left out. Blaze dappled kisses across my shoulders while he reached beneath me to stroke my breasts, squeezing the slopes and pinching the nipples until I moaned around Julius's shaft. On the other side of me, Garrison had edged down so he could tuck his hand beneath my belly. He teased it even farther down until his fingertips brushed the sensitive spot just above where Talon and I were joined.

The pressure against my clit sent a sharper bolt of pleasure through me than ever before. I bobbed my head over Julius's cock, tightening my lips around him, my moans reverberating through my mouth over his shaft. The crew's commander dug his fingers into my hair and guided my head at an even faster pace.

Talon bucked faster too, and the pleasure building in my core rushed through me like a speeding train. Blaze kept fondling my breasts, ducking his head right under me to lap one nipple into his hot mouth.

With all of us in sync together in this whirlwind of lust, I allowed myself to feel the full extent of my satisfaction. I noted the pulse of my heartbeat between my legs and the steady rhythm of the movement radiating through every part of my body. It was fucking glorious, and I reveled in every second of it.

Talon groaned behind me, and with one mighty thrust, all the pleasure within me built to a breaking point. My back arched further, and my cries became a muffled sound against Julius's skin. My vision whited out with the waves of ecstasy that washed over me one after another in a seemingly endless surge.

As a cry that really was a scream echoed from my throat, Julius jerked out of me and came with a hot splash across my shoulder. Talon gripped my hips with a nearly bruising force and roared his own release into the air. I panted beneath his brutal assault, yet another orgasm reverberating through me on the heels of the second.

We all shuddered to a halt, tangled, sweaty, and flush with carnal delight. Garrison slipped his fingers into his mouth as if savoring the flavor of me. Then he pressed his mouth to mine again.

"You're so fucking hot," he murmured, so much unstated emotion in those words that I trembled with them.

The others stayed close around me, wrapping an arm around my waist, stroking fingers over my hair, surrounding me in the blissful afterglow. A sense of certainty rose up inside me.

Nothing could come between us—not anymore.

SIXTEEN

Decima

THE FUR RUG beneath me was thick enough to insulate my body from the hard floor, and lying pressed into Blaze's body gave me all the warmth I needed to sleep through the night. When I did wake, it was to his fingers running down my back, back up it, around my shoulder, and then taking a similar path downward again. His touch brought shivers to my skin as I burrowed deeper into his natural heat.

The other men stirred around us. I didn't open my eyes to see who had ended up where. In the aftermath of our intense collision last night, we'd all dozed off where we lay.

Blaze's fingers crested my shoulder, tracing a smoothly curved line I knew cut across the skin there. When their motion paused, I opened my eyes to peer blearily at him.

He was studying the scar. "Where did you get this one?" he whispered.

I cleared the sleepiness from my throat before speaking, my voice still rough. "It was a torture attempt. The woman who momentarily restrained me managed to make that cut and break my pinky before I slipped my bindings."

"You've been tortured?" Garrison asked from behind. I peeked over my shoulder and found him sitting on the floor, leaning against the sofa with one leg extended and the other bent upright.

I wanted to laugh at the question. He'd seen the scars across my body, and he knew my history. It would have been more surprising if I *hadn't* been tortured at some point.

"Once or twice," I said with a shrug.

"Who did it?" Talon's deep voice echoed across the room. The ferocity in his tone held a clear threat, maybe one that would have unnerved someone else. But I wasn't that person. It warmed me to realize he'd have wanted to unleash that ferocity on my former tormenter.

"I don't know, but she's long dead now," I reassured him.

Blaze dragged his finger across another scar at the base of my back, a smaller but jagged line. "This one?"

Pursing my lips, I sorted through my memories. "An accident. I jumped through a window and didn't stick the landing. It was from the glass."

I knew the one that he'd eventually ask about—the most prominent of all of them. But he surprised me as he gripped my right hand and opened it, revealing the thin mark that spread across each of my fingers in a straight line. He didn't even need to ask as he ran his thumb across it and met my eyes in a silent question.

I didn't want to delve into that scar. It was more difficult than explaining the ones I'd obtained from missions. The missions didn't matter, and those people and places were a blip on my radar. Scars like the one across my hand—like the one beside my belly button—meant something different. They'd been given to me because of my failures and mistakes.

"Noelle," I admitted, clenching my fist as I thought about her. I broke away from Blaze's eye contact. "I wasn't doing as well using my left side as she'd hoped, so she made sure that my left side *had* to be my strongest one for a while."

"She did this to you?" Blaze asked, and I didn't have to look up to know that he was giving an utterly horrified expression. "She broke your *hand*, on purpose?"

"I hardly remember it. I was so young," I said, as if that made the situation better.

I wasn't lying. I remembered only the crunch when she slammed the edge of a cutting board into my fingers with all the might she could muster, claiming that I'd one day thank her for being a stronger fighter. And it *had* made me a stronger fighter, after all. I'd never had a difficult time using my left side after the weeks when it'd been my only option.

I hadn't realized how consuming the silence was in the

room until Julius finally spoke. "And the one on your stomach?"

I hadn't meant to upset them so early in the morning, but I could hear in Julius's voice how angry the thought of Noelle hurting me made him. It wasn't as if there was anything left to avenge now. She was gone, dead at their hands.

But of course, we still didn't know who'd hired her to train me so viciously.

I sighed. "It was another training mishap."

"I wouldn't consider having your fingers intentionally broken as a child to be a training 'mishap,' but please, continue," Garrison said, his usual snarky tone harshened by his own obvious anger—anger I knew wasn't aimed at me but my former captors.

I rolled to my back, tilting my head until I could see all of them. Julius had sprawled across the sofa, and Talon sat half upright at the other end. Garrison was the only other of my men on the floor.

They all watched me intently. Waiting for the story I didn't really want to tell.

I flattened my voice so it'd be as even as possible. "This one really was an accident. Noelle left me alone with a trainer who specialized in weapons, and he was teaching me the basics of the different styles of throwing knives. We got to the part of the lesson where I needed to learn to dodge the knives, and Noelle came barging into the room and distracted me. I didn't dodge one."

I took a deep breath, thinking back to the look of

horror on the weapons trainer's face. "They were practice knives, not fully sharpened ones, so it didn't go too far into me, but it lodged itself far enough that I needed stitches. And then I pulled the stitches twice during training in the following weeks, so that's why the scar is still so big."

What I didn't want to say was that I wasn't totally sure any more that it'd been an accident after all. Noelle had liked to surprise me to test my reflexes and instincts. Maybe she'd distracted me on purpose to see how well I'd dodge then. A ten-year-old kid in the middle of having knives thrown at her.

Blaze moved me closer to him and tightened his grip, slipping his other hand between us and stroking the place where the scar marred my skin.

"Do you remember where all of your scars are from?" Julius asked.

I shook my head. "Not all of them. Just the bigger ones. The small scars like this"—I pointed to a tiny scar on the side of my cheek and turned my head so they could all see. From where the other three sat near the sofa, I doubted they could even make out the pale mark—"I have no clue where it came from. I have tons like that."

"I can't remember where most of mine came from either," Garrison said.

Blaze took a deep breath, drinking in the scent of my skin, and I had the urge to kiss his bare chest. "I don't think I know where a single one of my scars came from," he admitted.

"What scars?" Garrison teased. "The ones that you get when you clean out your computer?"

Blaze narrowed his eyes and pushed himself up on an elbow, loosening his grip on me as he scowled at Garrison. "I guess I do remember one. You know, the scar I got when I was shot protecting your ass."

Garrison laughed. "Been there, done that, brother."

Julius spoke up. "I think Talon's the only one of us who *hasn't* been shot at least once," he said, gesturing to his ear with its ravaged lobe. I hadn't realized the injury was from a bullet, but it made sense.

"I think getting blown up is close enough." Talon rubbed at the flare-shaped scar on his thigh—barely exposed beneath his boxers. Looking at it, I guessed it'd been shrapnel from a mine or some other land explosive during his military days. He was lucky he still had his leg.

I cut in before their usual competitive natures could take the conversation on too far of a detour. "Scars don't matter." I sat up and looked over myself. With my nakedness fully on display, all four of them shut up. "What matters now is that we don't add to what we've already got and that we stop dwelling on the past."

I needed to take my own advice, especially when it was my *internal* scars that seemed to drive me forward these days. Although dwelling on my past was really all that I could do when my "past" wasn't completely history yet and seemed to be defining so much of my present.

I glanced at the clock on the rock wall and sat up straighter with a start. It was later than I'd realized. "I'm supposed to meet my dad for brunch at eleven," I said, scrambling to my feet. If I didn't get a move on diving into the shower, I'd either have to show up smelling of sex, nude, or late. I wasn't too keen on any of those options.

"Go do what you need to do," Blaze said with a small smile.

I stopped at the edge of the room just for a second, looking back at all of them as they enjoyed the view of me walking away. It didn't bother me, partly because their mostly naked bodies stirred up plenty of the same lust that I saw in their eyes in me... and partly because I saw just as much admiration and affection there as anything more carnal.

"You know, you're just as much my family as he is," I said firmly. "We've fought together and bled together—you've looked out for me even when you barely knew who I was... You mean a lot to me. I want a relationship with my birth family, but that doesn't mean I'm giving up what I have with any of you."

Julius gave me one of his measured but genuine smiles. "I'm sure we're all glad to hear that. The crew sticks together. Now go get your brunch."

I took the shortest shower in human history, threw on my clothes, and summoned an Uber to make the trip into the city proper. I made it to the café at eleven on the dot and found Damien Malik waiting just outside the wrought-iron fence that surrounded the large patio. He greeted me with a smile and a wave toward the gate.

"It's too nice a day to waste it sitting inside," he said as the hostess guided us to one of the patio tables. With the sun beaming down on us and cheerful music tinkling through the café's open door, I was inclined to agree with him.

"I'm not going to argue with fresh air," I said, taking my seat.

A waitress appeared with a flash of a smile. "Can I start you off with any drinks?"

My father ordered a coffee, but I figured I'd better forgo caffeine, since my nerves were already a bit jittery in his presence with the Hunter's insinuations and Anthea's unknown soil analysis hanging over my head. "Lemonade for me," I said, since I deserved at least a little sugar.

Damien leaned back in his chair, seeming more relaxed than usual. "It's good that you enjoy getting out and about," he said. "Keeps the mind sharp and the body healthy. And it's nice just being out in the sun for its own sake." He chuckled. "Not everything has to be for a purpose, of course."

"Always nice when the enjoyable things are good for you too," I replied with half-hearted amusement.

He tilted his head. "You know, you might enjoy the heat even more if you made use of our swimming pool. Your mother has mentioned that you always leave when most of the activity moves to the pool. We'd love to have you around even more, of course, now that you're getting settled in. There's no reason you shouldn't become a full member of the Malik family."

I curled my scarred fingers toward my palm, thinking of all the other scars I wouldn't be able to hide in a bathing suit. The Chaos Crew had viewed them with the curiosity of men who'd been through similar trials. Their only horror had been at the brutality I'd endured as a child. The Maliks would be horrified by everything about my marked-up skin. I didn't want to have to tell that many more lies.

As I groped for an appropriate answer, I glanced around the open patio. The patrons looked as well off as my father. Pearl necklaces and expensive suits abounded. The only person who stood out from the wealthy crowd was a kid in a T-shirt and jeans who couldn't have been older than fourteen, leaning against the restaurant's siding like he was waiting for someone.

"Chlorine really irritates my skin," I told Damien as I turned back to him. "And I burn too easily to enjoy just tanning." Two small lies to prevent a whole lot of bigger ones. "But if no one minds me hanging around by the side of the pool in regular clothes, I can stay later more often."

The waitress returned with our drinks, and my father sipped his thoughtfully. "I think that would be nice. The more you're around, the easier it'll be for you to find your place in the family legacy."

That word again—*legacy*. He talked about it as if that were the end goal of all these visits, as if there were something more I'd discover about the family once I'd gotten to know them even better. A prickle ran down my spine, the Hunter's insinuations rising up from my memory.

But surely Damien Malik wouldn't talk openly about any kind of legacy that he'd get investigated for.

As I gave some noncommittal answer that I barely paid attention to, the teen by the restaurant adjusted his position, sidling closer to the gate. The furtiveness of his movements put me on the alert. He was doing an okay job of being subtle, but I was trained to recognize when someone had a trick up their sleeve. What was he doing?

I got my answer a moment later when he brushed his hand across the back of a nearby woman's chair—and let his fingers snag on the strap of her purse.

Damien had swiveled in his chair at the same moment to check the board of specials. The kid was being sneaky, but not sneaky enough—he obviously wasn't any hardened criminal. As he jerked the purse off the chair, my father leapt to his feet with a shout.

The young teen looked terrified as my father rushed him and grabbed his arm in a death grip. My pulse stuttered even though I didn't exactly approve of making off with people's purses. It was just—he really *was* just a kid—and the whitening of his face with the tremor that passed through his body showed how ashamed he was at getting caught.

Something had driven him to this point, and I didn't think it was simply callous greed.

"Call the police," Malik shouted out, and turned to the victim of the theft, handing her the purse he'd pried from the boy's fingers. "He almost made off with this."

Someone at a nearby table gasped, and a few others pulled out their phones as if the petty theft required multiple reports. As if this kid really needed to be arrested. He was trembling now, looking seconds from wetting his pants.

I couldn't just sit there. My heart thumping, I pushed

myself to my feet and marched over. Damien dragged the boy toward the gate to wait for the police, and as I reached him, I realized his grip on the boy's wrist was even tighter than I'd assumed. He twisted his fingers, and the boy winced in pain. His fingers had balled into a fist.

"What else have you stolen, you little creep?" my father said under his breath in the harshest tone I'd ever heard him use. He jerked his hand down to pry the boy's fingers open, but there was nothing there. With a sharp exhalation, Damien twisted his grip again—and the crack of breaking bone made me flinch.

The boy yelped, tears welling up at the corners of his eyes.

"Garbage like you deserves what you get," Damien hissed. He turned and noticed my presence for the first time. His face reformed into its usual professional mask—he mustn't have thought anyone was close enough to notice.

"First he tries to rob people, then he thinks he can run off without facing the proper punishment," he said, as if the boy had been making a run for it. "He twisted his hand while I was pulling him back. No one to blame but himself. The police will sort it out."

That wasn't what had happened at all, but I had no idea how to challenge the 'facts' he laid out so easily. How would he look at *me* if I sided with the kid? Everyone around us was nodding in agreement, accepting his explanation.

If he'd been anyone else, I'd have torn him a new one right there and then. But this incident only proved that I really *didn't* know the man I was dealing with. And getting into a public altercation with a man with as much political clout as my father blind felt like a very bad idea. What if this was just the tip of an ominous iceberg?

The police roared up with blaring sirens. Malik handed over the kid, getting the woman to tell the story of her nearly stolen purse.

"He broke my finger," the boy said with a sob, cradling his hand to his chest. "He broke my fucking finger."

Malik rolled his eyes, giving the boy a small shove toward the officer who rested a large hand across his shoulder. "He was trying to get away, and it was all I could do to stop him. I didn't mean to break it, of course."

He sounded *so* convincing. Had I not seen it with my own eyes, I would have never believed that he'd fractured the boy's bones with malicious intent. How could he lie so blatantly without an ounce of hesitation in his tone?

The officer looked between them. "I can take it from here, Representative Malik. Your community is indebted to you once again."

The brilliant smile my father gave the officer sickened me. I stepped backward and moved swiftly to my seat. They exchanged a few pleasantries and a handshake as the other officer loaded up the kid in his car.

My father came back over, his mood darker than it had been at the start of our brunch. He looked at me with a grimace, and I wondered if he'd apologize for his actions and admit that he'd been out of line after all.

"I'm sorry that you had to be here for this," he said, dropping into his chair. "If you hadn't realized it before, the crime rates in this neighborhood are rising just like they are everywhere. It's tragic, but that's why it's essential that we crack down on the criminals whenever they pop up. That boy deserves everything that will come to him."

Did that include the cast and recovery for his injury?

I couldn't bring myself to respond. I took a sip of my lemonade and listened as Damien continued his rant about crime, not even considering that lying to the police and breaking a boy's finger was a heinous crime within itself. Did he think he was excluded from the law?

As long as he broke it punishing criminals, it seemed like yes.

As he simmered down and our food arrived, my stomach knotted. It was all I could do to choke down a decent amount of the meal. The truth of the situation was staring me in the face so hard I couldn't deny it anymore.

I was a criminal—one far worse than that kid. There wasn't a chance in a million years that he'd ever accept the true me or the men I considered family too. He wouldn't want to believe it, but when he did, he'd be sending me off to the electric chair. Maybe offering to throw the switch himself.

I'd known that, deep down. I'd been afraid of how he'd see the truth all along. But I'd let myself be lulled into complacency by how welcoming they'd been in general. I'd never had to face just how intense my father's dedication to his policies was until right now.

While the waitress cleared our plates, promising to bring the bill quickly, I debated simply walking away from this brunch and this whole situation. Never speaking to

Damien Malik or the rest of my birth family again. All the enjoyment I'd gotten out of having a family around me had soured with this unavoidable revelation.

What did I need them for if they couldn't handle who I really was? I didn't want to have to listen to any more of their rants or watch how they treated anyone they judged as unworthy of compassion.

I'd been foolish to think I could ever have a real relationship with this man at all, given his policies.

The urge to cut my losses and run wound through my limbs as Damien paid the check. It would be so easy. So freeing to put all the stress and pressure of trying to be Rachel Malik behind me. I could almost taste the relief.

But... I still needed answers.

As much as I wanted to leave and never look back, Malik and his investigators were in the best position to find the answers I needed about who had kidnapped me and why. Continuing to act like family with these people might be like playing with fire, but I wasn't done here yet for my own ends.

If my father found out the truth about me and my past before I learned what I needed to, he'd turn on me without hesitation. They all would. I knew that without a doubt. But it was a risk I'd just have to take.

SEVENTEEN

Julius

DESS HAD BEEN WORKING out for the better part of an hour. Even though the house didn't come with our typical exercise equipment, she'd gone through her usual circuit of floor exercises twice, jogged in place as if she had a treadmill whipping away beneath her feet, and worked through several sequences of combat moves.

None of that was particularly out of the ordinary, but the pace she'd set struck me as closer to frantic than focused. Sweat shone on her forehead and arms, but she didn't stop to so much as gulp water before throwing herself into the next set of exercises. Her eyes were glazed, focused on thoughts that had nothing to do with the house around us.

Seeing her like this sent a quiver of apprehension through me. Dess was usually nothing if not controlled. She could rival the best of us with her discipline.

When she started pushing herself this hard, it meant there was something she was trying to escape. Something she couldn't outrun by any normal means. I could take a few guesses at what that might be. The number of catastrophes in her life had been adding up for a while.

I got up from the sofa. "Dess," I said, but her head didn't so much as twitch in my direction. She just kept bobbing up and down in her whirlwind of stomach crunches.

"Dess," I repeated, a little louder, walking over as I spoke.

That time, her name sank in. She spun around and onto her feet in one smooth movement, then stayed crouched there, panting as she stared up at me.

"Is something wrong?" she asked.

I folded my arms over my chest. "That's what I was going to ask you. You look like you're trying to tackle a monster ten times your size."

She bit her lip, the gesture sending a flash of heat through me at the thought of taking that lip between my own teeth. I shook myself out of the memories of last night's epic encounter between the five of us.

She didn't need me lusting over her right now. She needed a confidante.

"It's nothing really new," she said.

I wasn't going to let her dodge the subject this time. "It's bothering you enough that you're going to dehydrate yourself with all that sweat. Why don't you grab a glass of water and then tell me what's bothering you? Even if it can't be fixed right now, there are other ways of letting it out than working yourself into exhaustion."

Dess let out a huff, but she got up and walked over to the kitchen, lifting the bottom of her shirt to wipe her damp face. I couldn't say I *minded* the brief view of her taut stomach. I had plenty of control too, but I wasn't any kind of saint.

She threw back the glass of water in a few long chugs, filled it again, and drank the second one more slowly. Then she set down the glass with a rap against the granite countertop. Her shoulders slouched just slightly.

"You know I had brunch with my dad this morning," she said. "There was a purse thief at the restaurant, just a teenager—I saw how Damien treated the kid, how he talked to him... I know this was obvious all along, but it really drove it home that I can never be who I really am with him."

"You can't tell him about the Decima part of your life," I filled in.

She nodded. "Even though I'm his daughter... I mean, he broke a kid's *bones* for trying to snatch a purse. Even if I switched over to the straight and narrow right now and stayed there from this day forward, if he ever got a whiff of the jobs I carried out before, he'd never look at me the same way again. He'd see me as a monster—the kind of monster he thinks he's fighting."

I hadn't thought that Dess would ever consider going entirely straight, but now that she brought it up, I realized it was an obvious option. It would certainly give her a better chance of integrating into the life she'd been meant to have. But imagining her walking away from us, saying good-bye to not just our company but all the skills that had made her famous among the most hardened of hitmen, wrenched at my gut.

She wasn't ordinary, not at all. She deserved to have that part of herself celebrated, not crushed.

And, damn it, I wanted to be there celebrating it with her.

"Would you *want* to go straight?" I asked, trying to keep my tone even and impartial. As much as I hated the thought of her leaving, it was her decision, and I needed to give her full rein to make the choice herself.

If I pushed her in one direction or another, she might end up resenting me later. After all the ways she'd had her life decided for her in the past, I didn't want to manipulate her now.

She sighed and clenched her jaw. "I don't want to, now. I'm not even sure I could if I decided it was worth trying to so that I could have a more open relationship with my birth family. I'm good at this. It *feels* good, pulling off a job, knowing I took one more prick out of commission who can't do any more harm..." She paused. "Now that I get to pick my jobs, I'm going to stick to the same code as you do—no one who doesn't deserve it. I can't quite believe that's wrong."

"There are a lot of those people," I muttered.

"Yeah. But there are also a lot of people like my father who can't imagine that anyone stepping outside the law could be anything other than a horrible villain."

Something about those words struck a chord in me.

Maybe there was something I could say that would help after all—not fix the struggle she was going through, but give her a perspective she hadn't had before.

I'd never talked with Blaze and Garrison about my history. I never even discussed it with Talon—he only knew because he'd been there. But the past existed for a reason: to inform the present. If I could use it to give Dess more tools to figure out the right path for her, then it was worth dredging up those terrible memories.

I motioned her away from the kitchen. "Come with me? There are some things I can tell you that might help you sort through this."

Dess cocked her head curiously and followed me over to the sofa. Talon and Garrison had gone off on a grocery store run, and Blaze was adding a few more surveillance cameras to his network in the neighborhood, so it was just the two of us. Still, my skin tightened before I spoke as if I had an audience of thousands.

The most important part had been my time in the military, but it was better to start right at the beginning, the incident that had set me on this path well before then.

"Dealing out justice was important to me from an early age," I said as Dess settled onto the sofa across from me. "When I was fifteen, I found out that my little sister —she was in middle school—was being abused by a teacher at her school." Even though Christy had gotten through that and no longer showed any lingering scars, just mentioning it brought a fresh wave of anger into my chest. "I didn't trust the authorities to deal with it properly. I was furious, and all I knew was that I had to protect her, so I got rid of him pretty much the same way I would a target now, just without quite as much finesse."

Dess's eyes widened. "You murdered him."

I raised my eyebrows at her. "Don't look so shocked. You were carrying out assassinations when you were, what, eight? By your standards, I was a late bloomer. I'm lucky I managed not to get caught."

She swatted my knee. "I was trained for it. You weren't."

"Don't underestimate the power of protective rage," I said with a small, wry smile. "Dealing out justice that way… It was more satisfying than I'd ever expected. So maybe I was always a little unhinged. I leaned into those impulses the best way I could, by joining the military. I figured I'd get the opportunity to defend our country through violent means, keep my appetite for brutal justice sated and do good at the same time."

Dess studied me. "But it didn't turn out that way," she said.

It wouldn't have been hard to guess that, considering she knew I'd started the crew more than ten years ago, when I still could have had an excellent military career if I'd wanted one.

I shook my head. "It didn't. I gave it a solid shot. Rose through the ranks and was recruited into a special ops team. That's where I met Talon. We were in the same squad, going out and working operations the regular forces couldn't have stomached."

"And then?"

I exhaled slowly. "And then we were sent on what was

supposed to be just an information-gathering mission. We were tapped for it because it was in an area with a lot of hostile activity from unfriendlies. It was a small town, people who didn't have much but were willing to work with us because they thought we could get them out from under the thumb of the local insurgents."

I paused to swallow and then went on. "You have to understand that in the military, everyone's expected to know their role and stick with it. And you don't question anyone who ranks higher than you—you just follow orders. So I was focused on carrying out my part of the job, but I couldn't help noticing that the commander seemed to be dropping the ball... not sending out as many sentries as I thought the situation warranted, directing us all into the same part of town instead of having us spread out..."

"So you spoke up, and he told you off?" Dess said.

I grimaced. "No. That's what makes this story so shameful. Well, I made a couple of comments to the commander, but he brushed me off and made it clear that he knew best, and it didn't seem worth arguing about. I thought maybe I was being overly cautious. It was my first year in special ops. He had way more experience than I did."

"But you weren't being too cautious."

"Exactly." The memories rose up, just as horrifying as they'd been fifteen years ago. "A contingent of insurgents swarmed the town. There weren't enough sentries to send out a warning quickly enough for us to be prepared. They shot several of us before we even realized what was happening, and then we spent the rest of the day and night locked in a bloody stand-off... Talon and I barely made it out alive with several of the townspeople we managed to help escape, but it was a near thing." I tapped my earlobe. "That was when this bullet came just a few inches from lodging in my brain."

"Just you and Talon out of the whole squad?" Dess murmured.

I inclined my head. "Everyone else with us, including the commander, died." A couple of cocky nineteen-year-olds who'd just started integrating into the squad. A woman who'd notified the command of her pregnancy earlier that morning. "As well as a hell of a lot of the civilians we should have been protecting." Elderly men and little kids, sprawled bleeding in the streets. I closed my eyes against the barrage of images.

"That's horrible," Dess said, reaching to squeeze my hand.

"It was," I agreed. "And it made me determined not to find myself in that position ever again. But that meant that I had to talk back when I disagreed with higher ranking officers. *Thinking* they knew what was right wasn't good enough. It had to be backed up with a plan where every piece was totally solid."

"I guess they didn't like the criticism very much."

I chuckled darkly. "No, they did not. I got written up a few times and then officially discharged. It wasn't the right fit. But I still had the urge to fight those who needed to be taken down. So I started the Chaos Crew with Talon, where I'd get to operate our missions according to *my* principles. And one of those is to surround myself with other people I trust—other voices who can help me see different perspectives. I don't want to ever start thinking that I always know better than everyone around me."

"That makes sense." Dess squeezed my hand. "I'm not sure I see how it relates to my father, though."

I held her gaze. "When I hear about men like Damien Malik, they remind me of the commander in the field that day. You can mean well and believe you're doing your best —and still be so caught up in doing things your way that you can't see when you need to adjust course. It's never wise to end up on a crusade like your father's where there's no room to pivot or notice the nuances of the situation. He's got tunnel vision... and that leads to people getting hurt who don't deserve it."

Dess nodded, worrying at her lower lip again. For a long moment, she was silent, and I started to worry I'd laid too much on her all at once. Then she rubbed her mouth.

"Thank you," she said, gazing back at me. "I'm sure it's not fun thinking or talking about all that. I hadn't looked at the situation quite that way before, though."

"I'm happy to both listen to other voices and be one when someone else might need it," I said, turning my hand so I could grip her fingers in return.

"You know, it's probably good for me to keep that idea in mind for myself too," Dess went on. "I need to keep an open mind and listen to everything people around me are saying if I'm going to piece together the evidence about my past and my family into a coherent picture. I can't get too stuck on assuming that one thing or another I haven't actually proven is true."

My smile came back. "That's very wise indeed. I'll give you full credit for that part."

She laughed, and her phone pinged with an incoming text. She fished it out of her pocket casually, but the second she glanced at the screen, her brow furrowed.

"What?" I asked.

Dess drew in a breath. "It looks like it's time to get some more of that evidence. Anthea just sent along the results of her soil analysis."

EIGHTEEN

Decima

THE DOCUMENT ANTHEA sent me was a list of minerals and other substances with figures and percentages that didn't have much significance to me. I had no idea whether what I was looking at was normal or concerning. Thankfully Anthea was sharp enough to realize that if I couldn't analyze the soil myself, I also couldn't analyze the analysis, so she gave me a call after I'd had a chance to look over the report.

"First off, there's nothing especially strange here," she said, getting right to the point. "I wouldn't blink twice at this sample if it came from a routine check rather than an analysis prompted by current suspicions."

I only partly relaxed at that remark. "But there's something that would give you pause because of the circumstances?"

"Yes. They don't prove any sort of crime, but they're

things I'd keep in mind as I weighed the other evidence."
She took a brisk breath. "First, you can see the ash content
listed. That's somewhat higher than average, but not
bizarrely so. Some people use ash instead of lime to
improve the soil, and mostly it appears to be wood ash.
Do they have a fireplace in the house or a fire pit?"

I brought up the image of the property in my mind's
eye. "They have a fire pit next to the pool."

"Then it's probably from their own fires, not
something they had to go out of their way to get. Totally
normal, if a tad old-fashioned. But the results suggest it's
not *all* from wood."

A prickle ran over my skin. "What do you mean?"

"You see the calcium level? That's again not incredibly
high, but unusual for a flower garden. In my line of work,
I most commonly see levels in that range when a body's
been burned. From the bones."

"A body?" I repeated, unable to hold back my shock.
That was the last thing I'd have imagined going into my
mother's garden.

"Don't get too panicked," Anthea said with a light
laugh. "As I said, it wasn't a tremendous amount. There are
totally innocent explanations, like the cremation of a
family pet whose ashes were scattered there. Or possibly
smaller animals could have died under the ground and
decomposed enough that their remains mixed with the
ash. It isn't a red flag, more like a yellow one. Something
to be aware of if other pieces start to point you in a
worrying direction."

"Okay," I said, my stomach sinking. Her report put

me basically back in the same place I'd been before, knowing something might be wrong but not being able to prove it one way or the other. I resisted the urge to fidget and had to confirm, "But if you saw these results from a garden no one thought was a problem, you wouldn't assume anything bad had gone down."

"Not at all. It's absolutely possible that there's nothing at all... untoward going on. But I thought you should be aware of the possibilities. Are you satisfied that your favor has been repaid?"

Her tone had gotten brisk again—probably she had plenty of other things to take care of rather than reassuring me.

"Yes," I said quickly. "Thank you for taking the time to explain." I didn't want her to think I was ungrateful. She was clearly good at what she did—who knew if I might need her help again?

Good will and personal opinion were their own kind of currency in both my father's world and the criminal circles I was learning to navigate.

I set down the phone and stared at the stone wall, barely registering the lingering cocoa scent in the air from the mugs Garrison had made before he'd left. How much of a chance was there that anything other than a pet had been cremated and tossed in the Maliks' garden? Even if they'd done *something* wrong, I couldn't wrap my head around them being murderers. They hated petty thieves— how would they have been able to justify stealing people's *lives*?

But the Hunter had known I'd turn up something

revealing in the soil. He'd specifically pointed me to the garden. It might not have been terribly unusual, but it'd been unusual all the same.

There could be other explanations that were unnerving but not as far as murder, right? Or, hell, maybe the Hunter had planted that evidence somehow.

I really didn't know, and that fact made me itchy.

Julius had gone off to the other end of the room to consult something on his phone while I'd talked to Anthea. When I got up, he glanced over at me. "Going somewhere?"

I rolled my shoulders, trying to work the restlessness out of me. "I think I'm going to drop in on my family. They're not expecting me. Maybe I'll find out more if they're unprepared." Blaze still hadn't picked up anything from their electronic communications, but a political family would probably be savvy enough not to say anything at all incriminating where it could be digitally recorded. I had no idea what they said to each other when I wasn't around.

Julius inclined his head. "Do you need anything from me?"

I shot him a quick smile. "No, but thank you. I should be back pretty soon."

I summoned an Uber and spent the entire ride stewing over what I'd heard. When we approached the house, I had the driver drop me off a block away so I wouldn't draw my family's notice. My father would be at work now —he'd talked about the meetings he had to get to after our brunch—but there almost always seemed to be at least a couple of Maliks at or around the house. This late in the afternoon, my mother should be back from her work, and Carter didn't have a summer job.

I'd only just set off toward the house, keeping an eye out for any family members who might spot me, when a woman wearing a courier vest sped up next to me on a bike.

"Rachel Malik?" she said, sounding a little breathless.

I stiffened. "Yes."

"This is for you." She thrust a small package into my hands and raced off again before I could ask her a single question.

What the hell? I tore open the package, braced in case it was something dangerous, but all I found inside was a basic headset. I studied it, and sound crackled from it, just loud enough for me to hear a voice. "Put it on, Rachel."

Even as tinny as the voice was through the small speakers, I recognized the Hunter at once. My stomach clenching, I slipped the headset over my ears and stepped back into the shadow of a tree at the front of a nearby lawn.

"What do you want?" I demanded under my breath, abruptly pissed off as well as confused. The only reason I was here at all was because of the garbage he'd stuffed into my head that might not have any truth to it at all. And how had he figured out I'd come to the house right now? Had that woman been hanging around waiting for me to arrive for my next visit—or had he tracked me somehow?

My skin crawled, and I rubbed my arms.

"Ah, Miss Malik," the Hunter said, as if this was a

totally normal call. "It's wonderful speaking with you again."

I was done playing his game. "Wonderful for you, maybe," I said. "I've got better things to do than listen to you ramble on about your delusions."

"Oh, you've decided they're delusions, have you? Didn't bother to do your research all that well."

"Or maybe there's just nothing to find."

He guffawed. "There's so much to find when it comes to Damien Malik that I'm starting to think you're willfully blind."

"And yet for some reason you can't tell me any specifics or offer up any proof," I shot back. "I don't work for you. I don't know you, and it's obvious you have your own agenda. If you're using me for whatever goal you have, I'm not interested in being your puppet."

"Then you're just interested in being theirs," the Hunter said.

"I'm nobody's puppet," I spat out.

"Well, the evidence that I told you about should speak for itself, and you can decide what to do with it. Have you dug it up yet?"

I opened my mouth to respond, but I closed it. He didn't need to know what I'd learned. I wasn't working for him, and he claimed to be an investigator. He could do it himself.

"The more you learn, the more you'll see," he went on. "You can't let your desire to have a family close your mind to what's really going on here."

I didn't like having a stranger tell me of my biases,

but his remarks echoed what Julius had said to me a couple of hours ago too closely. I did need to listen to people other than myself, because even if I knew I could never have a full relationship with my family, part of me still balked at believing they were awful in ways I hadn't discovered.

But that didn't mean that one of the people I listened to had to be this total creep.

"You don't know anything about what having a family has done to me," I snapped. Then I tore off the headset and tossed it into a set of nearby bushes.

Let the Hunter come and retrieve it if he wanted it. I owed him nothing, and he wouldn't continue using me—not without giving me real information.

But I still had my own mission here.

I walked carefully toward the Maliks' home. A second car was parked in the driveway—not one belonging to either of my parents. It took me a moment to place it as one that belonged to an aunt and uncle. My mom had company.

Well, that meant more people to be having conversations I might want to overhear. If I wanted to get facts, this was the place where I should be able to do it.

I slipped across the lawn and flattened myself to the exterior of the house. The summer day was warm enough that the windows were open to let in the breeze—perfect.

I listened at one window and then another, slinking around the house, prepared to jump away with an excuse if someone happened to step outside and notice me. It didn't take long to determine that most of them were in the family room while my mother puttered around in the kitchen nearby.

When I peeked inside, I saw Aunt Mabel and Uncle Henry were sitting side by side on the loveseat across from my brother, no sign of my cousin Margaret today. But five mugs had been set out around the teapot and the plate of squares on the coffee table. Maybe they were expecting her later—or one of the other relatives might be on their way. I'd have to keep my ears pricked for cars.

Right now, I was more interested in the voices traveling out to me. When I'd first homed in on their voices, they'd been talking about a golf tournament, but it seemed the conversation had shifted. My aunt was saying something about "proper preparations." She tsked her tongue. "I mean, it really isn't the sort of thing you want to spring on someone if they're not ready."

Carter slouched in his armchair, what I could see of his face grim. "Are we *really* going to bring her into all of it? The rituals and everything? She's barely part of the family."

"She's as much family as you are," my mother said firmly from the kitchen, where I couldn't see her at the moment. "But it could be a difficult transition when she didn't have the full upbringing to help her form the right mindset... Your father was able to explain it to me well enough, though. We'll have to see how it goes."

The hairs on the back of my neck stood on end. They were talking about *me*, weren't they? But what "rituals" was Carter talking about? Why would I need a special mindset to understand them?

Uncle Henry cleared his throat. "We have time to sort that out. No need to rush anything. But she's a Malik. She deserves the chance to claim her full birthright if she's up for it."

"As long as it doesn't threaten the rest of us," Aunt Mabel said, twisting her napkin in her hands.

"Right," Carter put in. "I'm just saying we should be careful."

Threaten them? Be careful? They were talking like I was some kind of danger to them.

Did they know more about me than I'd realized? But the second that thought passed through my mind, I shook it away. If they'd realized I was a killer for hire, I'd have expected much harsher words than what I'd just heard. Hell, I'd have expected them to already have called the National Guard on me.

"We'll see," my mother repeated, and then, to my frustration, changed the subject. "Mabel, how was that convention last weekend?"

As Mabel loosened up and started gushing about some event she'd attended about "data retention" or some other concept that related to her job, my gaze drifted through the room from where I was crouched. It snagged on a movement only just visible through the family room doorway.

Margaret had appeared in the hall—next to a door that she nudged back toward the wall with a very deliberate motion. And the second it'd slid back into place… suddenly I couldn't see the edge of it anymore.

The striped wallpaper behind her looked as impenetrable as if no one had ever passed through it.

I stared for several seconds before yanking myself down below the window ledge as she headed toward the family room, where she'd have been facing the window. My heart was suddenly beating faster.

That spot in the hall—it was where I'd noticed the faint wear in the carpet when I'd investigated the house before, wasn't it? The signs that I'd thought pointed to furniture that'd once been placed there.

But if my eyes hadn't just deceived me, I'd been correct in my first impressions. The wear *had* been caused by a door, just one that was concealed so well you couldn't find it or open it unless you knew the secret.

What kind of family needed an entirely secret doorway within their own home? And where the hell did it lead? No one had mentioned it during their tours of the house, so it obviously wasn't a fun quirk but something they purposefully kept hidden.

Did it have something to do with the rituals Carter had been talking about?

I rubbed my hands over my face. The more I searched for answers, the more questions I seemed to get instead. How did all the pieces I'd been seeing and hearing fit together? Were the Maliks hiding even more?

Was this what the Hunter had been warning me about?

The second that question crossed my mind, I grimaced. I was all tangled up because of the way he'd been egging me on when I hadn't noticed anything more than mildly awkward before—and that was mostly my *own* awkwardness. There could be totally innocent explanations for all of this. The Maliks were in a position with a lot of scrutiny because of my dad's political standing. Of course they'd keep some things private.

That private, though?

I stifled a groan. Was I getting played by a man I'd never met, or were these secrets just as important and dangerous as the Hunter had claimed?

The one thing I knew for sure was that I needed to see what was in that secret room.

NINETEEN

Decima

"WE WERE NEVER PARTICULARLY CLOSE, but I wouldn't have thought he'd outright screw us over," Julius said as we stalked through the streets with the rest of the crew.

"Are you sure it *is* a trap?" I asked, glancing around. "Maybe he really does have something important to talk to you about."

Garrison let out a huff. "And he really needed to talk to us about it in some random alleyway? If it's a dead end, I say we leave without even sticking around to find out what mess they're trying to pull us into."

Earlier today, Julius had gotten a call from a guy he'd worked with briefly a few years ago, asking for a meet-up with only a vague explanation. Julius had agreed, but he'd suspected from the start that it was some kind of set-up. I guessed it was hard not to be paranoid about that kind of thing when our enemies had already turned several of the mercenary teams he'd once seen as colleagues against the crew.

We were all well-armed with both guns and knives, braced for a confrontation. My senses prickled with alertness as I scanned the buildings around us. We wanted to find out exactly what this was about, but we weren't throwing caution to the wind, that was for sure.

"He sounded nervous," Blaze said. "It could be that he needs help. And either way, we have to get to the bottom of it."

"As long as we don't end up in the bottom of a grave," Garrison muttered.

Talon cast a baleful look over all of us. "Maybe we should shut up and focus if we want to avoid that outcome. We're almost there."

Julius nodded with a self-deprecating smile, and we fell into silence.

At the mouth of the alley, we paused in a defensive formation and peered down it. The passage turned farther in, just as Blaze had expected from the satellite imaging he'd pulled up. No one had blocked it off in any way that was visible from here.

Julius made a brisk motion, and we all followed him, spreading out even more as we strode along the cracked concrete between the looming brick walls. We didn't want to make it easy for anyone to surround all of us at once.

The shadows wrapped around us like a damp sheet,

and my nose itched with the sour smell trickling from a nearby dumpster. Julius and Talon rested their hands on their hips over their holsters. Blaze outright withdrew his gun, less confident in his quick draw than the others.

We paused at the bend, looking both ways to where the streets showed at either end. We definitely weren't cut off. But there was no one here yet, and we were right on time. That didn't bode well.

I stayed in the alley we'd entered through next to Garrison. Julius and Talon ambled a few paces down each direction of the longer alleyway. Blaze stopped right in the middle of the T, knitting his brow.

And we waited.

For a long stretch, nobody came—not to speak to us or to descend on us with guns blazing. I stayed tensed, conscious of every sound that came from the quiet warehouse district. Other than the distant grumble of passing traffic and the hiss of a plastic bag caught in the breeze, it was silent.

When it was twenty minutes after the meetup time, Blaze shifted on his feet. "Maybe *he* got ambushed on his way to meet us."

"I don't think we should stick around any longer," Julius said grimly. "If he's got something to say, he can reach out again."

At the same moment, a faint scraping sound reached my ears from behind a door in the side of the building next to me. I stepped closer, my fingers curling around the hilt of one of my knives—

And the door burst right off its hinges into me, slamming into my body and knocking me onto my ass.

Sudden footsteps and gunshots thundered all around me. I shoved at the heavy metal slab that was pinning me down and then squirmed to maneuver myself out from under it.

"Keep her down!" someone shouted, and a figure that I realized was braced on top of the detached door stomped on my hand, making my fingers release my knife before he kicked it away.

Clenching my jaw against the jab of pain, I aimed a punch and managed to clock the guy in the groin—hard. With a strained noise, he swayed on his perch, and I wrenched myself out from under his and the door's weight.

The scene I escaped into was total mayhem. Bullets ricocheted off the walls, bodies heaved this way and that, and voices hollered back and forth. I couldn't tell which were from my men and which from the enemy. Grabbing my gun, I moved to charge into the fray—when yet another opponent charged into me.

I lashed out at him, smacking him in the head with the butt of the gun, kneeing him in the gut. He shoved me backward, barely touching me other than that. Like he was just trying to get me out of the way rather than attack me.

A few more men converged on me. I raised my hand to shoot, and the nearest one knocked my aim off course. Several fists flew at me, but none of them hit me that hard —except the one I couldn't quite manage to dodge amid the barrage, which lost me my pistol too.

For fuck's sake. I whipped out my other knife and fell into a fighting stance, glaring at my four attackers. But they just stood there, equally poised but not closing in. Again, I had the sense that they were trying to keep me *out* of the fighting rather than drag me into it.

Just like the men during the attack at the hotel had hesitated to fight me.

An uncomfortable chill pooled in my gut. I took a few testing swipes at the blockade, and the men simply fended me off with their own blades. A couple of them had guns at their hips that they weren't even trying to use. But there were too many of them together for me to make a full attack on one without leaving myself vulnerable to too many others.

I peered past them at the rest of the battle and spotted Julius ducking to the side as he fired his gun. He hurtled backward toward me, and then stopped, his head jerking to the side and his eyes widening as he stared at someone farther down the alley.

"Petrov?" he said. "What the hell—"

He cut himself off to fire another couple of shots and swing his knife with the other hand as two more men rushed at him. Behind them came a stern, bulky guy with a broad forehead that had a scar angled across it. He was looking at Julius with a strange expression too.

Did Julius know that guy? Petrov wasn't the name of the contact we'd been expecting to talk to. What the hell was going on?

"Someone get to Dess!" Talon's voice hollered from a spot I couldn't see.

I squared my shoulders and prepared to take care of myself. These pricks might *want* to keep me out of the fighting, but we didn't always get what we wanted. A lesson I was happy to teach them after how many times I'd learned it.

I eyed my opponents again and identified a flaw in their formation. My fingers tightened around my knife. Then I sprang into action.

As if I meant to try to stab a guy in the middle, I lunged forward. But just as he moved to deflect me, I swerved in the opposite direction. My slashing blade cut across another man's arm—not enough to take him out of commission, but significantly weakening his stronger hand.

The men shifted to adjust their positions to compensate, and I flung myself at the nearest wall. Using momentum and speed, I rebounded off it and leapt right over the pricks' heads.

They definitely hadn't expected me to end up behind them. Before they could do more than grunt in surprise, I'd punctured two of their hearts from behind. The third guy whirled around, and I slit open his throat. He crumpled into a pool of blood.

That was what they got for thinking they could contain me.

The constraints of the alley had worked against our enemies as much as ourselves. They must have been hoping to take us more by surprise. Bodies littered the concrete around me, and thankfully none of them belonged to the Chaos Crew. I saw Blaze get in a shot that caught one guy in the head, and Talon wrenched his favorite knife through another opponent's belly.

A man sprang at Garrison, the closest of the four to me. I yelped a warning and sprang to help as Garrison leapt out of the way with his gun hand jerking upward. The guy raked a knife across Garrison's forearm, and then ducked and rolled just as Garrison fired at him. Before I could make the attacker pay for the injury, he backed away, panting.

He wasn't the only one retreating. They must have realized they weren't winning this fight. Only three of our attackers were still standing, one of them the bulky guy with the forehead scar. He waved his own knife, smeared crimson, and they took off down the one route open to them without obstacles.

I would have charged after them, but as I raced around the corner, my gaze caught on Blaze, who'd fallen back against the wall with his hand pressed against a cut on his chest. My heart lurched with concern. I dashed to him instead.

"It's okay," he said in a voice that was only slightly strained. "Just a minor flesh wound."

When he lifted his hand, I saw he was right—it was a long cut, but shallow. Maybe not even bad enough to require stitches. When I spun around, our remaining attackers had vanished.

Julius cursed. All four of the men gathered around me, watching the shadows warily in case there'd be another attempt.

"You knew one of them, didn't you?" I asked Julius. "You said his name."

"There's no time to talk about it," he said brusquely. "People will have heard the shots and called the cops. We need to get out of here fast."

With him in the lead, we hustled out of the alley and made it to the rental car we'd arrived in just as sirens pealed in the distance. We dove inside, Garrison behind the wheel, and peeled away from the curb.

Squashed in the back between Blaze and Talon, I kicked the back of Julius's seat. "We're out of there now. Who was that guy you called Petrov?"

To my surprise, it was Talon who answered. "Former special ops. We were on a base with him for a while during our military days."

I stared at him. That was an even bigger coincidence than I'd have imagined. "And he just happened to show up with a bunch of jerks trying to kill you?"

"It obviously wasn't by chance," Julius said, anger thickening his already deep voice. "Whoever's behind these attacks, they know more about us than they should. And they're using every tactic they can against us."

"He won't know much about our current abilities," Talon pointed out, but his tone was somber too.

"Who would know about your connection to him?" I asked. "How do the people who sent him even know that you were in the military?" It wasn't like the Chaos Crew kept a business website with a list of its members and their biographies.

Blaze grimaced. "If these are people who've come at us before, they may have seen enough of us that they could have been able to use their own facial recognition software, or fingerprints, or something like that to make a connection."

Garrison coughed from where he was sitting behind the wheel. "I'm more interested in the fact that they tried to shove Dess off to the side. They didn't do a thing to hurt you once they had you out of the way, did they?"

A flush that was mostly frustration coursed under my skin. "No. Not until I forced their hand, and then they didn't get away with much."

"And who would care so much about keeping you safe while slaughtering us?"

It wasn't hard to see what he was getting at. We'd already discussed this theory the last time.

I rubbed my face. "It could be Damien Malik. I know. But there are other explanations too." Even if I couldn't think of them off the top of my head. The enemies who'd come after us back in the crew's hometown hadn't treated me so gently.

All this had started when I'd reached out to my birth father. Where did it end?

I had no idea, and every passing day brought more questions without answers. The Hunter had told me to dig deeper. I didn't want to follow his instructions—but it was starting to seem like that was the only possible route I could take if I wanted to get through this with my *other* family alive.

An idea twined through my thoughts until it felt solid enough for me to speak out loud. "I need to crack open all the Malik family secrets—and none of us has found any way we can do that on our own. I think it's time I set up another job to exchange a favor."

TWENTY

Blaze

DESS STRODE through the door after her mission looking both exhausted and fulfilled. I studied her as she flopped onto the sofa next to where I'd set myself up with my laptop and a plate of pasta I'd already polished off. She'd refused to tell us exactly what the mission was, handling this one completely on her own.

There were no obvious signs of combat on her clothes or skin. Her leggings and form-fitting top—which showed off some of my favorite assets—suggested work that required precise physical movements, but that covered a lot of areas. All I knew was that she looked content now that it was over.

"How was it?" I asked, setting my laptop on the coffee table in front of me and leaning back into the sofa.

Dess kicked off her shoes and grinned at me. "It couldn't have gone better."

Seeing her like that brought a warm sensation to my chest. Proud and content were two emotions that didn't seem to come naturally to Dess, so I treasured every glimpse of them I got. She deserved to take pride and happiness in what she was capable of.

Seeing her stretch out on the cushions as if she owned the house—as if she belonged with us—only exemplified that warmth.

"Has your search brought up anything?" she asked me, and I jerked my mind back to my own mission.

"I did a deep dive into all the Malik family holdings," I said. "Properties, vehicles, bonds, bank accounts. Everything they own, everything we could delve farther into. Unfortunately, they either don't have much outside of the house we know about and its insured contents, or they're very good at keeping whatever else they own off all the records I can access."

A little of her shine faded. "So there's nothing?"

I wagged a finger at her. "Have a little faith. I said there isn't *much*. I did discover that there's a safety deposit box at a separate bank from where they handle most of their finances in your grandmother's—Damien's mother's —name."

"Grandma Ruby," Dess said, sitting up straighter. She used the name with a familiarity that sent a weird twinge through me. She was suspicious of these people and she knew they'd never accept her, but she'd become a part of their collective all the same. "What do you think is in it?"

I shook my head. "There's no way to know. But the fact that it's at a separate bank suggests that it might be something more secret than your typical safety deposit contents. It's the best lead I turned up."

"And you're the best at turning up leads," Dess said, with a softly sly smile that heated me up in very different ways. She rubbed her mouth, her expression turning pensive. "Getting into a bank would be pretty difficult, but I think the guy who owes me can handle it. Garrison said he's an expert robber and safe cracker, known for getting at just about anything you could need that's locked away… I wanted to keep my options open since I didn't know what you'd find."

She picked up her phone and dialed the guy up. The conversation didn't last long—maybe two minutes of exchanging information and setting a time to do it— before she ended the call and gave me a mischievous look.

"Good news," she said. "We can go tonight. He said a tech expert would be an asset, so it'll be you, me, and Echo. I hope you're ready."

———

While Dess and I showed up a half-hour early in the still of the night, the man who called himself Echo was already waiting at the meeting spot down the street from the bank building, smoking a cigarette where he stood in the shadows between the beams of two streetlamps.

"Isn't the first rule of robbery *not* to leave DNA behind?" I murmured to Dess. I hoped Garrison had done his due diligence on this guy.

She shrugged. "Not our DNA, not our problem.

Anyway, what are the chances the police would make anything of ash on the sidewalk a block away from the place. If this goes well, no one will even know the bank was broken into."

I had to admit she had a point.

The guy was certainly a character. He stood taller than both of us, but his height seemed to be all he had going for him. His arms and legs were skinny enough that I wondered if he'd been through a food shortage—and whether he couldn't have stolen himself some meals if he needed them so badly. His tortoiseshell framed glasses looked like they were meant to be a fashion statement, but they slid down his nose as he lifted his head to look at us. Even his clothes hung loosely on him.

Should I buy this guy a cheeseburger when we finished here?

Dess nodded to him. "Echo."

He grinned awkwardly down at her, showing a mouth of nicotine-stained teeth, and tossed his cigarette butt into the gutter. "You're early."

"So are you. Are we ready to go?"

He clucked his tongue. "I need to explain first."

Dess held up her hands. "Of course. We're ready to listen."

"Good." He gave a little twitch of his shoulders that made me wonder if he had a few screws loose in some literal sense as well as being half-starved. "Security guard, cameras, silent burglar alarms at every door, window, and room entrance, control panels at the vault and each secure door. That is this bank's security. We can't get into the vault without setting off an alarm, so no money. You can't steal money from this bank. You *can't*."

I was starting to get a bit annoyed. Did this guy think *we* were amateurs? "It's a good thing none of us is looking to steal any money, then, isn't it?"

Dess nudged me gently with her elbow. "Echo has broken into hundreds of secure buildings. Without setting off any alarms like we did the last time we did a major break and entry. He's never been caught."

I shut my mouth at the mention of the near-debacle we'd faced at the genetics storage center, an embarrassed flush crossing my cheeks—I still didn't know where my instructions had gone wrong to trigger that alarm—and tipped my head to the other guy.

"You're just looking to get at the safety deposit boxes," he said. "I know. That is doable. But I highly recommend against taking anything out of them too. We can get to them and get out again, but as soon as you remove contents, you alert your target that they have an enemy."

That consideration at least made sense. "Got it," I said.

"Can you walk us through the steps for getting to the boxes?" Dess asked.

Echo started flicking off points on his fingers. "We need to take out the security guard, but you can't kill him. Fred is a good man. The cameras need to be diverted from the outside. Your tech man can help with that. The motion-detecting alarms are at knee level, so we can avoid those. The control systems are turned off with a key swipe, and the guard has the key card for most rooms. We lift it from him. I can handle the inner doors and the box itself by my own means which I prefer not to share." He looked between us. "Shall we get started?"

"Absolutely." I pulled out my tablet. "I may be able to handle the outside cameras from right here."

It turned out that I needed to walk a little closer for the signal to be strong enough, but then I hacked into the feed quickly enough that this dude *had* to be at least a little impressed—not that it should matter to me whether he was. Examining the setup, I winced. "I'll have to 'adjust' them one at a time as we pass them. Mess with them all at once, and the guard in the camera room's bound to notice something."

Echo shrugged. "Do what you have to do. Just make sure no one sees us."

He strode ahead of us and went straight to the back door. It opened easily in his grasp, and he glanced back at us with a twinkle in his eyes. "I took care of this one earlier."

Okay, maybe the guy did know what he was doing.

I continued looping and resetting the feeds as we slipped into the building and made our way through the narrow, darkened halls at the back of the building. Echo pointed to four small panes low down on the wall. "Sensors."

We stepped over them no problem, swinging our knees high, although I couldn't see the lasers that we were avoiding. Tension wriggled down my spine. I'd never been the most coordinated of the crew. It would *really* suck if I somehow broke Echo's perfect record my first time on a mission with him. I'd never live the infamy down.

"How do we know if we activate a sensor?" I asked, switching the cameras again as we hurried onward.

"We'll hear sirens," Echo claimed nonchalantly, continuing forward with quiet footfalls. When we reached a door, he bent next to it with some gestures I couldn't make out and disabled the lock on that one with a faint click. He closed it behind us after we'd darted past it.

He paused before we turned a corner, and the thump of footsteps reached my ears. "Fred's doing his patrol. You want to take care of that?" He glanced at Dess with a confidence that made me wonder again what favor she'd done for him to earn this one in return.

Dess slipped around the corner without hesitation. We waited in silence. The footsteps halted with the briefest rustling of a scuffle, and then there was nothing. Whatever Dess had done, it'd taken her only a matter of seconds.

She returned from hiding the unconscious body in less than a minute, brushing her hands together like she did this every day. Which I guessed was almost true, at least in her previous career under the household's control. She flashed the key card she'd grabbed. "He's fine," she reassured Echo. "He'll wake up in a few hours."

Echo didn't bother speaking again as we approached the room that we most needed to enter—the one that held the safety deposit boxes. He stopped us in our tracks and pointed to the invisible sensors that would have sent us straight to prison. Lifting his scrawny legs high, he walked through them without much effort, and I went second this time, trying to move with extra caution.

Part of me expected it not to work when Dess used the

guard's keycard to swipe into the room, but the lights flashed green. She glanced over a shoulder, giving me a look of absolute confidence. We'd made it to the room with her grandmother's deposit box, just moments from figuring out what lay inside.

I hoped it made all this trouble worthwhile.

Echo stepped into the room first. "Which one?" he asked under his breath.

"476," I said automatically, reciting the number I'd ingrained in my memory.

He turned to the smallest set of lockboxes on the wall and pulled a tool from his pocket. Apparently he was truly worried about someone stealing his techniques and, I don't know, making a fortune by showing them off on TikTok or something, because he placed himself very deliberately between us and his hands so I couldn't see what he was doing with the thing. But he jammed it into the compartment somehow or other, and the next thing I knew, it was popping open.

Echo motioned Dess over to open the drawer behind the door he'd opened. I followed her, pulling out my camera. We might not be able to take the contents with us physically if we wanted to keep our intrusion here a secret, but we could steal away any evidence we found in other ways.

Dess shone the beam of her small flashlight into the open drawer. The first couple pieces of paper at the top of the pile were nothing all that exciting: something to do with stocks or bonds, very official looking and nothing salacious. Dess nudged those aside and froze, staring.

The Polaroid photograph beneath the papers showed a little boy, no older than seven or eight, lying naked on his side. His staring eyes and the bluish pallor of his skin made it clear he was dead.

But it hadn't been an easy death by any means. His body was mottled with vicious wounds. I'd seen a lot of gore in my life, but nothing quite like this. My stomach heaved.

Who would do something like that? Who would keep a *record* of it?

Damien Malik's mother, it appeared. At least as the answer to the second question.

Dess had closed her eyes, her lips pressed tight as if she was resisting the urge to vomit. I wouldn't have blamed her if she'd given in to that urge, even though it would have made our exit a lot trickier. She drew in a few shaky breaths and forced her eyes open again.

Together, we sorted through the photos. There were five of them in total, each of a different child. The youngest I'd estimate was four and the oldest maybe ten. All of them were dead; all bore similar wounds that spoke of horrifying torture.

By the end of it, I didn't want to steal the contents of the box. I wanted to burn it out of existence. And preferably out of my mind too, if that'd been possible.

Dess was still staring at the last photo, which showed a girl who looked to be about six years old. Her blond hair was streaked with her own blood, two of her delicate fingers chopped right off her hand where it'd stiffened against the floor in death. Dess drew her forefinger over one of the wounds on the corpse's side, a jagged one that gaped open.

"The knife they'd have had to use to do that kind of damage," she said in a strained voice. "And the way they must have dragged it through her body to make that kind of mark... It would have been excruciatingly painful. I'm not sure I'd do it to my worst enemy, let alone a kid. And they all have cuts like that, more than one. How could anyone be *that* cruel to someone so helpless?"

A memory flickered up in the back of my mind of a different broken body, and I swallowed thickly. "Some people are just horrible."

"And why does my *grandmother* have them?" she added, that additionally horrible layer to this situation sinking in.

Echo glanced at the photos and shuddered. "That is fucking sick," he muttered, and pulled back toward the door as if he couldn't stand to even be near the images. I gave him a few points for having some sense of morality.

With my jaw clenched against my nausea, I snapped my own photos of each of the Polaroids. The thought of having those images on my phone made me want to set *it* on fire too, but we needed to be able to examine them later. There might be clues we didn't have time to pore over right now... and I'd like to be able to have a bucket at the ready when I did, in case my stomach finally heaved itself up my throat.

None of this made any sense. Yes, we'd had our suspicions that there was something fishy going on with the Maliks, but never in a million years would I have thought it'd involve torturing children.

Of course, the torture and the deaths themselves might not have anything to do with any of them. Maybe these were images from crimes they'd discovered that they were trying to fight back against.

If that were the case, though, I didn't know why they'd have kept the evidence in a safety deposit box instead of giving it to the police.

As soon as I'd gotten my photos, Dess shoved the box shut. Echo scurried over for just long enough to lock the door that hid it. Then he ushered us out of the room with as much urgency as if it were filling with poisoned air, which I hoped wasn't actually the case. The mission had gotten noxious enough as it was.

We dodged the same security measures on the way out, Echo moving with ruthless efficiency. As soon as we were back out in the night air, which tasted unbelievably fresh washing into my lungs, he shot a glance at Dess. "I want nothing more to do with this," he said, and marched away without another word.

I couldn't say I blamed him.

Dess was silent all the way to the car. When we reached it, she got into the back instead of the front and dropped her head into her hands. I slid in next to her, not sure whether she'd want to be touched. Not sure whether I could manage to touch her in a way that'd be comforting when I was so twisted up inside myself.

"Why did she have those pictures?" she whispered.

"Where did they come from? What's this supposed to mean?"

"We'll figure it out," I said, my voice sounding distant to my own ears. "We'll get to the bottom of it."

"Five of them." Her head jerked up, her eyes widening with panic. "What if it's still happening? What if whoever hurt those kids is still doing it?"

I knew the right answer to that question. Resolve hardened inside me, pushing down my queasiness. "Then we'll stop them," I said firmly.

Dess's forehead furrowed. "How can you be so sure?"

"I just know we'll find a way. *I'll* find a way." I paused, and then let the story spill out, as much of it as I was willing to say. "You know what I'm like—how hyperactive I am. I was even worse as a kid. I got on people's nerves, and a bunch of kids in the neighborhood bullied the hell out of me for it. The worst of it was—"

The words stuck in my throat despite my intentions. Dess frowned, gripping my hand. "What happened?" she asked softly.

The obvious concern in her tone unlocked my voice. "I had a dog. A mutt, no special breed—fox terrier mix or something. He was the only thing I had back then that didn't mind how I was. And one day the bullies—they grabbed him out of my yard—I found him in the back alley, all battered and bloody. Dead. It looked like they'd kicked him back and forth until his bones broke, and then they smashed his skull with a rock."

Fury flared in Dess's gaze. "That's more than bullying. They were psychopaths."

I shrugged. "They were vicious kids. I don't know how much they even understood what they were doing. Maybe they thought of it like a stuffed animal. Whatever. It doesn't help anything for me to rage about it now. But when it happened—I was so mad at myself that I hadn't managed to protect him. That he'd gotten hurt like that because of me. That was when I swore to myself that I'd never be so powerless I couldn't save the things and people that matter to me again."

"You don't even know those kids in the photos," she pointed out.

"I do know that I've seen them," I insisted. "And I sure as hell care that it doesn't happen to anyone else. So you'd better believe I'm going to fight until we destroy whoever's responsible."

And it wasn't just the kids. Did Dess even realize that she now topped my list of people who mattered to me?

If uncovering the story behind those children would help her, I'd walk through Hell itself to figure out what happened and how it was connected to the Malik family. I wouldn't let her meet a similarly horrific fate.

I *would* protect her, no matter what I had to give to do it.

TWENTY-ONE

Decima

I'D TRIED to sit a few times while Blaze worked silently on his laptop, but the lack of movement unsettled me. If I wasn't in motion, my mind could only dwell on the tormented childish figures that I'd seen in the photographs.

I couldn't walk away from them, but at least staying on my feet kept the most crippling sense of horror at bay.

Blaze stirred with his usual restlessness and shot me an apologetic glance. "With kids, there are a lot fewer images available, and those photos didn't give the clearest view of their faces. I'm doing my best to find at least partial matches."

I nodded. "It's okay."

But it wasn't, not at all. If Grandma Ruby had those photos in a safety deposit box, they must have been important, and she must have wanted them hidden. But for her to have them at all…

What if the Hunter was disgustingly right about the Malik family, beyond any crime that'd ever occurred to me?

I stalked toward the kitchen, where Talon was drinking from a bottle of kombucha while he sharpened his favorite knife, and then strode back across the living room again. My hands clenched at my sides. I really wanted to punch someone, but I didn't have anyone to punch.

Who were the villains here? Could this have been some kind of setup? Maybe the Maliks were being framed.

Blaze let out a pleased sound, and I hurried over to join him. "You've got something?"

He waved at his screen. "These are partial matches, like I said, but I think I've identified a couple of the kids. A boy, aged five, and a girl, aged eight. Both of them had missing child reports filed with their local police departments."

"Local departments," I repeated. "You mean they weren't from here in DC?"

Blaze shook his head. "The boy was from Jersey City and the girl… Detroit. Not *too* far away, but whatever was going on, it wasn't restricted to this state."

"Whatever *is* going on," I corrected. "For all we know, this is still happening. When did they go missing?"

"The boy… three years ago. The girl, twelve." He grimaced. "Whether it's still happening or not, the murderer has been at it for a while."

I frowned, my stomach twisting even tighter. "You said there are just the missing child reports. No documentation of a definite crime? Did no one ever find the bodies?"

"It doesn't look like it. I haven't turned up any articles or records of unidentified bodies discovered in that condition. Although there are always remains turning up here and there that've deteriorated beyond recognition and were never identified."

"Or the killer disposed of them in a way that wasn't discovered." After taking those pictures as the sickest of mementoes. My fingers flexed and clenched again. "What about the other three?"

"I haven't located them at all so far. Maybe they were from farther abroad or longer ago, and they'll pop up eventually. Or maybe they weren't even reported missing, at least not with a photograph to go with the report."

A sour taste entered the back of my mouth. The kids had been so alone that nobody had even realized they were taken, tortured, and killed? How could anyone let a child remain missing without reporting them? Didn't their schools or neighbors notice when they disappeared without a trace? More importantly, shouldn't their parents have known?

But if they'd been that neglected, maybe that'd made them ideal targets.

I let out a frustrated sound and buried my head in my hands. "How could the Maliks have anything to do with this? It would ruin all of them—everything they're so committed to working toward. It doesn't make any sense."

"I agree," Blaze said gently. "It's a lot to swallow."

"But the evidence is right there. Maybe I'm too biased —of course I don't want to be related to people who'd do something that horrific." I groaned. "How can I trust my judgment about them? The actual evidence points right to them. No one could have known I'd find that safety deposit box. What would be the point of planting evidence where it wouldn't be used?"

Blaze got up and rubbed my shoulder. "There are so many factors we can't account for. I don't think we can draw any definite conclusions yet. Other than there's at least one very sick murderer out there, and they're connected to your family in one way or another."

"I didn't get more answers. I only have more questions —worse ones. Where do we go from here?"

I wasn't aware of Talon crossing the room until he came up on my other side. He gripped my elbow firmly, grounding me with his solid presence. "We'll keep looking and keep digging until we have the answers," he said. "No one's beaten us yet."

"And you're not being biased," Blaze put in. "It *is* a bizarre idea that your family would be responsible for crimes like these. If I come across any indication that they're being set up, I won't be remotely surprised."

"But you haven't come across anything like that so far," I said.

"No, but I haven't come across anything that gives further proof that they committed the crimes either."

"Other than the photos being in a box in my grandmother's name."

"That's just one piece of proof without any context," Blaze said.

I let out a growl of frustration and raised my head. "I feel like there's nothing I can do. If I knew who'd done it, I could go destroy them and make sure they never hurt anyone again. But I have no idea and no way to figure it out. And more kids could be dying right now because I can't."

"You're doing your best," Blaze said, but his reassurance bounced right off me.

Talon turned me toward him. He tugged my hands away from my face and fixed me with his impenetrable gaze. "You're stronger than this, Dess," he said. "Stronger than those fears. Stronger than the asshole who killed those children. If you need help remembering that, come at me. I know you could take me if you really tried."

I stared at him. "Hurting *you* isn't going to prove anything."

The corner of his mouth curled up with a hint of a smile. "You won't hurt me. I'm made of pretty tough stuff. But I think you need a reminder of just how much you can tackle. Now come on. Don't tell me you're afraid of a little sparring all of a sudden."

I made a face at him, and he pinned me with those cool blue eyes that would have sent anyone else running. Instead, they brought a warmth flaring up inside me. "Let's see all that power you've got in you," he taunted.

A surge of defiance raced through me, and I swung a fist at his shoulder. Talon dodged and tapped my side with his knuckles. He didn't hit hard—it was a dare to fully commit to the fight.

My competitive nature rushed to the surface. It felt *good* to focus on this, to feel the power he'd talked about. I sank into that sensation and came at Talon with twice as much determination as before.

We bobbed and circled each other, exchanging blows, our breaths roughening as our movements sped up trying to catch the other off-guard. I almost forgot about Blaze until another fist rapped against my shoulder blade.

I spun around and shoved the hacker down on the sofa, pinning him there before I'd fully processed what had happened. He just grinned up at me, not a hint of worry in his bright eyes.

"What are you doing?" I demanded. Talon loomed behind me.

Blaze tipped his head to the side with a slyly innocent expression. "I figured if you feel better beating up on one of us, two would be even better. Although…" He shifted his position beneath me where I'd straddled him with one hand to his throat and the other on his chest, and I was abruptly aware of his erection brushing my sex. Heat had pooled there without my realizing it. "Now I can think of other ways you can dominate us that might be even more fun."

A tingle of desire passed through me, but at the same time something in me balked. "I don't think I should be having *fun* right now."

Blaze reached up to place his hand over mine where it still loosely held his throat. "Don't think of it as fun, then.

Think of it as showing your strength and remembering who you are. You're having trouble even thinking clearly— you need a break. More than that, you need to believe in yourself, and I know that you do when we're together."

I raised my eyebrows "You're awfully confident that you can make me feel that way."

Blaze chuckled. "I don't think anyone can make you feel that way. But I know that you can make yourself feel strong if you're in control of both of us."

In control of both of them. The thought provoked an eager quiver despite my initial doubts.

I glanced back at Talon still braced behind me. Handling all the guys the other night had been a rush, one that sent a heady flush through me just at the memory.

Maybe this *was* what I needed—a reminder that I wasn't as weak and powerless as I felt. I'd ordered Blaze around before, but with Talon I'd only encouraged his own aggression. What would it be like to take control over a man that domineering? To have both of them totally under my sway?

The thrill that came with the idea made up my mind for me. Before I could second-guess the impulse, I leaned back to grab Talon's bicep. With a heave, I yanked him down on the sofa next to Blaze. Then I adjusted my position so I straddled one of each of their thighs, my knees sinking between their legs.

"Stay still," I ordered both of them, with a push of their chests toward the back of the sofa. Then I gripped the front of Blaze's shirt and captured his mouth.

He kept his hands to himself, but he kissed me back

with all the passion I knew he was capable of. I finished with a flick of my tongue over his and turned straight to Talon, who was watching me with smoldering eyes.

First I buried my face against his neck, taking in the masculine scent of him and grazing my teeth against his skin in a way that made his hips jerk toward me. "I said 'stay still,'" I murmured, and raised my head to nip his earlobe. "You've done a good job at fucking me in the past. But this time, I'm going to show you what it's like to be fucked by me."

A flicker of emotion passed through Talon's normally impassive face, lust and admiration and more that I couldn't identify. It definitely wasn't true that the man didn't feel, no matter how emotionless he tended to present himself as.

I ran my fingers over his smooth scalp and dug them into the back of his neck as I pressed my lips greedily into his. He met me with just as much fervor. The unrelenting passion in the kiss had my toes curling. My hand worked its way between us and began pulling down the joggers that he wore.

He managed to pivot his hips and allowed his pants to slide down his legs at my coaxing. His boxers followed, and I traced my finger up his thigh with an intensity that felt immoral. I moved it so, so slowly that I saw his attention split between me and the finger that I trailed up his leg.

It must have been a noise from beside us that drew my attention back to Blaze. His name had never fit him more with the hunger that shone from his face. I couldn't neglect my other lover.

"I want both of you," I said in a voice that came out huskier than I expected. He reached for his jeans, managing only to unclasp the button before I stopped him with a hand on his wrist. "That's my job."

I pulled myself up and allowed my one finger to trail down Talon's still clothed chest, all the way to the base of his impressive length. As I stood, I twirled my finger around it slowly and meticulously before releasing him.

The heat that roiled through my body had my limbs trembling. I pulled Blaze up so we stood chest to chest with each other and reached a hand into his pants—surpassing the fabric entirely as I gripped him beneath the belt. He dipped his head backward and groaned toward the ceiling as I stroked him just as slowly. Despite being the one theoretically in control, I couldn't help but still feel completely out of control at that moment.

I hooked my other hand through his pants and tugged them downward, but he didn't seem to notice in the slightest as I continued my teasing motions. Fuck, at this moment, Blaze was one of the most attractive men I'd ever seen. The way his light red hair hung back as his breathing increased in tempo—as I increased the rhythm of my motions—was almost godlike. His fists, balled at his side, showed the restraint that he was exercising.

I wanted more than that. But I could make that kind of command too, couldn't I?

"Don't hold back on me," I said. I might be in charge of this encounter, but I didn't want them to treat me like I was fragile and incapable. "I want everything you can give me. Show me just what you want to do to me—no holds barred."

Blaze's eyes flung open, and I saw the restraint there too. I knew he was doing whatever he thought would make me feel the most in control, but more than anything, I wanted to know how *he* wanted this moment between us to unravel.

Blaze's eyes flashed with uncertainty before he placed his hands on my hips. "Are you sure?"

I smirked. "Positive."

He didn't waste any time considering his options. One of his arms dipped around my back, and the weight of his body forced me to fall backward. I clutched the fabric of his shirt as he slowed my fall and draped me across the coffee table. Blaze immediately went for my pants, tugging them down my legs and trailing kisses in the wake of the fabric.

The tender treatment might have raised my hackles in another context, but I knew Blaze so well now that it stirred no memories of the villain who'd violated me before. And after all, this man was doing exactly what *I'd* told him to do.

And oh, was I pleased with the result. The hacker hooked his arms under my legs and tossed my feet over his shoulders. In an instant, his tongue had slipped inside of me, devouring my core.

I thrashed, my cry of both surprise and pleasure reverberating through the room as Blaze feasted. He seemed to know intuitively where it would be best to devote his tongue and lips. Then he inserted a finger into the mix and pumped it inside of me with the same tempo as his tongue had offered a second before.

I panted beneath him as the waves of my pleasure grew and eddied. With each swell, the bliss intensified until I was near my breaking point. But Blaze wasn't finished with me yet. He sent me right up to that edge before letting me drift back down just shy of release.

"Blaze," I growled. He only looked down at me through lowered lashes as he inserted a second finger into me and went back to work. I tightened my thighs around his head and gave a direct command. "Make me come."

The second I'd spoken, he started working me over even more relentlessly. He put every ounce of knowledge and experience into his fingers and his tongue to bring me to that edge once again—before tossing me even higher and allowing me to plummet over it.

With a cry, I released everything I'd been holding back —all the pain and uncertainty, all the sadness and frustration. I replaced it all with the feeling of this man wreaking blissful havoc on every inch of me.

I didn't even have a moment to wind myself down before Blaze moved to the side and Talon bent over me. "Do you still want to be the one to fuck me, or can I have the honor of fucking you instead?" he asked in a tone that practically made me come just like that.

"Why not both at the same time?" I said, still breathless and dazed from Blaze's claiming. "Give me everything you've got. I'll meet you there."

"I know you will," he rumbled, and tugged my legs

toward him to wrap around his hips. I pushed myself upright to yank him to me, and his cock slid into me so perfectly we both groaned.

We rocked together, both of us bucking into each other's bodies. Talon glanced down at the place where our bodies met, and his voice turned even more heated. "There's nothing like fucking you. Watching you go almost cross-eyed when I push inside of you. And then all the ways you move, all the sounds you make."

He demonstrated, pulling himself out and then thrusting back into me. I couldn't help but gasp as that complete feeling of fullness took over my senses—as the lingering satisfaction from Blaze pulsed inside of me, enhanced each time Talon moved.

I glanced over at where Blaze watched, his breathing just as fast as ours. I didn't speak, instead gesturing for him to come to me in an unspoken command. As he came up beside me, I reached to clasp his cock in my hands. "You're mine too," I informed him, and opened my mouth, licking the head.

With a groan of his own, Blaze braced himself against the coffee table—which I hoped was *very* sturdy given all the action it was seeing today—and aligned himself in front of my mouth. I drew him in between my lips, still rocking against Talon at the same time.

He tasted delicious, warm and musky, exactly the flavor I'd imagine desire would be. Giddiness swelled in my chest as he moved with the motions of my mouth, as more pleasure raced through me with each crash of my and Talon's bodies against each other.

I *was* strong—strong enough to master both of these men. Strong enough to handle four lovers who were the most powerful men I'd ever known. And I'd have them with me every step of the way, supporting me with their own power.

Together, it was hard to believe anything could stop us. We'd do whatever needed to be done.

Blaze's hand gripped my hair as I sucked on him. Talon's rough palms on my hips held me with him, and I found myself on the verge of another climax. Unlike before, it didn't come in waves. It hit me at once, taking me mercilessly as my body pulsed around both of them.

I moaned against Blaze's erection. "Oh, fuck," he muttered, and pulled back just in time to let loose his own release across my chest and neck. He gazed at me with total adoration, panting but beaming.

I could feel Talon getting closer and closer with each thrust that I met. He bucked into me faster and harder until he gave one final slam of his hips and clutched onto me like a lifeline. I sagged into his embrace for the long moment before he finally pulled out.

It'd been good. It'd been *fantastic*. But even as the sense of power continued to resonate through me as I smiled at my lovers and swiped the sweat from my face, a tendril of uneasiness crept up inside me.

No matter how strong I was, we still had a horrible villain to bring to justice. One more enemy on top of the others we'd already accumulated. And I couldn't help wondering if this was even the end of it, or if there was even worse to come.

TWENTY-TWO

Decima

FOR THE FIRST TIME, I'd been conscripted into helping with the serving of dinner in the Malik household. As Grandma Ruby, Grandpa Bo, Aunt Mabel, and Uncle Henry chattered in the dining room, I grabbed serving spoons and potholders in the kitchen on my mother's instructions.

Carter dumped a small pan of green beans into a serving dish, and a few drops of melted butter spilled across the marble countertop. Iris had her back to him, but she seemed to innately sense the mess, turning with raised eyebrows.

"I know, I know," he said, grabbing a paper towel.

She tsked her tongue. "Try to be more careful to begin with. Rachel, dear, would you scoop the potatoes into a dish?"

It was still weird being called by my birth name. I

wondered if I'd ever get used to it. It was even harder now that I had all these suspicions about the family crowding my head.

I moved past Carter to deal with the potatoes, glancing briefly out the window in the direction I knew Garrison and Talon were waiting just out of sight. My brother glanced over at me. "You're roped into the chores now too," he teased.

"I'm going to eat, so it's only fair that I help dish it out," I said with forced cheer. I picked up the tongs and started moving the crisped potatoes from the baking sheet to a decorative white bowl.

"I thought you worked in a restaurant," Carter remarked. "You kind of suck at that."

I wrinkled my nose at him with what I hoped was suitably sibling-style annoyance as my heart stuttered briefly hearing my cover story questioned. "I'm a hostess. I lead people to their tables and take reservations, no food handling. But if you think you can do a better job…" I waved toward the tray in offering.

Carter snorted and took the beans over to the dining table. But by the time we'd all joined our relatives in the dining room, me seated next to my brother as usual, he turned to me with a bit of an arrogant air. "You know, now that you're part of the family, you don't have to keep a menial job. You can start working toward whatever career you want. Mom and Dad would obviously be happy to help you financially to get you on the right course."

Before Iris could jump in and agree, I gave a little

laugh. "I'm sure they would, but I like paving my own way. Anyway, the job I have suits me just fine for now."

Carter frowned. "Don't you want a career that *matters*? I'm going into law enforcement, and I'll make a difference there. I know I will. It's a lot more important than pointing people to the right restaurant table."

I forced a casual shrug. "Sounds a little too dangerous to me. I've had plenty of that in my life already."

A bit of a hush fell over the rest of the table at that remark. I'd thought the reference to my kidnapping would stop Carter in his tracks too, but he seemed determined to push my buttons, even though I doubted he'd ever find himself facing anything as dangerous as I'd done in my real job a hundred times over.

"But you'll never accomplish anything with a life working at some restaurant," he blurted out. "You'll never get to do anything meaningful. That would be such a sad life."

"Carter," our mother chastised. "Your sister is allowed to do whatever she wants with her life. As long as she's happy, that's all that matters. Plus, you don't have to have a career in law enforcement to support your father and advocate for putting away criminals."

"As long as she supports the family legacy, that's really all that matters," Aunt Mabel said as she dabbed at her mouth with her napkin.

Grandma Ruby chimed in. "Protecting the country from evil-doers is our curse and blessing, and it may be yours one day, too. If you decide to stick around with this crazy crew, that is."

Right. Because the only possible meaningful work had to be throwing criminals behind bars—or breaking their hands, or whatever, I supposed.

My mother smiled in agreement. "We don't expect you to fully commit to all of this right away, dear. It's something that we'll introduce you to over time."

I bit into one of the potatoes I'd dished out, trying not to show how uneasy the conversation was making me. The tone the conversation had taken sounded even more cultishly obsessive than when my father had brought up the family legacy the other day.

But if the Maliks were this dedicated to the cause and so willing to do everything to defeat crime, I couldn't imagine how they'd ever be involved in what we found in the safety deposit box. It didn't make sense. Maybe they'd gotten those photographs to remember just how horrible criminals could get?

But there wasn't any record of the murderer being caught or the bodies being found. Where had they gotten the pictures *from*? Why keep them locked away like that?

My head was spinning again. My gaze instinctively followed Uncle Henry as he straightened up over the baked chicken and lifted the butcher knife to carve off some more meat. He plunged the blade into the breast, twisting his wrist in a circular sawing motion that made my breath catch in my throat with a jolt of horror.

The motion looked just like the kind that could have marked those jagged wounds that'd gouged the children's flesh.

I blinked, and then he was cutting through the meat

in totally normal slices, as if he always had been. I watched, looking for any indication of that same twisting cut, but he didn't do it again.

For fuck's sake. Had I imagined that because I was so horrified by the pictures, so desperate for answers? This quest was turning me paranoid.

Grandma Ruby must have caught something in my expression that I hadn't quite been able to hide. "Are you all right, Rachel?"

The words brought me back to the moment, and I nodded, plastering a fake smile on my face instinctively. I knew from experience that they wouldn't be able to see through it.

"I'm great. I just got a little lightheaded for a second. I probably haven't drunk enough water today." I set down my fork and took a gulp from my glass. "Do you mind if I excuse myself for a moment and go use the restroom?"

A worried expression crossed my mother's face. "All this talk about legacy and crime would be enough to overwhelm anyone. I'm sorry. You go take care of yourself, and let us know if you need anything."

I dipped my head graciously and hurried out of the room. As soon as I'd passed out of view into the hall, I tapped a quick message into my phone—the message the men were waiting for. They were going to buy me more time than a simple bathroom excuse could manage.

I strode toward the bathroom and slipped inside, my ears pricked. It only took a matter of seconds. Then a bizarre squawking sound pierced through the walls, like there was a flock of rapid chickens congregating right outside the house.

What the heck had the guys orchestrated? As my relatives' voices faltered and then their footsteps hustled over to the back door to see what was going on outside, I had to resist the urge to join them. The crew could tell me all about it later. I could just imagine how much Garrison would enjoy conveying the story.

Instead, I darted out of the bathroom and over to the spot opposite the family room doorway where I'd seen Margaret emerge seemingly through the bare wall. My fingers slid over the striped wallpaper, testing it with years of honed experience. I couldn't expect the crew to keep my family distracted forever. If I took too long, my relatives might return and catch me in my stealthy investigation.

My fingertips caught on the faintest of grooves and traced it up and down, confirming that it was straight and tall enough to mark the edge of a door. My pulse kicked up a notch. There.

But there was no knob, no obvious way of opening it. How had Margaret done it? I hadn't seen her go in.

There were a few basic mechanisms to concealed doors, so I just had to figure out which one this operated by. Trying not to let the voices filtering in from outside distract me, I gave the door a general shove with my shoulder. Nothing. Then I ran my fingers along the edge of the seam again, pressing every couple of inches.

At hip height, the surface depressed just a fraction. Something in the wall gave a small click, and the door swung open.

My breath caught in my throat. I peeked through the doorway and found a plain flight of stairs leading down into the darkness of a basement room.

Without hesitation, I slipped inside and found a handle that let me pull the door shut. At least no one would be able to figure out where I'd gone, even if they noticed I'd been gone for a while.

I pawed at the walls on either side of the stairwell until my palm hit a light switch. When I flicked it upward, brilliant light spilled into the space at the bottom of the stairs. All I could see was polished wood flooring and the edge of a maroon rug that looked as thick as the ones in the main rooms upstairs.

As I eased down the stairs, a crisp scent—smoky and herbal—tickled my nose. It reminded me of the incense in churches and temples I'd occasionally had to carry out missions in or around. I couldn't place the exact scent—it might not have been quite the same as any I'd encountered before.

There was no sign of its source when I reached the bottom of the stairs. I came to a halt and stared at the room that opened up beyond the steps.

It looked like a large den. Bookshelves lined two of the walls, stuffed full with thick volumes and antique-looking decorations. In the center of the room, on top of the rug I'd seen the corner of, squatted a large desk piled high with more books and various other documents. A large leather office chair sat behind it, with a few more traditional wingchairs scattered through the rest of the space.

Damien already had a home office space upstairs. Did

my mother work down here? I hadn't gotten the impression that her job would require anything so elaborate. And why would she have kept it hidden?

I slunk closer to the bookshelves and scanned the spines. Most of them appeared to be volumes on law, politics, and criminology. I found one row with stranger titles, things like *Channeling the Inner Spirit* and *The Energy of the Great Beyond*. No one in the family had mentioned any kind of spiritual interests, but I guessed they could have those books more out of an academic interest rather than because they believed in the contents.

I snapped pictures of all of the shelves and then studied the items placed here and there in front of the books more closely. Some of them were antiques as I'd thought, a fancy old candlestick here, an intricately carved trinket box there. Others I had a lot more trouble making sense of.

Knitting my brow, I paused over a small shoe that must have belonged to a child. It was a dress shoe, but not particularly fancy or pretty, just a glossy black shell that looked like it was made out of plastic and a narrow strap with a tiny flower over the snap. The toes were lightly scuffed.

Normally when people kept mementos from their children, they bronzed them, didn't they? And I didn't see how this could have belonged to me or Carter. It was too large to have belonged to the toddler I'd been when I was kidnapped, and too girly for me to imagine a five- or six-year-old Carter donning it. But the style was fairly modern, so I couldn't picture it belonging to my parents' generation either.

Maybe it'd been Margaret's? But then why would it be here in my parents' house and not at Aunt Mabel and Uncle Henry's?

The shoe wasn't the only oddity. There was a little figure with a face roughly carved into the wood and a scrap of fabric as clothing. What appeared to be a hair clip in cheap metal shaped like a butterfly. A thin, folded cloth that might have been a napkin or a handkerchief.

Why would my parents have used things like that as part of the décor? It didn't match the rest of the room at all.

By the time I turned to take in the far wall, my skin was already creeping. What I found myself staring at didn't exactly comfort me. It held a few more framed parchments like the one I'd found in Damien's office, but these looked progressively newer and less worn, which fit with the numbers I was now more convinced were years. They continued on in a steady progression until they reached the 2000s, at which point they started to double up, two of the same before going on to the next.

The rest of the notations next to them looked like the same unfamiliar code as on the matching document upstairs. As far as I knew, Blaze had never managed to crack it.

Maybe he'd be able to with more examples to work with. I took pictures of those parchments too, holding my hands as steady as I could.

I'd seen a lot of horrible things in my time. I hadn't

actually uncovered anything specifically horrible *here*. But the whole vibe of the secret room—and the fact that it was secret at all—was making my skin crawl in a way I'd never experienced before. I couldn't shake the sense that *something* was very, very wrong.

At the end of the row of parchments, there was one more framed picture. This one was a faded photograph of a house with a broad front porch and vines crawling up one side. It sat on a wide, open property with no near neighbors, like it was out in the countryside. I didn't recognize anything about it either, and my parents hadn't mentioned owning a country home. Blaze hadn't found a deed or other record for it in all his searching.

So what was so special about it that they'd framed this photograph and hung it here?

I frowned at it and added it to my phone along with the rest. Then I turned my attention to the desk.

The papers I could see were printouts of news articles marked up with a few notes in what I could recognize as my father's handwriting. There was nothing particularly odd about them—they were reports on recent crimes here in DC, with things like the police response time circled. He was analyzing the performance of local law enforcement, which seemed like a totally Damien Malik thing to do.

I would have dug deeper, but just then a floorboard creaked somewhere above me. My nerves jumped, and I froze in place.

The family had come back inside. If I went back up

now, they might spot me using the hidden entrance. They might already be wondering where I was.

My hand darted to my phone. I tapped out another quick text to Garrison that an additional distraction was needed ASAP.

I'll take care of it, sweetheart, he shot back with a blowing kiss emoji I couldn't help seeing as sarcastic. A moment later, whatever he'd done, the footsteps above creaked away in the opposite direction.

There was no time to examine anything else right now. I dashed up the stairs, placing my feet as quietly as I could, and pressed my ear to the door. When I heard nothing on the other side, I nudged it open and squeezed out.

I shoved it back into place and was just starting down the hall toward the dining room when Grandma Ruby appeared from the back of the house. I swiped my hand over my hair, hoping I didn't look too rattled.

"Well, you certainly know how to miss a party," she said with an eye roll that didn't seem particularly hostile. I relaxed just a tad. If I'd been even a few seconds slower…

"What happened?" I asked in as casual a tone as I could summon.

She shook her head. "I'm still not even sure. We heard the strangest sounds, like there was a whole farmyard out there, and then some shouts for help, but we couldn't figure out where they were coming from. Then just as I'd come back inside, because really, it's dinner time, your mother shrieked like they were being murdered." She let out a huff. "It was only a rock that landed in the garden and crushed a few flowers. Nothing worth fretting about."

Somehow I thought she'd have taken a different tune if it'd been her own garden assaulted. "How strange," I said innocently.

I joined her back at the table. In less than a minute, the rest of the family poured back in, exclaiming to each other with their theories about what had been going on— neighbors acting out, poultry escaped from a delivery truck, a prank from a political opponent.

They were all so engrossed in their speculation that I didn't have to say anything at all, just eat the rest of my dinner in silent reverie. My body might have been at the table, but my mind was stuck in the room downstairs, trying to make sense of its strange contents alongside the photographs we'd found in the bank.

Noelle and Anna had always claimed that they were protecting me, that they'd taken me in to shelter me from the cruelty of the world. I knew that was at least partly a lie... but what if there was some truth to it too?

My parents hadn't died, obviously, but maybe the household really had seen kidnapping me as a way to protect me. Because I was starting to think that whatever my birth family was up to was way worse than anything my former captors had done.

TWENTY-THREE

Decima

"A SHOE?" Garrison said, leaning into the counter with an expression that told me he was thinking just as hard about the situation as I was. He looked down at the printed-out photos I'd set between us, shaking his head. "That is pretty weird. And the papers and symbols are just as bad."

I grimaced. "I just wish I understood what all of this means—if it means anything, you know?"

"Did you snap any pictures of the desk before you left?" Julius asked, scanning the photos of the bookshelves.

I shook my head. "I ran out of time. Maybe I can go back down there the next time I visit."

Talon's eyes shot up and captured mine. "You're not going back."

I frowned at him. "I have to."

He gestured to the photos. "Not until we know what

all of this means. It's definitely disturbing, especially after what you found in the lock box. We're not sending you into a potentially deadly situation for information. You're not a spy."

I narrowed my eyes in challenge. "No, but they *are* my family. It's not like any of you could waltz in there and get access anywhere near as easily."

"Talon's right," Julius said. "It would be reckless to go back without more information. We won't tell you where you're allowed to go, but please, give us a chance to see what we can make of this first."

"I wasn't planning on heading right back there today," I said. "But even if I did, I can take care of myself."

Garrison nudged me with his elbow, his tone wryly affectionate. "Sweetheart, nobody claimed that you couldn't. But you do have a bit of a blind spot for your family, and we won't let them exploit that—exploit *you.*"

I wanted to argue that I didn't have a blind spot, but it would be a lie, and all of them knew it. No matter how much evidence arose against the Maliks, a part of me still wanted to believe it wasn't possible. I couldn't help searching for ways to deny the facts that had been laid out before me.

Blaze pulled the photo of one of the coded documents toward him, running his finger below each of the numbers that looked like years. "If these are dates, as the numbers suggest, it's possible they'll match up with some factor to do with the missing kids that I've found... Now that I have this, I might be able to break the rest of the code. I'll see what I can do."

He switched back and forth between the photos and his laptop, so immersed that he didn't even glance at the rest of us. A weird tremor formed in my stomach, both anticipating the answers I'd worked so hard to get and dreading them at the same time.

"Was there anything else strange about the basement room outside of these pictures?" Julius asked.

"I took pictures of everything that seemed at all significant." I lifted the photo that showed the image of the country home. "Any idea what this could be about when there's no record of them owning another home? Why would they keep a picture hanging on the wall of some random house?"

"It could be one that used to belong to them and passed out of the family," Talon suggested.

I hummed to myself. "I guess it could be that. Something they lost somehow and want to remember. No one's ever mentioned an old house that they miss to me, but obviously there's a lot they haven't revealed so far."

"They're definitely keeping a lot of secrets," Garrison muttered.

But what did it all mean? We didn't know what the dates meant, just like we didn't know anything about the house or the odd items on the bookshelves. There wasn't nearly enough proof to draw any kind of conclusion. The only hope we had of finding evidence was Blaze, and he was currently frowning at his laptop with no sign of cracking the code yet.

"Where do we go from here?" I asked when nobody else offered any insight. "We have all of these clues, but we have nothing to connect them to. We don't even have a working theory."

Julius leaned into the countertop and swiped his hand across his face. He didn't know either. Whatever the Maliks were hiding, they kept it hidden too well. What if Blaze couldn't figure out what the parchments meant? We still wouldn't have gotten anywhere.

Garrison straightened up and took on a brisk tone. "It's no good standing around here brooding while the tech head does his work. Staring at the pictures isn't going to make them speak to us." He tapped my arm. "Why don't you and I go scope out the place where Malik's wife works? You said she takes Fridays off, right? So she won't be there to notice. I can chat up her colleagues and see what they'll let slip about her, and you can pickpocket a few phones we can scan for texts and emails exchanged with her."

My legs itched to move, to have something more to do, but I hesitated, biting my lip. "I don't know. Iris hardly talks about her job. It doesn't seem like she's that invested." All I knew about it was that she worked in insurance.

Garrison shrugged. "What's more likely to turn up something—standing here doing nothing or trying out a little more scouting?"

I had to admit he had a point. And now that he'd proposed the idea, the thought of sitting around in the house made me want to explode.

I glanced at Julius, and he gave me a nod. "You'll want to be careful about it, but you already know that. As does

Garrison." He shot the younger man a pointed look. "Be quick. We don't want anyone realizing why you were nosing around."

I bounced on my feet, restless energy coursing through me. "All right. Let's see what we can find."

"We won't do anything that you wouldn't do," Garrison said to Julius with a wink, and headed with me to the doorway. Once it'd firmly closed behind us, he smiled wickedly down at me. "Now, Julius has done a lot of reckless things, so if you want to jump into something crazy before we go to the office, the option is still on the table."

I let out a genuine laugh for the first time in what felt like forever and bumped shoulders with him. "I think we should wait until after if we want to do anything too wild."

Garrison looked down at me as we started our walk, and when I met his eyes, I found unrestrained joy there. It was almost as if coming out here with me had cleared his mind, and now he gazed at me as if I were the most valuable thing he'd ever seen.

"Are we thinking skydiving, bungee jumping, maybe stealing a police car for a joyride?" he asked.

I threw a mock punch into his arm. "I don't think that Julius has ever stolen a cop car."

Garrison shrugged. "I wouldn't put it past him under the right circumstances."

"I don't think we have the right circumstances going for us right now," I teased, and glanced toward the driveway. "Do you want to take the rental car? Or we could get an Uber if we don't want the license plate caught on street cams in the area. It'd be a long walk." I imagined it'd take at least an hour, although in my current state of frustration, I wasn't sure I'd mind that much exercise.

Apparently, Garrison felt the same way. "I'm okay with walking a few miles if you are," he said. "I've barely gotten much chance to stretch my legs in the past few days."

"Other than arranging phantom farmyards and fighting for your life."

He shrugged and smirked at me. "Yeah, other than those minor adventures."

We turned the corner to walk past a couple of old industrial buildings, and the screech of tires made my head jerk around.

A van roared into view and skidded to a stop right next to the sidewalk. In the space of a heartbeat, three men in ski masks had leapt out, clamped their hands around Garrison, and hauled him into the back.

I leapt after him, my hand snagging on one guy's shirt. The guy kicked back at me at the same time, and in my startled panic I didn't dodge quite well enough. The heel to my gut sent me staggering to the side.

As I threw myself forward again, the van was already peeling away from the curb and racing away, the back doors clanging shut with Garrison behind them.

My body reacted on pure instinct. Some part of me believed that if I just pushed my legs fast enough, I'd be able to catch the van, even as the engine roared.

I sprinted after it faster than I'd ever run in my life, my feet pounding on the asphalt. A yell of rage lodged in my throat, but I couldn't spare enough breath to let it out. My gaze darted over the few cars parked along the road, but if I stopped for long enough to break into one of them and hotwire it, I'd lose sight of the van and have no way of chasing after it. The license plate was covered, so I couldn't even use that to believe I'd be able to track it down later.

So I kept running, propelling my body forward with all the strength I had in me. My hands darted to my hips. I hadn't brought my gun for this excursion, but I did have my usual concealed knives. I'd started carrying two in light of recent events.

I drew out one and then the other and hurled them at the tires of the van, praying that I could hit one well enough to deflate a tire and force the vehicle to slow. But the driver must have noticed in the rearview mirror that I was up to something. The van swerved left and right on the wide road, and my knives clattered uselessly against the pavement.

Swallowing a curse, I raced onward, searching the ground for anything else I could use to try to stall the van in its tracks. As I passed the places where my knives had fallen, I scooped them up without breaking my stride. Then I veered toward the curb and grabbed a chunk of concrete that'd tumbled there.

In one last-ditch effort, I heaved the chunk at the van's window. The vehicle swerved again at the last second, and the concrete only dinged the bumper. The van roared around the corner.

I dashed after it, sweat trickling down my back from the exertion. My legs were starting to feel numb from how hard I was pushing my muscles. I sped around the buildings onto the cross-street—

And found the van was gone. The engine sounded somewhere beyond my view, but it was dwindling too fast for me to catch up.

"Fuck!" I shouted at the sky, coasting to a stop.

I couldn't do this on my own. I needed the rest of the crew—Blaze would be able to check traffic cams—Julius had contacts in the city. We'd figure this out.

Wouldn't we?

As I hurried back to the house, my stomach knotted. What had the men in the van wanted with Garrison? Who had they even been? I had no idea if they were related to the attackers we'd faced in the city before, or our various earlier opponents in the crew's hometown, or maybe they were some totally new force we hadn't known about.

The look he'd given me a minute before the car pulled up—full of happiness and pride—reverberated through my mind. I swiped my hand across my face, but the gesture couldn't shake my anguish.

They might be torturing him, even killing him, right now. While I loped along here unable to do anything about it. If I'd grabbed at him just a little sooner, reacted just a little faster—

I pushed my legs harder again. Any extra second could help Blaze find the van before it disappeared forever. I didn't allow myself to consider the breathlessness or the exhaustion that wreaked havoc on my limbs. I just sprinted until the house came into sight.

I burst through the doorway, my breath so ragged it

took me a few moments to gather myself enough to form words. "Garrison," I gasped. "Some men grabbed him. Black van. Took a left on Meridian Street."

"Hey, hey," Julius said, striding over with his arms reaching for me.

I shook my head and pushed him away. "They took him! Don't worry about me. We have to find him."

Blaze stared at me with wide eyes. Why wasn't he already pounding away at his laptop's keyboard?

"We know," Talon said, his tone chilly with anger. "We just got a text message from his phone."

"What?" I sputtered. "What did it say?"

The men exchanged a look. They were calm—too calm. I'd seen that measured stillness on their faces before missions. This was the calm before the storm. I braced myself for what they were about to tell me.

Julius cleared his throat. "It said that unless we track him down in the next twenty-four hours, there's no chance we'll find him alive."

TWENTY-FOUR

Decima

"THAT'S IT?" I demanded as Julius's last words rang in my ears. "What do they want? Did they even say for sure that he *will* be alive for twenty-four hours?"

Blaze got up from his chair. "No. They didn't say anything else. But it's obvious they want us to try to find him."

"And if we don't soon enough, they'll definitely kill him," Talon said flatly.

Nausea curdled in my stomach. "It's a trap," I said. "Obviously, right? They wouldn't be sending us on a manhunt just for fun. They want to get us someplace vulnerable and take out the rest of us."

Julius tipped his head in acknowledgment. "It looks that way. Whoever's responsible, they must have realized we're too strong all together for them to tackle us that way.

So they've picked off one of us and are hoping it'll set the rest of us off-balance."

I rubbed my face, the images of what Garrison might be facing at the hands of his attackers rising up again. "We can't just abandon him. We have to find a way around their stupid trap and get him back."

"Of course," Julius said, so firmly a tiny bit of my distress subsided. "We're a family. We don't leave each other behind, no matter the consequences. But we have to do this carefully, or we're all dead meat. They've given us a timeline. We'll figure out as much as we can so we can go into this trap prepared to destroy it."

"The first part is who's behind the operation in the first place," Talon said, and paused.

My stomach sank. I already knew where that line of thinking was leading.

"The Maliks," I said. "That's where the evidence we found before pointed, even if it wasn't much. And now this happens right after I broke into their secret room? Maybe it's a coincidence, or maybe they realized someone had gotten in there, and they're striking back."

Blaze made a face. "Unfortunately, I have to agree. If I could just get this code worked out... I'll see if I can track the van's route too." He gave a small growl under his breath and went back to his computer.

Julius folded his arms over his chest. "All right. Assuming Damien Malik is responsible, where can we think of that he might have taken Garrison to?"

"He could just keep him in the van," Talon said.

"Possible, but risky. If they keep driving around, they'll

need gas soon, potentially exposing them to bystanders. And they must suspect Blaze will be able to search for matching vehicles. I think they'd want to stash him away somewhere more secure." Julius glanced at me. "How about that secret room? That seems like a reasonable place to hide away someone you don't want found."

I thought back to the study-like space I'd crept into and balked at the suggestion. "It wasn't like a dungeon. It was too cozy—like it's used for family meetings and sitting around reading rather than their dirty business. I can't imagine them bringing him there. Besides, it'd be awfully risky having him right there in the known family home. They've got to have other properties somewhere."

Blaze shook his head without looking up from the computer. "I didn't find anything under any of the Maliks' names except the houses they're currently living in. I guess they might have brought him to your grandparents' house or one of the aunts and uncles'?"

I frowned. "That still has the problem of being too easily tied to the family—and I don't know if the other houses have secret rooms too." That seemed like a bit much, although I couldn't dismiss the possibility entirely. But there was another option. "What about the house in the basement photograph? Have you run an image recognition search for it?"

Blaze sighed. "Yes, but nothing's popped up based on that picture. It obviously isn't in a high trafficked or photographed location. But that secluded location could be anywhere in the world for all we know right now."

"Damn it," Julius muttered, pacing the room in a rage

that I'd never have thought I'd see from the controlled commander. Witnessing his unrestrained frustration made the situation feel more real. More terrifying.

Garrison was counting on us, but we had no solutions. No way to find him. No leads. I could tell from Blaze's increasingly despondent expression that following the van wasn't getting him very far either.

But I had to do *something*.

Just as I thought that, my phone vibrated in my pocket. The guys went still and silent as I pulled it out, other than the clacking of Blaze's fingers on the keyboard. I studied the text message that had appeared on the screen, gritting my teeth as I processed it.

"It's from the Hunter," I said, glaring at the phone.

"What does he want?" Talon loomed next to me, and I knew that if he faced any opponent right now, he'd come out victorious. He'd kill anyone with his bare hands if it meant finding Garrison alive, and I couldn't say I didn't share the sentiment.

"He wants to meet," I said. "He's mentioned a place nearby that he wants me to go to."

"Give me the spot, and I'll give him a piece of my mind about how he's put you through the wringer," Julius grumbled, striding toward the door. I leapt forward and caught his arm, holding him back.

"He said he only wants to speak to me. That he'll leave if anyone's with me." My chest constricted.

"Like hell," Blaze said. "We can't send you out there alone to meet a guy who's essentially a stranger, especially not this Hunter who has been leading you in circles for weeks. We lost Garrison today, and we're not losing you, too."

"I'm going with you," Talon insisted, walking to join Julius and me by the door.

I pushed both men back a step. "None of you are thinking straight. Get off your high horses and consider what this means. Of all the times the Hunter could have sought me out, he chose the moment when I needed answers the most—the day that Garrison was taken. If I don't follow his demands, do you think he'll tell me anything? I can't risk losing whatever information he's willing to share. It could make the difference between whether we find Garrison or not."

Julius's muscles flexed, but his mouth pressed into a flat line rather than arguing. He understood the stakes just as well as I did. "What if he's the one who took Garrison?" he said finally.

"Then he'll definitely know where to find him, won't he?" I shot back, and let out a huff of frustration. "But most likely, he noticed something about the Maliks with his surveillance that tipped him off to what they've done. Look, so far every time we've been attacked here in DC, I've been ignored and even shoved out of the fray while they focus on you guys. I'm the one who's the *most* safe out there. If I see anything remotely suspicious, I'll leave. I won't take any risks I don't have to."

Talon's jaw worked. He marched away and returned seconds later with a pistol in his hand. "You're not going out there unarmed," he said, and I knew he'd accepted my plan.

I accepted the gun with a nod of thanks and tucked it into the back of my sweatpants. "I wouldn't dream of it."

Julius exhaled roughly. "For the record, I don't like this at all. But you're right. Just—don't get too close to him and keep an eye out for anyone else suspicious nearby. And if you're not back in ten minutes—or if we hear shots fired—we're coming after you."

I let out a humorless chuckle. "If he doesn't manage to say anything useful in ten minutes, then I'll already be leaving. Maybe after shooting him for wasting my time all over again."

Confident that my self-appointed bodyguards wouldn't stand in my way any longer, I tucked my knives back into their usual places and quickly donned a second gun in an under-shoulder holster that I hid beneath a lightweight hoodie. Plenty of options was always a good thing. And my bare hands were weapons all on their own. I couldn't get much better armed than this.

Looking at the men around me, I gathered my resolve. The message said to come alone, but I wasn't completely alone. They were with me in every way they could be.

The Hunter had probably known where I was staying from the moment I'd given the address to the Uber driver he'd conscripted. He'd asked me to come a few blocks down the street from the house to a parking lot beyond an old office building that was now boarded up.

As I approached, I heard the rumble of a motorcycle's engine before I saw anything. Coming around the building, I found a tall, broad-shouldered man sitting on a thrumming chopper. A helmet covered his head, the visor reflecting the mid-morning sunlight back at me rather than revealing his face. I could only make out the vaguest shapes of his eyes and nose when a tuft of cloud briefly passed over the sun.

I walked closer, keeping my hands in easy reach of my weapons. There was no sign of any other figure around. It was just me and him.

When I was about ten feet away, he held up his hand. "That's close enough," he said, and his voice confirmed my suspicions. Even slightly muffled by the helmet and the drone of the engine, I knew it immediately.

This was the Hunter himself.

I stopped, setting my hands on my hips. "You called me out here, and now you're acting like I'm a threat?"

A hint of amusement came into his tone as he pitched his words over the engine's rumbling. "I have to be careful, you understand. I don't know where your loyalties lie. You are a Malik, after all."

I grimaced at him. "Just because I was born a Malik doesn't mean I am one."

If I'd expected him to lead with information about Garrison, he was just as disappointing as usual. "Have you done any more investigating to substantiate what I told you about them?" he asked.

Was that all this was again? Another excuse to badger me, at the worst possible time?

My teeth set on edge. "Are you here in person because that way I can't just hang up on your shit?" I demanded. "I'm done with this game."

As I spun on my heel, his voice stopped me in my

tracks. "Then you haven't found any concerning photographs?"

I froze, unable to decide whether I wanted to entertain this conversation after all. Whether I wanted to give away what I *had* found to this man.

But he must have already been able to guess. "You did, didn't you? You're sharp enough to have gotten that far. Then you saw a little blond girl along with the others."

The memory of the photo smacked me with enough horror to make me glance back at him. "What about her?" I said, the question coming out raspy.

Even though I could barely make out his face, I felt his stare boring into me through the helmet's visor.

"That was my daughter," he said. He kept his voice even, but rage reverberated through it all the same. "The Maliks stole her from me and killed her as brutally as you saw. I've never been able to prove it definitively, but I know it was them. That's why I've been investigating them, and it's why I was worried about you coming into the fold."

My stomach roiled with the urge to puke. He was confirming my worst nightmares about my family—but I still didn't know for sure if I could trust him. It still didn't make any sense. But then, how could he have known about the photographs if his story wasn't true?

How could I focus on that right now when Garrison's life hung in the balance this very second?

My back straightened as I realized that there was one answer that would help me solve both problems. "Do you know where the killings might have been carried out?

Where they took the kids?" It'd have to be someplace they felt was secure. Someplace that'd work just as well to hide a kidnapped hitman.

The Hunter paused. "I think the family must have a property nearby—one under the radar and isolated. I've been searching, but I haven't found it yet."

Before he could say anything else, his phone chimed loudly in his pocket. He glanced at it and revved the engine on his motorcycle. "I've got to go," he said, and tore out of the parking lot without giving me a chance to respond.

"Wait!" I hollered after him. "I have more questions." But he was already roaring down the street. I couldn't tell if he'd even heard me.

He'd told me nothing at all about Garrison. He didn't have any more idea about where the Maliks might be hiding him than I did.

Actually, that wasn't totally true. I pushed down my hopelessness as everything he'd said sank in. We hadn't found any other properties the family owned, but the Hunter was sure they had another one—one in the area. All I had to do was figure out where.

But the only people who'd know were my birth family, and they hadn't mentioned anything about it so far. If it *was* where they murdered children and stashed kidnapping victims, it wasn't likely that they'd tell me in a casual conversation.

They were my family, though. They'd been talking about bringing me into the legacy, about me being one of them. Was there some way I could use that?

As I hurried back to the house in the hill, my mind whirled, and my thoughts centered on Garrison in a different way. He was the one in the group who got information out of people rather than computers. I didn't have him to guide me, so I had to figure this out myself. How would he have convinced someone to cough up an address? I'd watched him in action before.

He'd get people talking. He'd catch them off-guard and set them up to reveal more than they meant to before they even realized how much they were spilling. He might act like he knew all about what he was fishing for already to put them at ease with confirming or correcting his suggestions.

What if I could do the same? If I wanted to save Garrison, I'd have to become him for one phone call.

I took out my phone and scanned through the limited numbers. Who would be the most likely to fall for this kind of gambit? Someone who didn't already have decades of experience pretending *not* to be a mass murderer, presumably. But someone who was familiar with the family's "rituals."

After a moment's debate, I tapped my brother's number and raised the phone to my ear.

Carter answered after just a couple of rings, nothing in his tone giving any indication that he knew I had a reason to be upset. "Hey, Rachel. I wasn't expecting to hear from you." He sounded mildly surprised but not concerned or shifty. Maybe he wasn't in on this particular part of our parents' plans. Or maybe he was a very good actor.

I'd just have to be better.

"Hey," I said in a brisk but warm tone. "Dad wanted me to meet him out at the country house so he could show me around. I'm excited to find out more about everything the family's involved in, but I seem to have misplaced the address. Can you remind me where I'm going?"

Calling Malik "dad" sent shivers down my spine, but I held up the ruse through my whole spiel.

Carter answered automatically, just as I hoped. "It's just off Eckleberry Lane, if you've made it that—" He caught himself, and his tone turned abruptly wary. "Dad wanted you to *meet* him there? What did he say he wanted to show you?"

"Don't worry about that," I said. "You've told me enough."

I hung up the phone and dashed back to the crew with the street name on my lips.

TWENTY-FIVE

Talon

THE RENTAL CAR sped down the country road, frequent potholes jarring Dess and me in the backseat. It was obvious not many people drove down this way, which made sense if the Maliks had set up some kind of torture home out here.

As soon as Dess had come rushing back to report on her conversations with the Hunter and her brother, Blaze had identified the only Eckleberry Lane remotely in the vicinity. From there, it'd taken a matter of minutes for him to skim through satellite footage and identify a house just off it with a footprint and roof that appeared to match the Maliks' photograph.

With the threat to Garrison in mind and the knowledge that Dess's brother could alert the rest of the family to her likely arrival, we'd jumped into the car without much preamble—though of course we'd paused long enough to grab some necessary equipment. Dess and I were quickly and efficiently loading up the assortment of guns we might need to bring to bear. I had my usual knife strapped to my hip, and I knew Dess had at least a couple of blades concealed on her body.

If our brother-at-arms was hidden away on that property, there was no way in hell we weren't bringing him back, no matter how many bodies we had to drop along the way.

Julius jerked on the wheel and swerved around a turn, and Dess swayed with the movement. My hand instinctively rose to her back, but she continued loading one of the semi-automatics, hardly even seeming to notice the movements of the car or her own body. She was so far in her own head that I wondered if any of us could really get through to her.

Garrison was usually the one who could break her hard exterior, even if sometimes he did it by heckling her until he got a rise. I had no idea what to say. Out of all of us, I was the worst choice as an emotional support guide. I barely knew how to feel my own emotions, as few of them as I noticed having at all.

"I'm going to kill all of them," she murmured as she set the last gun atop the pile between our seats. She paused for a second, her hands flexing, and reached for one of the earlier ones to give it a brisk cleaning.

"We'll kill them together," I replied firmly. It shouldn't need to be said that I'd have her back—that all three of us would. These people were worth nothing to me after what they'd done to our crew and to her. Seeing them dead would bring me a shitload of satisfaction.

That emotion I'd definitely feel when it came.

Blaze let out a triumphant sound in the front passenger seat where he'd still been hammering away on his laptop. Both of our heads jerked in his direction.

"I've got it. Fucking finally!" he crowed, and swiveled for a second to catch our eyes. "It was the parents, not the kids. That's what threw me for so long."

"The parents what?" Julius said gruffly. "Why don't you back up a bit for those of us who weren't code-breaking alongside you."

Blaze blinked at him as if it hadn't occurred to him that we couldn't read what was going on in that restless brain of his and then launched into an energetic explanation. "The code in the documents the Maliks have in Damien's office and their secret basement room. I suspected they had something to do with the murdered kids, and I was right. But I was expecting the symbols to match up with the kids' names, and that was a dead end. I finally realized there's a parent named for each date instead."

Dess leaned forward in her seat, the weapons momentarily forgotten. "What do you mean?"

Blaze held out his laptop so we could see it from the backseat. He zoomed in on part of one of the parchments and ran his finger along a line of data that still looked like scribbles to me. "The part on the right is a full date. This one is May 27th, 2019. The name next to it is Harvey

Little. He's the father of one of the kids in those pictures that I found a police report on."

I frowned. "Why would they have listed one of the *parents* when it's the kids who were murdered?"

"I'm not sure," Blaze said. "I have the computer automatically translating the rest of the entries now. I'll look up the other names and see what I can make of them."

We waited in tense silence while he tapped away, the rumble of the car's engine filling the cramped space. Dess didn't tear her eyes away from the back of Blaze's head. He sucked a breath slowly through his teeth, tapped some more, and then let out a thoughtful noise.

"What?" Julius prodded.

"I'm finding a bit of a common theme," Blaze said. "Some of these people appear to be ordinary citizens, but at least half of them so far have had criminal records. Significant ones. Armed robbery, extortion, multiple counts of assault, that kind of thing."

"Oh," Dess said, that single syllable so pained that my gaze shot straight to her. She'd turned to stare out the window now, her face pinched with tension, her jaw tight.

I wished I could peek past her guarded expression into her head, but she made it so difficult to see anything that she didn't want to show us. It'd been obvious before that she was unsettled by all the information we'd been uncovering related to the Maliks, though. The fact that she was withdrawing even more meant she was under increasing strain.

The only way she knew to survive was by hiding herself.

Finally, she glanced at the rest of us again. "That's the missing piece. The motive. They're killing the children of criminals. I'd be willing to bet that even the ones you didn't turn up a record for, the Maliks found out they were involved in some illegal stuff. I guess, in their eyes, murdering their kids must be some kind of punishment or revenge, or balancing the scales—an eye for an eye..." She shuddered. "Or maybe they think the kids will turn out the same as their parents and that it's better to cut it off at the root. I could believe it from the way they've talked."

Blaze let out a low whistle. "That's fucking psychotic."

"It's *sick*," Dess spat out. She rubbed her eyes with the heels of her hands. "*They're* sick."

And they were her family by blood. The more we learned about them, the more this had to hurt her. The cuts from this revelation, I realized, would go deep and never completely fade. She'd witnessed and dealt out a lot of violence in her time, but clearly nothing on this level.

Maybe the household had done her a disservice in more ways than one by sending her after businessmen and politicians rather than criminals. She wasn't totally prepared for how depraved the worst of society could get.

I wouldn't deny that the Malik family was a rare breed, but it was one that I recognized. I'd met plenty of psychopaths who justified beating up on the most fragile members of society. Hell, I'd been raised by two of them.

Had my life gone a little differently, I could have become one of them.

Julius continued the drive without a comment, but I knew he was silently processing the information, marking it to his memory as he drove. Blaze was occupied with tracking down the other entries on the coded lists. I was the only one who could see how off-balance Dess looked. It didn't fit the woman I knew at all.

How could I get her back on track?

"It's awful, but we'll put an end to it," I told her in the most reassuring tone I could offer. "We'll end *them*, and not one more kid will die at their hands."

Dess completely buried her face in her hands and gave a shaky sigh. "It's not just that. If it was just that, I wouldn't feel like this."

I hesitated and then forced myself to ask, "How are you feeling?"

Her shoulders drooped, but the muscles in her arms flexed at the same time. "It's just—" She took a deep breath. "I hate them with everything in me. I hate that the Malik family has apparently been killing innocent children for a century, and I hate that they've gotten away with it. I hate that they're sick and demented, and I want to kill them for taking Garrison from us."

She stopped again, almost as if she was done speaking. I could tell she wasn't really finished, though.

"But?" I prompted.

She cleared her throat and lowered her voice. I didn't know if it was because she didn't want to be heard or if it was because she felt guilty saying whatever was about to leave her lips. I leaned forward, intent on hearing every word of it.

"I just found them," she whispered. "I thought I'd get a chance at having an actual family, the way I was supposed to if the household hadn't kidnapped me, and it almost happened. They welcomed me, they were so happy to have me back... and the whole time they were *monsters*. It'd give anyone whiplash, wouldn't it?"

"Of course it would," Julius said in an even voice.

I studied Dess's face, sensing that she hadn't quite finished spilling her guts. She looked too agonized still.

She dropped her hands into her lap and looked down at them. "They're not *that* different from me. I go out and kill criminals, and say it's fine because those people were hurting innocents. They're killing in order to hurt criminals."

"It isn't the same," I said with a rare surge of anger. "We attack the people who are the actual problem. Those kids couldn't have done anything wrong. They torture and murder the innocents *we* would be protecting. It's the opposite."

"I know. It's just... a lot to take in. And I have to deal with them as soon as possible, I have to look at them after everything..." She growled to herself.

If it'd been anyone else responsible for those deaths, I was sure she'd have been ready to mow them down without any hesitation. But she'd been drawn in by the dream of having a loving family, and it had to be hard not to want to try to put the pieces back together even after that dream was shattered. She'd finally found her relatives after more than twenty years, and now she had to kill them to stop something even more horrible from continuing.

For her not to feel conflicted about that, she'd have to be made of steel and stone. Like me.

I'd been out of my depth for this entire conversation, but suddenly it occurred to me that I might be the best person to tackle her current dilemma. It meant dredging up memories I preferred not to dwell on, let alone talk about, but for her, I could ignore the minor discomfort.

It was just the past. Julius already knew the basics. I didn't mind if Blaze did too. They were my family now—the truest family I could ever want.

"I'm going to tell you a story," I said.

Dess peered at me, knitting her brow, and waited.

I leaned back in my seat, holding her gaze. "My parents died when I was a toddler—not much older than you were when the household took you. I was sent to live with my maternal grandfather and his new wife. They were... not happy about being saddled with me. Or maybe they weren't happy about much of anything."

"They didn't treat you well," Dess filled in, and stiffened. "Your scars."

A humorless chuckle fell from my lips. "Yes. I don't think a day went by without them yelling at me and beating on me in some way—smacks and kicks from my grandfather, pinches and cigarette burns from his wife. Occasionally they went off in a wild enough rage that I ended up bleeding or with a broken bone. I'm probably lucky they didn't kill me."

Dess winced. "I'm so sorry."

I shrugged. "It was a long time ago. But it's shaped a lot of who I am today. They were most often set off by any sign of emotion—if I laughed at a funny TV show. If I cried over a bee sting. Shit like that would definitely mean a beat-down. So I learned not to show what I was feeling." And after a while I'd stopped feeling much of anything in the first place.

But that wasn't what I was telling Dess this story for. I pushed onward. "No matter what I did, they used me as a punching bag. The most I could control was just how bad it got. It took me a long time to realize that kind of treatment wasn't normal. I couldn't remember being 'parented' any other way. But even before I realized just how awful they were, I knew I hated it. As I got older, I threw myself into training—muscle-building, fighting techniques, weapons—anything I could find through videos on the internet or other means that gave me back a sense of power."

"That makes sense," Dess said quietly. The compassion shining in her eyes woke up a strange ache inside me that I didn't know what to make of.

"But it wasn't just to get a sense of control," I said. "I wanted to know I was *stronger* than them, so that—when I was old enough that I didn't need their support anymore, I paid them back for all the pain they'd inflicted on me for all those years, all at once. They got what they deserved, and that was the end of it."

I didn't have to spell out what I'd done any clearer than that. I could tell Dess caught my meaning.

I braced myself for shock or horror. I'd chosen to

remove the bastards from my life—carefully enough that I'd never been pinned with the crime—and nothing would convince me that I hadn't made the right decision. But that wouldn't make it easy to see her recoil from me.

All she did was shake her head and reach out to squeeze my forearm. "I don't blame you."

Those four words cracked open a wall I hadn't even known I had inside me. My breath came out in a rush. For a second, I was so overwhelmed by the unfamiliar sensations sweeping through me that I couldn't even speak.

I groped for a steadier sense of calm so that I could finish what I'd meant to say to her. I hadn't been looking for her sympathy. I wanted her to understand that I wouldn't blame *her* either. No one in their right mind would.

"The point is," I said, "family means nothing. You don't choose who gives birth to you or who raises you, and sometimes they're awful people. Sometimes they need to be taken down, just like any other random person might. You didn't ask to have these pricks as your family, and you'll be doing the whole world a service by taking them out of it. So feel whatever you feel, but don't for one second think there's anything wrong with you for doing what has to be done."

Dess squared her shoulders. Her mouth still slanted at an uneasy angle, but her eyes held a resolve that hadn't been there before. "Thank you. It helps knowing you've been there before in your own way."

My lips formed a smile that didn't often come

naturally to them, warmth spreading through my chest despite the lingering awkwardness of my confession. I didn't know what it meant, but I didn't care. All that mattered was that I'd given everything I could to make sure this incredible woman made it through the next few hours unscathed.

TWENTY-SIX

Decima

MY SPINE STIFFENED when Blaze gestured to a dirt lane up ahead. "That's the turn-off," he said. "Another half a mile and we'll reach the house."

Julius took the turn with ease, and a white-walled building immediately came into view in the distance, expanding gradually as we zoomed toward it. I couldn't see it perfectly yet, but I could already tell it was the house from the basement photograph.

And that wasn't the only thing we could see. At least six cars were parked outside the building. I recognized Damien's, Aunt Mabel and Uncle Henry's, and my grandparents'. The other three might have belonged to other relatives I'd spent less time with.

"Looks like we have plenty of company," Julius said, taking them in.

Talon handed one of the pistols we'd cleaned and

loaded to Blaze and brandished another himself. "Nothing we can't handle."

Were all of those family members in on Garrison's kidnapping? My stomach knotted as we reached the end of the lane.

How had they justified *that* crime to themselves? Saving me from bad influences? Did they know what the crew did but somehow didn't realize that I was in the same line of work? Or did they just figure they could bring me over to the "right" side once they'd gotten rid of my men?

My jaw clenched. It didn't matter what they wanted. They were sick, child-murdering psychopaths, and every kindness they'd ever offered me was tainted by that fact. I knew I wouldn't feel at peace until every one of the Maliks who'd had a hand in the murders was six feet under themselves.

Talon was right about one thing: some people needed to be taken out of this world before they could do more damage. Who better than me to deliver that sentence?

Julius parked at the side of the lane a short distance from the official parking area where the other cars stood. So far there'd been no signs of movement. No one stirred in or around the vehicles. The house's windows were dark. A small barn stood beyond it across about twenty feet of scruffy grass, its tall double doors shut and latched.

"Everyone ready?" Julius asked.

I slung a holster over my arm, tucked another gun into one at my hip, and wrapped my fingers around a third. We couldn't go into this too prepared, as much as a small part of me, the part that'd craved a real family, still balked at the idea of firing the weapons at the people I'd thought of as that family. "I am."

We got out onto the dusty earth, the guys similarly armed. The wind swept over us, carrying a dry scent that itched in my nose, like stale hay.

We'd only just walked past the cars, starting to cross the stretch of patchy grass between the parking area and the covered porch, when the front door swung open. The four of us halted, guns at the ready.

Nearly every person I'd met at that first reunion spilled onto the porch before my eyes. Aunts, uncles, and cousins, my grandfather, and of course, my father. The only people missing were Carter, Grandma Ruby, and my mother. Had my brother spilled the beans about my call, or had the rest of the family been waiting here already in case we figured out where they'd taken Garrison by some other means?

I stepped a little ahead of my men, my finger curled around the trigger of my gun. If any of the men and women before me were armed, I could blow them away before they so much as set their hand on their weapon.

"Where is he?" I demanded.

My father pushed to the front of the crowd, resting his hands on the porch railing. I couldn't read his expression, it was so stern and yet haunted at the same time. His gaze slid from me to the men around me, and his forehead furrowed. Had he expected me to come alone? As if the crew wouldn't stand by their lost member.

"Who the hell are these people?" he demanded.

As if he didn't already know. "The closest thing to a

family I actually have," I said. "Now answer the question. Where is he?"

Damien's attention jerked back to me. "Your brother? I told him and your mother to stay home after he told me you'd found out about this place. I don't know what led you to it, but I promise you, I can explain."

Fury seared through me so fast it burned away everything but my horror at everything else I'd discovered. "Explain what?" I spat. "Why you torture and murder little kids for your own enjoyment?"

If I'd still had any doubts about whether the Maliks were responsible, Damien's flinch was enough to dismiss them. The rest of the family stirred around him with restless murmurs. Aunt Mabel made an uncomfortable grimace. Margaret's eyes flashed as if she was eager to have this secret out in the open. Grandpa Bo shook his head as if he was disappointed in *me*.

"That's a vast simplification of a complex and honored process," the older man said.

"An *honored* process?" I said. "Are you kidding me? I've seen pictures. What you did to them is nothing but sick."

Damien raised his chin. "It's the opposite of sick. The Maliks have a divine mandate going back over a century to *stop* the spread of the criminal sickness through this country. We offer up the pain and lives of the tainted children to a higher power to prevent more pain and lives lost at the hands of those who'd turn to unlawfulness and sin."

I stared at him. It took all my willpower to stop my jaw from gaping open. "You seriously think that some sort of god wants you to torment innocent kids as a way of stopping crime? You're fucking insane."

"Insanity is in the eye of the beholder," Margaret muttered, as if that was helpful.

"We don't enjoy the process," Uncle Henry insisted, though from the look on Margaret's face, that wasn't true of everyone. "Only the outcome we're working toward."

My father nodded. "It has to be done for the good of everyone in this country. Sacrifices must be made to set the energies among us on the right course."

Suddenly the supernatural-sounding books in the library made a lot more sense. Where had the generations of Maliks before them first gotten these crazy ideas? What had convinced them to keep acting on them?

It didn't matter. The people in front of me had been carrying out their horrific legacy their whole lives. I could see from the flash of determination in my father's eyes that they had no intention of stopping even with my discovery of it.

But I had to try anyway.

Bile had risen in the back of my throat. I swallowed it down and fixed him with my firmest stare. "You're an educated man. Can't you hear how ridiculous this sounds? How could killing children possibly have any impact on whether other random people commit more crimes?"

"You'll understand," Damien said. "I promise you, once we bring you into the rituals, you'll see how it all connects. It *is* an honor, being chosen to carry out this divine calling—"

I couldn't stand to listen to him anymore. I took

another step forward, and Aunt Mabel flinched. "I'm *never* going to understand, and I'm sure as hell never going to be a part of this psychotic cult of yours. I'm going to ask you again. Where. Is. Garrison?"

My father's brow furrowed, and I expected him to dodge the question again, continuing this stupid game of not knowing what I meant. But at the same moment, a clanging sound reverberated from the direction of the barn. My gaze shot straight to the other building.

From this angle, I couldn't help noticing another, smaller structure tucked next to the barn. A big brick chimney with a wrought-iron belly... A furnace.

The nausea gripping my stomach expanded up through my chest. Ash. Calcium levels in the soil. Signs of bodily remains.

Just like that, I knew that furnace was where they burned the results of their "offerings." That was why no murders had been reported—no bodies had ever been found.

And then the Maliks took a little of the ash and scattered it in their garden back home to fertilize their precious flowers of justice. My gut lurched, and I thought I might actually vomit.

But the sound had come from the barn itself. Was that where they'd locked Garrison away? What state had they left him in?

The urgency of my worry drowned out my queasiness. Turning away from the house, I set off toward the barn with the rest of the crew at my heels.

It seemed the Maliks didn't like that. They all poured down the steps, hustling to get between us and the barn.

"You've gone far enough," Grandpa Bo said in a growl.

My father's gaze flicked over the men with me again. "We can't have strangers poking around in our most private and sacred business. We can't have them *knowing* what we do here."

Margaret snickered. "You gave them a death sentence."

Who did she think she was? I ignored her, glowering at Damien. This confrontation was going to end in death, but I wanted to make sure that Garrison's life was no longer on the line before blood got spilled… if I could.

"You don't want to start this fight," I warned him.

A tremor ran through him, but then his expression set with determination. "There are only two options now that you've come this far, Rachel. Either you accept your role as part of the family—or we can't let you leave here alive."

"I think she's already made her position perfectly clear," Uncle Henry said with a flash of dark metal as his hand leapt up.

Julius saw it too. Before my uncle even took aim, the crew's commander blasted him away, a clean shot through the center of his forehead. And then the scene erupted into total chaos worthy of the crew's name.

The rest of the family charged us, whipping out guns and knives, from little paring blades to blocky cleavers. Most of them threw themselves at the men, aiming to close the distance before the crew could take any easy shots.

My father lunged at me.

Shots boomed and grunts and groans filled the air all around me. I didn't have time to look and see who was responsible for which sounds. Damien snatched at my hair, and I had to dodge faster than I expected to escape his grasp—which sent me colliding with one of my uncles. I whirled around, and a boot slammed into my calves. My legs buckled.

I landed on my hands and knees and immediately rolled to the side. As I sprang back onto my feet, my father barreled into me, knocking me back to the ground.

When he loomed over me, there was a moment when I could have shot him. I still had a pistol clutched in my hand. But my damn heart stuttered, I hesitated for a split-second, and the next instant he was kicking the gun from my fingers.

He shoved me down with a knee on my abdomen and the muzzle of his own gun pressed to my forehead. My pulse lurched for a totally different reason. But it seemed Damien Malik wasn't all that keen to kill the daughter he'd only just discovered was still alive.

"This could have been so different," he said in a ragged voice. "I didn't want it to come to this. If you'd given me time to ease you into it, to show you everything…"

As if there was anything he could have shown me that would have convinced me that killing kids out of a delusional sense of divine justice was a-okay. But I kept my mouth shut, knowing that one twitch of his finger would add me to his list of murders.

One of my knives was just inches from where my hand lay. If I could just get him distracted enough to give me the space to make a move—if I could get him to withdraw his gun just a tad…

"I don't want to do this," he went on. "It was a miracle to have you returned to us."

"You don't have to do anything," I dared to say, shifting my fingers a smidge to the left at the same time.

Damien gave no indication that he'd noticed. He leaned more weight onto my chest with his knee, the pressure turning my breath shallow and sending an ache through my previously-broken ribs. His hand trembled, but he kept the gun pressed right against my skin.

"We wanted you to join us, but we've been doing this for too long to let you destroy our legacy now," he said. "Blood doesn't matter if you can't fulfill our calling."

"I thought blood was everything to this family," I said. "Is it so different with me just because I was gone for so long?"

"It has nothing to do with you being gone," he shouted. "You've desecrated everything we stand for with your dismissive words and the violence you've brought here. If I have to kill my only daughter to keep our legacy alive, I will do it."

He clearly meant it. I relaxed my body as well as I could to give me a wider range of motion, but I let my voice come out taut with hurt. "You kept me in the dark for so long. What was I supposed to think when I stumbled on the evidence? You have to know how it looks. To believe in some kind of higher power guiding all this… You never really gave me a *chance* to understand."

His gun-hand shifted just slightly. "I'm trying to

now," he rasped. "If you'll join us, if you'll open yourself to the energies and the mysteries we celebrate and the mission we're fulfilling, it'll be even better than when you didn't know. All you have to do is show you'll give it a chance."

I latched on to that opening with everything I had in me. "Of course. I didn't see at first how devoted you all are. There must be something more to it." Damien's hand wavered while I spoke and then dipped to the side, away from my head. I kept talking, my words covering the faint rustle of my clothes as I slid out the knife. "I'll do whatever I can to make up for the things I said, to show you—"

Relief spread across his face as my fingers tightened around the hilt, and in that moment, I didn't feel the faintest trace of regret. I slammed the blade upward, raising my voice into a yell. "—to show you there's no fucking way I'll ever buy into that insanity!"

The knife dug into my father's throat before I'd finished my defiant exclamation. I wasn't sure he even heard all of it.

Blood gushed down over me from the artery I'd severed, and Damien sputtered, his body already going slack with the life rushing out of it. As his body sagged, I shoved him off me. He lolled on his back, his eyes hazing as even more blood pooled beneath him. Then he was totally still.

There was silence all around me. More bodies littered the ground—every member of the Malik family who'd joined this confrontation. Julius, Talon, and Blaze stood among them, breathing hard and with a few small scrapes here and there, but nothing concerning.

Of course not. My birth family hadn't known how to fight a crew of highly trained hitmen. Their typical opponents had been literal *children*.

I stared down at my father's corpse, the blood that'd soaked my shirt and hair cooling against my skin with the breeze. Somehow I wanted to feel at least a tiny stirring of guilt, a reminder that I was still human. But all I could think of was those pictures of the children, mutilated far beyond anything I'd done to him.

The only thing that mattered now was finding Garrison. Making sure they hadn't given him the same treatment.

My gaze jerked toward the barn, where that sudden sound had come from. The building the family had tried to cut us off from.

I motioned to the crew, praying all the while that my instincts were leading me right. "Come on. Let's get our man back."

TWENTY-SEVEN

Garrison

FUCKING PATHETIC.

I twisted and jerked at my hands, trying to find any way to maneuver myself out of my bonds in the barn where my captors had left me, but I was getting nowhere. My arms had been extended too far above my head, and the ties were too tight to slip through them. I could lift my legs if I tried hard enough, but the only thing that stood below me was a wobbly barrel. If I knocked it over, I'd be left dangling by my arms, gagged, and unable to yell for help. That'd be even less fun than this.

I paused to take a breather—as well as I could breathe with the sour-tasting rag stuffed in my mouth. The men who'd brought me here had disappeared what felt like ages ago. As far as I knew, I was completely alone in the building.

An ache was spreading through my wrists and down

my arms. It brought an awful sense of resignation over me. I had to wait for the crew to find me. I'd always been the most reluctant fighter of the bunch, and now I was the weakest link in another way.

If I'd been better able to fend off the pricks who'd grabbed me—make some kind of break for it—

But no matter how I'd thrashed and struggled, I hadn't been able to stop them from trussing me up like a fucking pig. And now I was being used as bait in what was obviously a trap. I didn't even know what Dess and the guys would be walking into when they came after me.

Part of me almost hoped they wouldn't. Better that I faced the consequences for my incompetence alone than that they all suffered for it too. I was the newest member of the crew—unless you counted Dess—along with being the weakest link. They didn't have to be as loyal to me as they were to each other.

I had the feeling they'd come anyway, though. Dess would insist on trying to rescue me. Julius would see it as a point of honor. Talon went wherever Julius led, and Blaze probably jizzed himself at the thought of solving whatever puzzle our enemies had laid out.

I tested my arms again, but I already knew that situation was hopeless. I was stuck in this position until someone cut me down. The best I could do was take stock of as much of my surroundings as I could in case something about them would prove useful later.

Only a few streaks of muted sunlight drifted through a high window somewhere behind me. I studied the walls of the barn in the dimness. Symbols I didn't recognize but that looked arcane enough to unnerve me marked the wood all around the space.

Was this some kind of cult thing? I thought of the symbol tattooed on the back of Dess's neck that connected her to the organization that had kidnapped her, but none of the carvings looked anything like that teardrop with its diagonal line.

The Maliks had their weird code that Blaze had been trying to decipher. Maybe these connected to their bizarre "legacy" somehow?

I had no idea which of our enemies might have kidnapped me. The men had all worn ski masks to conceal their faces. None of them had said so much as a word to me.

The smell of the musty hay that scattered the floor around me filled my nose. No sounds reached me except the creaking of the rafters. Then several car engines rumbled outside.

I stiffened. The engines cut out somewhere nearby, and it sounded like around a dozen people tramped across the ground in the near distance. But they didn't come my way, and their urgently muttering voices were too quiet or too far away for me to make out any words. Hinges squeaked, and a door thumped shut. Then it was quiet again.

I couldn't tell how long it was before another engine growled up. The car doors slammed, and more feet rasped across the ground. The door hinges squeaked again. A voice pealed out loud enough to reach my ears, instantly recognizable.

"Where is he?"

Dess. And if she was here, the rest of the crew was too.

I closed my eyes against the wave of relief that rushed through me. I shouldn't be *happy*. It was a fucking trap, and they'd walked right into it for me. The thought of Dess getting injured, even killed, because she'd been determined to find me constricted my innards from my throat all the way down to my gut.

Specifically Dess. I didn't want anything to happen to the guys either, but with her—with her it was a sharper pain than I could remember feeling in ages. Maybe not even since the aftermath of my family's car accident, fifteen years ago.

It had been my fault that they'd died, and if I lost Dess because she came for me...

I couldn't think like that. Dess could kick just about anyone's ass, and it wasn't as if the guys were any slouches either. But the fear kept wrenching through my body, and a startling realization dawned on me.

I cared about that woman more than I'd cared about anyone or anything since I'd lost my parents and my brother as a kid. More than I'd thought I was capable of caring for anyone with all the walls I'd put up. I'd been so sure that really connecting with anyone would be dangerous somehow—for me, for them—but it'd happened anyway...

And I was okay with it. It fucking hurt, but I'd take all the agony in the world just to see her walking past the barn door with that little smile of hers and the triumphant gleam in her eyes that'd say she'd kicked even more asses today.

A clattering sound jerked me out of my thoughts. It'd come from somewhere behind me, but when I twisted my head, I couldn't make out the source. The barn held at least one side room. Were some of the men who'd kidnapped me still lurking around, planning a surprise attack to turn the tide?

I grunted against my gag, but I was hardly in a position to shout out a warning. It sounded like the people outside had caught on as it was. The voices rose, sounding closer than before—Dess arguing with her father, other voices I didn't recognize tossing out ridiculous comments.

Then a gunshot reverberated through the air. I flinched, and the next second dozens more shots thundered outside, along with thumps, wordless shouts, and pained noises that set my heart thudding faster.

The crew had better know what they were doing.

Even though I could tell it was hopeless, I strained at my bindings again, trying with all my might to break free. Then the gunfire stopped. I inhaled shakily through my nose, fear clamping chilly hands around my lungs.

The footsteps pounded toward the barn now. My heart leapt to my throat, but an instant later the door flew open to reveal the exact four figures I'd wanted to see on the other side, none of them looking all that worse for wear. Well, other than the fact that Dess appeared to have poured a bucket of blood over herself. From the steadiness of her gaze and her posture, it wasn't hers.

At the sight of me, she let out a little yelp and ran over, the guys rushing with her. Dess hugged my legs while

Talon hauled a crate over to stand on so he could slice the ropes that bound my arms. The next thing I knew, I was tumbling fully into Dess's damp embrace.

Someone yanked the gag from my mouth, and the meaty stink of fresh blood flooded my throat as well as my nose. Normally it'd have turned my stomach, but right then it was the perfume of victory. I hugged Dess back, reveling in the strength still radiating from her body and the little noise of relief she made at having me in her arms.

"Are you okay?" she murmured. "They didn't—"

"All they did was tie me up," I said quickly. "Nothing's damaged but my ego."

"And we know you had more than enough of that anyway," Blaze teased, and a ripple of startled but joyful laughter rippled through our group.

"I heard a noise in one of the back rooms," I added with a jolt of memory. "If there's anyone else lurking around…"

Talon strode over to check the rest of the building with his usual ruthless calm. He returned in a moment with a grim expression. "There's no sign of anyone around. I think we got them all."

"Good. We don't want to stick around here too long," Julius said in his typically commanding way. "I don't think there are any neighbors near enough to have heard the shots, but I'd rather not tempt fate by thumbing our noses at it. Let's get cleaned up so we don't *look* like we've just carried out a massacre and then get out of here."

Dess nodded, drawing back enough that I realized the blood was smeared all across her neck and the ends of her hair as well as drenching her shirt. What the hell had *she* been through to get to me?

The set of her mouth told me she didn't want to talk about it—and I got a clear enough story when we marched outside, her arm still wrapped tightly around mine.

The bodies of several people I recognized from the Malik family—and a few I couldn't recognize at all because of bullets they'd taken to their faces—scattered the stretch of grass between the barn and a house I recognized from the photograph Dess had shown us. Right in the middle of them sprawled Dess's father, his throat slit, a puddle of blood seeping into the soil around him. I had no doubt at all who had delivered that killing strike.

I reached down and grasped Dess's hand in a show of solidarity, not minding the prickles of receding numbness that bit into my nerves at the motion. Dess swallowed audibly and squeezed my fingers in return.

"It had to be done," was all she said, and that was all I needed to know.

The door of the house was unlocked. We pushed inside, and Julius motioned Dess upstairs. "You need a whole shower," he told her. "I'll see if I can find some clothes around for you to change into." He and the other guys had a few splatters of gore on them, but nothing compared to her drenching.

Dess glanced at me and made a face. "I made you a mess too. I'm sorry. Come on." Her fingers curled even more firmly around mine as she tugged me toward the bathroom. "Look for something new for Garrison!" she called over her shoulder.

She didn't let go of me until we'd reached the large bathroom with its pearly gray walls, as if she was afraid she'd lose me again along the way. There, she pulled back the shower curtain and sighed happily. "There's plenty of soap." She turned on the shower hot enough for steam to immediately start fogging the air.

When she turned back to me, I still barely noticed the blood coating her skin and shirt. All I could see was *her*. This strong, stunning woman who'd destroyed her own family to save me.

An impulse gripped me that thrilled and frightened me at the same time. My hand moved of its own accord, my thumb swiping a scarlet drop off her temple while my palm lingered against her cheek. Dess's gray eyes turned a bit puzzled as she gazed back at me, maybe wondering if I'd suffered a hidden brain injury.

I needed to say it. She needed to know. If today had proven anything, it was how quickly our circumstances could turn sideways.

Next time I might not be bait. Next time I might be dead. The thought of leaving this life without her knowing how much she meant to me scared me more than being so whole-heartedly genuine.

"I love you," I said, not giving myself another moment to think about the words. I forced my masks to drop in the hopes that she could see all the emotions that ran through me as I spoke the words. That she'd know how true I was being in this moment.

Dess's eyes widened. She placed her hand over mine against her face and leaned into my touch, but her expression was as uncertain as it was appreciative. My gut started to twist with apprehension as she opened her mouth and closed it again, no sound in the room but the hiss of the water.

"I—" she started, and swallowed audibly with a little shake of her head. "I don't know if I can say that back. I feel like I'm still learning how to be a normal person overall. I hardly even know what love is supposed to mean."

My throat tightened, and I had the urge to yank my walls back into place. To toss out a snarky remark that would turn the situation around and make it seem like I'd only been joking. But I held myself firm against it. I felt what I felt, and I would own it no matter how she responded.

"That's okay," I said. "I didn't say it because I expected anything from you. I just wanted you to know how much you matter to me. How much I'd have hated to lose you if something had gone wrong today." A self-deprecating laugh slipped from my lips. "From the moment those pricks grabbed me, that was pretty much all I thought about."

A soft smile curved Dess's mouth. "I can talk about *that*. Maybe I don't know what love will be for me, but you and the rest of the crew are more important to me than anyone else in the world. I'd kill for you. I'd die if I had to go that far to protect you. I wouldn't hesitate for a second."

The honesty of those words rang through her voice and washed away any trepidation I'd felt about my confession. How many people offered that level of devotion when they did say, "I love you"? Her declaration meant more than those three little words would have.

"That's more than enough for me," I said, my voice getting rough, and pulled her into a kiss.

I didn't care that a hint of metallic flavor lingered on her lips or that my fingers slid through still-damp blood as I tucked my hand around her neck. She was *my* woman even if she was the other guys' too, and in that moment I needed to confirm that fact in every possible way.

Our mouths crashed together with a ferocity that grew more heated by the second. Dess gripped my shirt and arched into me with another groan. She was making me even more of a mess than before, but I didn't give a shit about that either. I had her, and that was all that mattered.

I hefted her onto the sink counter and pushed between her legs without breaking the kiss. As I kicked off my shoes, I yanked off hers. Then, ignoring the rest of our clothing, I whipped her around and stepped over the edge of the bathtub.

Dess growled eagerly as I pinned her up against the tiled wall, nothing supporting her but one of my hands and the pressure of my hips. The steam billowed around us, the warm water pelting us, and our mouths grew slick as we kissed again and again. I couldn't get enough of her.

The blood that had smeared her skin and mine streamed off us into pink trails that wound through the bottom of the bathtub toward the drain. As a path cleared,

I moved my lips to the crook of her neck and left nipping kisses down its length.

"We're still dressed," Dess murmured around an amused gasp.

"We weren't getting back into these clothes anyway," I reminded her, my mouth brushing her shoulder as I spoke. "But believe me, I am planning on taking care of that."

Keeping one hand on her thigh, I used the other to tug up her shirt. It took mere seconds to unclasp her bra. Then I was massaging her breasts skin to skin, running my calloused fingers over each of her tender nipples. Dess's head dipped backward as she gasped out her pleasure.

When I'd had my fill—for now—of her gorgeous breasts, I trailed my hand downward and dipped it beneath her waistband. She ground into my finger the moment it brushed her clit, and I smirked against her lips. I curled that finger right inside her and groaned at the slickness waiting for me there.

"So fucking wet for me," I muttered.

A giddy giggle fell from her mouth. "In more than one way."

True. I lowered her for just long enough to strip her soaking shirt right off her and then tug off her pants. She yanked at the buttons on my shirt in turn. As she delved into my jeans next, she ran her hands up and down my rigid erection until I practically went blind with pleasure.

Then she grabbed the bottle of body wash and held it up. "We're still kind of messy. Are you going to wash me?"

Holy fuck, could she have gotten any sexier? The slyly

seductive question made me want to shove her back against the wall and thrust into her there and then. But taking her up on her offer would be even more enjoyable in the long run.

I poured a generous amount of soap into my palms and rubbed them together, eyeing the canvas of her body before me. Then I got started, lathering the soap meticulously across the front of her, paying extra close attention to the most important areas. She dipped her head back beneath the water as I massaged all her curves with the floral-scented soap, her breath quickening at my attentions.

"Turn around," I demanded, and she did exactly as I asked, exposing her entire back and ass to me. I gripped her hips and moved her toward the back of the shower until she placed her hands against the wall. Dropping to my knees, I began washing her just as I'd been doing before, running my hands over each calf, and then her thighs. I reached her ass in no time and rubbed the soap into it with rough palms before standing and starting on her back.

She swayed toward me in anticipation, but I continued washing her back as if I didn't notice. My own motions went jerky from lust as she brushed her ass against my jutting cock. I slapped it, and she whimpered encouragingly.

"Put your arms up," I demanded, and she did as I instructed, resting both of her forearms against the wall above her head. "Bend over."

She bent, pushing her ass up toward me. I rinsed the

suds from my hands and pressed one between her thighs. She ground into my touch. I couldn't wait any longer.

I lined myself up and plunged into her slick cunt as far as I could go. Dess's welcoming cry pealed through the air, and if the other guys hadn't figured out that we were doing more than washing up in here, they had to know now. The thought only drove me faster.

God, she felt so good around me. I thrust again, placing a hand on one of her hips and using the other to press her into the wall with the force I knew she liked, maybe even needed to fully surrender to the moment. The feeling of her skin against me and her heat around my cock sent me so close to the edge that I feared I'd barrel over it before she could find her own satisfaction.

I slowed my pumping, bringing myself deeper into her rather than rocking faster against her. Dess let out another moan. She was close—almost as close as I was to finishing.

I pulled myself out and gripped her hips, turning her toward me. Then I pushed her back into the shower wall facing me and thrust so deep into her that her eyes went out of focus, her mouth falling open.

Planting my forearms over her head, I trapped her body with mine and pressed my lips against hers. A tremor ran through her, her channel clenching around me. I could feel every inch of her when she came for me, and I pounded into her harder, drawing her release out with each motion.

I couldn't hold on for long. She ran one hand into my hair and scratched her fingernails down my back, and I stiffened with my own release.

My lips remained cemented to hers as we both came down from the frantic fucking. I kissed her again, more gently this time, and took in the emotions whirling in her stormy eyes.

I'd swear I could see my whole life in that pensive, passionate gaze, and I wouldn't have wanted it any other way.

TWENTY-EIGHT

Decima

"RIGHT," Julius said into his phone as Talon drove us back into the city. "Take care of all the bodies and wipe down the house and barn. Leave everything else as is."

I sank into the back seat between Blaze and Garrison, grappling with mixed feelings about our leader's instructions to the local clean-up crew he'd gotten in touch with. On one hand, we didn't want to risk leaving any evidence at all of our involvement once the murders of my family were discovered. But on the other, there was probably evidence of all the murders *they'd* committed on the country property, and the cleaners might erase that too.

Well, they were dead. I wasn't sure their crimes needed to come to light now that their legacy could end here. Surely the few remaining Maliks couldn't keep up such a horrific conspiracy on their own?

We'd just passed the city limits when Blaze's phone pinged. He fished it out and glanced at the screen.

"Huh," he said, and glanced over at us like he had something he wanted to say but wasn't sure the news would be welcome.

I elbowed him. "What is it?"

"Well, not to send us off on another chase after all of today's excitement, but... I did get a partial license plate for the Hunter's bike when he met you this morning. I had it running through the system, and I've just gotten a match from some street-cam footage in downtown DC."

I jerked over to peer at his phone. "Really?" I might have been exhausted from everything we'd been through, but the news set my nerves on high alert all over again.

Blaze motioned to the screen, which showed a man getting off a motorcycle outside what looked like a nightclub from the exterior décor.

I frowned at the image. "That's not the guy I talked to." He was too thin, and when he pulled off his helmet, he was clearly too young as well, not much older than I was.

Talon had tuned into our conversation. "It's not uncommon for an organization to have a pool of vehicles if they don't want any individual member to be easily tracked."

"Or he could have stolen it and returned it," Garrison suggested.

"He's supposed to be law enforcement," I reminded him, but my need to say "supposed" reminded me of how little we still knew about the man who'd reached out to me with his ominous warnings.

"It doesn't make much sense to me," Julius said, his forehead furrowing as he turned in his seat to join the conversation. "How a man with the kind of resources he obviously had and a clear enough idea of what the Maliks were doing couldn't manage to prove it."

Blaze nodded slowly. "You're right. Not to downplay how brilliant we all are, but we put the pieces together in just a few weeks, partly because of the tips he gave us. Sure, Dess had more access to their house, but anyone could have broken in. I haven't matched an entry to the girl he said was his daughter yet, but I've IDed the kids from the last five years, so it's farther back than that. He must have been investigating this for a while."

I rubbed my arms, abruptly chilled. "It's a loose end. I don't like not knowing how he really fits into the whole situation. Why don't we go over to the club and just see what we see? Even if he's not there, maybe we'll find something out about the people he works with if that guy with the bike is a colleague of his. And if not, it wouldn't be a bad thing to have a drink and unwind, right?"

"Here, here," Garrison said in a mildly sardonic voice, and knocked his knuckles against my hand as if offering a toast. I grinned at him, the gleam of his eyes sparking renewed heat in me after the interlude we'd just shared and the emotional declarations made on both sides.

Whatever we found, whatever we faced, the five of us had each other's backs. That was a hell of a lot more than I could say for the "real" family that'd kidnapped Garrison and tried to murder the rest of us today.

By the time we reached the club, the sky had darkened with the setting of the sun. We parked a block away and walked over, scanning the street as we went.

Garrison stopped us a few storefronts shy of the club itself. A few patrons were standing outside, being waved in one by one.

"It doesn't look like a public event," he said. "The bouncers are checking something—looks like some kind of invitation."

Julius took in the club-goers and then us. "I think we can blend in if we find an alternate entrance. They're dressed a little fancier than we are, but nothing that should make us stand out too much."

I nodded. I'd ended up decked out in linen pants and a silky blouse since there hadn't been anything *less* fancy on offer in the Maliks' country home. "We'll just take a quick look around then?" I suggested. "In and out?"

"In and out," he agreed.

Being five mercenaries with plenty of experience penetrating buildings without being noticed, we found a moment to slip through a back door with barely any trouble at all. Inside, we slunk through a hall and out into the main room of the club.

It was a pretty upscale place with a sleek steel bar counter, mahogany tables in the booths, and marble tiles covering the floor. Amber lights fixed along the middle of the ceiling gave the room an atmospheric glow. Servers circulated the room with flutes of champagne, weaving between the crowd of party-goers who were laughing and chattering with each other energetically. The whole event had a celebratory vibe.

It was mostly men, I realized as I studied the crowd. There were women here and there, hanging off the guys' arms in skimpy dresses, but they appeared to be there for the men's entertainment rather than their own. The back of my neck prickled.

"I wonder what they're celebrating," I said.

Garrison tipped his head toward the crowd and snatched a champagne flute off a passing tray. "Let's see if we can find out. Nudge us if you see the Hunter."

I wasn't sure I'd recognize him at a glance. Maybe if I heard him talking. I'd only seen him with his motorcycle helmet on.

I took a glass of my own and held it in front of me as I made my way into the festivities. I tapped the arm of one younger guy I passed and gave him my best innocent smile.

"Hey," I said, pitching my voice over the bass of the music. "What's the big celebration? My date didn't tell me what's up, and now he's gone off somewhere."

The guy chuckled. "Beats me! I'm just here for the babes and the booze."

I forced a laugh and moved on. Maybe one of my fellow women would be more helpful.

I fixed my attention on a redhead who moved from one man to another as confidently as if she owned the place and eased over beside her. When she glanced over at me, I motioned to the room around us. "Crazy party, isn't it? What are we celebrating anyway?"

She shrugged but grinned. "All I know is the boss is very happy about something. That's good for all of us." She flicked her hand toward the bar.

There were several men gathered there, but as soon as my gaze settled on them, I could tell which one had to be in charge. There was a guy with his back to me who stood a few inches taller than the others, the artificial light gleaming off his silver-and-blond hair. All the men around him were facing him, jostling like puppies eager to catch their master's attention.

He pushed himself a little away from the bar, grasping the beer bottle the bartender had passed to him, and my heart skipped a beat.

Those broad shoulders, that posture, and that height— the way he moved… And the blond parts of his hair were the same color as the little girl in the photo, weren't they?

I was abruptly sure that I was looking at the Hunter, fully revealed. He was "boss" over all these people, not just an investigator in a larger organization?

And he was hosting this celebration *now*, right after the family he'd been working against for years had fallen… Could he already know what we'd done? How? Or was it just a coincidence and there was some other special occasion?

I glanced over my shoulder toward the guys, who'd followed me from a discrete distance. At my look, they drew in closer around me.

"The older blond guy by the bar," I said, tilting my

head in his direction without looking right at him. "I swear that's the Hunter. And someone just referred to him as the 'boss'—that he set up this party."

Garrison knit his brow, taking in the room again. "If he's got all these people working under him, it makes even less sense that he couldn't tackle the Maliks without getting you involved."

"There's only one person who can explain that," I said. "Let's see if he'll talk to me properly for once. Or maybe we'll overhear something useful."

We moved through the crowd toward the Hunter, who'd turned so that I could make out his profile. He had a craggy face like it was sculpted out of rough granite, with a high forehead and a strong jaw. I etched it into my memory as I pushed my way closer.

Our intentions must have been obvious, because we were only five feet away when another man broke from the Hunter's side and intercepted us. He held up his narrow hand, his close-set eyes flashing. "Now isn't the time to petition the boss with your problems. You can wait until tomorrow, whatever it is."

He spoke with an air of authority—he must have been a close associate of the Hunter's. But he didn't seem inclined to answer any questions himself.

I raised my chin, putting on my best appearance of assurance myself. "We're not petitioning him. He specially invited us, and it'd be rude if we didn't at least say hello."

The man snorted. "I know everyone he'd have 'specially' invited, and I have no idea who you are. Now scurry along and stop with the bullshit. This isn't a game of Candyland."

Behind me, Garrison sucked in a sharp breath. I might not have backed down if his obvious reaction hadn't worried me. I stepped back from the man who'd interrupted us and turned to face the crew.

Garrison grabbed my wrist before I could say anything and dragged me several steps farther away. The other men followed, looking confused. "What's going on?" Julius asked in a low voice.

"That Candyland line," Garrison muttered, his expression tense. "You remember our contact for the household job? He went by the code name Viper? I talked to him a few times after because of their supposedly missing "property," and I'd swear he used almost the exact same phrase a couple of times. It's not the kind of thing you hear all the time, either."

A chill condensed in my gut as a vague memory rose up of the voicemail message he'd played for us one time. I'd been too upset to commit the exact words to memory, but the "Candyland" part did send a tremor of recognition through me.

"The household job," I repeated. "You think that guy is the same one who hired you to slaughter everyone in the household?"

Garrison inclined his head, his mouth flattening. I glanced back toward the man in question, who was now standing right by the Hunter's side, his eyes narrowed as he fended off another possible petitioner.

What were the chances of that? The man who'd

approached me about investigating my family was also the boss of the man who'd destroyed my captors' home? And not just that. Like Garrison had said, 'Viper' and his people had wanted to get their hands on me too. We'd had every reason to believe they were behind the attacks on us back in the crew's hometown.

Nausea coiled through my abdomen. This all felt way too wrong.

And then, as my gaze darted through the room, my eyes caught on one of the skimpily dressed women, a young brunette who was perched on an older man's lap. He caught up her hair in his hand and tugged her head toward him, and a dark blotch showed just above her hairline at the back of her neck.

My pulse hiccupped. Unable to think, barely able to *breathe*, I stalked through the room straight to her and lifted her hair higher.

The woman squawked and jerked away from me, and the man started to sputter, but I'd seen enough in that brief glimpse. She had a tattoo imprinted at the back of her skull—a tattoo of a droplet with a line slicing through it diagonally, just like the one on my own neck.

The mark of the organization behind the household. What the hell was going on?

The thumping of my heartbeat had drowned out most of the noise around me, but the commotion I'd caused had drawn other patrons' attention—including the boss's. I glanced up, locked in my daze of shock, to find the Hunter striding toward me.

The crew pulled close around me in a protective

formation. The Hunter didn't look remotely fazed. He walked in a straight line, trusting that those around him would dart out of his path if they were in his way—and they did. It was only a matter of seconds before he came to a stop just a couple of feet from where I stood, his expression impenetrable.

Had he stolen that woman from another location like the household, the same way he'd tried to steal me? Or was something even bigger going on here? I was too off-balance to sort through everything I'd just discovered.

The accusation tumbled out of me. "You had them killed. The people who kidnapped me. You were behind the massacre at the household."

He cocked his head slightly to the side as if trying to feign confusion, but his voice came out too steady for me to believe he didn't understand. "I believe you'll find that Damien Malik was responsible for that incident."

What? I might have been bewildered, but I knew that one statement was impossible. My birth father had clearly had no idea whatsoever that I was alive when I'd first approached him. He'd still believed that I'd died in a car crash as a toddler.

As the Hunter stared me down, the understanding sank in that I might be in the middle of a game much vaster than I'd ever suspected. I had no idea where I stood or what the rules were.

And the man in front of me, standing tall amid his crowd of underlings without any sign of concern that I'd found him, could be an even bigger monster than the one I'd just killed.

ABOUT THE AUTHORS

Eva Chance is a pen name for contemporary romance written by Amazon top 100 bestselling author Eva Chase. If you love gritty romance, dominant men, and fierce women who never have to choose, look no further.

Eva lives in Canada with her family. She loves stories both swoony and supernatural, and strong women and the men who appreciate them.

Connect with Eva online:
www.evachase.com
eva@evachase.com

Harlow King is a long-time fan of all things dark, edgy, and steamy. She can't wait to share her contemporary reverse harem stories.